The Chaiwallah

A Novel

by

TIM VAN ES

Copyright © 2025 Tim van Es

ISBN: 978-1-7640024-2-4

To my twin sons Dean & Jordan,
born under the Mumbai skies

Chimbai

WHO IS THIS *chaiwallah?* the newspaperman thought, parking his bicycle.

It was still early morning, and Chimbai Square was dark and quiet. The newspaperman, always the first vendor to open up, stood next to his simple stand. Wooden planks atop two thick tree branches that spread horizontally beside the wall of a nearby house. The makeshift tarpaulin roof was originally dark green but was now rust-colored from years of accumulated street dust. It looked as weathered and worn as the newspaperman's jeans and checkered khaki business shirt.

After a few careless swipes of an old cloth to wipe down the platform, he walked to his bicycle and unloaded the papers, stacking them onto the wooden board. After going back and forth a few times, he removed his cracked brown leather sandals and settled down cross-legged on the platform to fold his papers one by one.

Glancing to his right, he investigated the chaiwallah's cart, watching the man's tea-making process. From his metal spice box, his *masala dabba*, the old, white bearded man pulled fresh ginger, cinnamon sticks, black peppercorn, cloves, nutmeg, and green cardamon and tossed them into a large shiny aluminum pot full of water.

"Good-morning, sir!" the chaiwallah called enthusiastically.

The newspaperman hesitated, surprised by the old man's energetic greeting. "Oh, hello. Welcome to Chimbai," he replied in a friendly tone. He continued folding his papers, staring at a few lazy street dogs in the otherwise deserted square, and decided to try a cup of chai when he was done.

Chimbai Square, where four roads intersected, sat beside the Arabian Sea in Bandra West, a well-known residential suburb southwest of Mumbai. Apartment buildings with shops below blocked the unassuming square from having a water view. The square and surrounding roads were paved with small bricks that time had burnished to a rust color, like the roof on the newspaperman's stand. Except for a few, most of the weathered beige and brown apartment buildings surrounding the square and connecting streets were just a few stories high.

Neighborhood residents often referred to two key landmarks in Chimbai Square: the century-old white crucifix statue near its center and the large ancient bodhi tree at the east corner of the square that connected it to St. Joseph's Road. This was a short road housing the area's government school and several residential apartment buildings. The other three streets, all named Chimbai Road, branched out from the square.

On the southern end, between the road and the sea, were Bandra's Koliwadahs, a four-hundred-year-old fishing community residing beside the beach. Despite rapid urbanization, the Koli people's lifestyle was mostly unchanged. Koli men were usually around the beach repairing boats and nets to prepare for their next fishing trip, which could last days, weeks, or even months depending on the season. The Koli women took care of the household and sold their husband's catch along the southern Chimbai road or to wholesalers.

By the time the newspaperman finished folding half his

papers, sunlight had started to filter into parts of Chimbai Square from between the apartment buildings. A man and woman wearing sneakers passed by. A moment later, the newspaperman saw the early morning delivery truck park in front of the supermarket underneath one of the apartment buildings and wait to unload.

On the left side of the supermarket was a hairdresser, and on the right was a hardware store, a pharmacy, a liquor store, and a doctor's office. The supermarket always opens first with the other shops opening at various times later in the morning.

The newspaperman saw three young men get out of the truck to help supermarket staff unload the goods. As they unloaded rice, dal, water containers, and other items, two black and yellow rickshaws parked behind the newspaper stand, awaiting residents headed for work. Then another couple speed-walked across the square. When the men finished unloading, the three truck drivers walked across the square to the chaiwallah's cart.

"His first customers," the newspaperman mused out loud, as he folded his last papers. He watched the fruit seller next to the bodhi tree open up, with the owner loosening the ropes around his stall. "Done," the newspaperman said. He stretched his legs, slipped on his sandals, and strolled to the chaiwallah's cart. "Let me be one of your first customers," he said.

"Thank you. I am grateful, sir," the old man replied politely.

"First time in Chimbai?" the newspaperman asked.

"Yes, I like moving around." The man smiled and picked up a cutting chai glass from his rack. "I am a bit of a nomad," he laughed softly.

As the newspaperman watched the chaiwallah pour the filtered chai from his *patila*, a smaller pot, he noted the old man's neat white beard and dark, deeply wrinkled facial skin and radiant light brown eyes. *This man looks old and young at the same time,* he thought. The chaiwallah wore a bright, white, well ironed business shirt with a white lungi and shiny light brown leather sandals. *Keralite or Tamil?* the newspaperman guessed as he accepted the glass of chai.

"Thank you, sir." The newspaperman examined the rich, caramel-colored concoction then lifted the glass to his nostrils, inhaling its aroma. "Fragrant!" The chaiwallah waited for him to take his first sip. "Rich, complex, and delicious," the newspaperman complimented.

Wonderful to hear that, sir," the old man replied happily. After letting the newspaperman enjoy a few sips, the chaiwallah asked, "Tell me, what are the headlines today?"

The newspaperman glanced back at his stand, gathering his thoughts. "Umm… this year's flourishing agricultural sector after a great monsoon," he began.

"Some highlights from the Durga Puja and Navaratri festivals across the country, and updates on India's countrywide solar panel expansion."

"Interesting," the old man responded. "I'll buy one. And I'll make sure to share today's headlines with each one of my customers to help you sell a few more.

"Oh," the newspaperman said, surprised, "that is very generous of you. Thank you, *dada*," kindly referring to him as grandfather.

The chaiwallah smiled warmly. "You're welcome, *beta*," he replied, calling him son.

Aditi

IN THE MAZE of narrow, dusty dirt road alleys in the Koliwadahs, Aditi woke up just before the alarm. She lived in a simple ground-floor studio in a low-rise, brick building in the midst of the fishing community. The room was filled with the scent of damp earth and salty sea air. While basic, her studio was much better than many of the self-made shacks the majority of the Koli community lived in nearby.

Aditi turned her head to see Vishal sleeping beside her. *Such a wonderful boy,* she thought fondly, but then felt some guilt that he would soon need his own room. *He's growing up so fast.*

Suddenly, a deafening bang from the adjacent wall shattered her thoughts and made her sit up straight. "*Are macchi!*" she uttered aloud, using the Koli expression meaning "oh fish," to out her frustration. *I can't take this noise much longer,* she thought.

Her gaze fell once again on Vishal, who had turned but slept through the noise undisturbed. Her eyes locked onto the golden-colored photo frame on the wall between her kitchen and dining table. Inside was a picture of her parents, taken before Aditi was born just a short stroll away. They were standing proudly beside their fishing boat.

She slipped out of bed and padded past the mandir attached to the wall. The small altar, facing northeast, was draped in saffron cloth and held three small brass statues. Lord Ganesha, the remover of obstacles, Goddess Mahalakshmi, and the great King Rama. In front of the three gods stood a gold-plated incense burner Aditi got from her grandparents, an oil lamp, and a small brass bell. Most of their *poojas*, their prayers, however, were held in her auntie's home in a nearby alley.

Aditi turned on the light of the bathroom, which was absent of natural light, and closed the flimsy plywood door. Dark green tiles lined the bathing area with a hole in the floor for drainage. On the tiles stood a white plastic bath stool next to a large plastic bucket beneath the tap, with a small plastic mug inside. Brushing her teeth, Aditi looked in the mirror that hung above the sink. *Maya will probably make a decision within the next two weeks,* she thought. *We can move to a slightly better place.* She stared into her own eyes with defiance. *Yes, Diti, but you need to do better…*

She changed into a classic, modern navy-blue cotton *kurti* that fell just below her knees. Tiny lilies were stitched onto the collar in a darker shade of blue. All other edges along the dress were stitched in contrasting light blue. Underneath, she wore bright white leggings and light brown sandals. Her thin, feminine, golden necklace gleamed, matching the gold bangles decorated with colored glass gemstones she wore on her left arm. The glistening gold and bright colors contrasted with her rich, deep skin tone, radiating warmth and beauty. Before reaching over to Vishal, she walked up to their to-do list on the whiteboard above the dining table to check on progress.

After a brief moment, she whispered, "Wake up, *baala*. Today is your lucky day."

Vishal sat up, yawned, stretched his arms, and leaped out of bed. "Lucky?" he asked, as Aditi walked back to the kitchen.

"I'm making your favorite *poha.*"

"I'm starving!" Vishal said, ambling toward his mother.

"You are always starving, baala," she laughed, looking back across her shoulder.

"Something special today?" Vishal asked, observing her from behind.

"Why, baala?" Aditi asked, cutting the last chilies.

"Well, you look like that."

She turned around, smiled, and reminded him, "You know what I always say...."

"That the way you look impacts the way you feel," he swiftly answered.

"Yep," she nodded.

"But I wear the exact same school uniform every day!" He laughed.

"How is your research going?" she asked, now sautéing the chopped chilies and red onions.

"A bit boring. Why you are always giving me these kinds of assignments?"

"They are not assignments," Aditi chuckled, adding asafetida to the pan.

"I just want you to create the habit of reading and thinking critically."

"Extra jaggery, please!" Vishal requested, before walking into the bathroom.

Aditi added boiled potatoes, green peas, carrots, turmeric, salt, and extra jaggery to the pan.

Vishal walked out of the bathroom in his school uniform. Aditi said, "The assignments, as you call them, give us interesting discussions in the evenings, don't you think?"

"Yes, very interesting," Vishal replied, his tone somewhat

sarcastic. "When are we going to the Elephant Caves?" he asked.

"Maybe next weekend, baala. It depends on my workload. Come, sit. I'll be right there." Aditi dished out two bowls of poha and sat down. After the first scoop of the soft, spiced flattened rice flakes, she opened her laptop. "Sorry, Vishal, I need to check if anything is urgent."

Vishal ate silently.

"Oh, come on!" Aditi suddenly exclaimed aloud in frustration.

"What happened?" Vishal asked.

"Nothing. It is just this email." Aditi continued to read, trying to hide her disappointment and surprise. *I really thought I would be invited for an interview. I am more than qualified,* she thought. She updated her file showing a long list of jobs she got rejected from in various stages of the application process over the last few years.

"*Chal,* Vishal!" Aditi said closing her laptop, telling him to hurry up and go.

Vishal closed the warped aluminum door behind him and climbed onto Aditi's old, white kinetic scooter, flattening the back tire.

"Ready?" she asked.

"Yep," he answered.

She maneuvered them through the narrow alleys, rocks and sand skipping from the tires, until she finally stopped short of the southern Chimbai Road. She looked for traffic and turned left, heading toward Chimbai Square. Now it bustled with shoppers, cars, and rickshaws. As she waited for a car to pass by, she spotted the chaiwallah's chai cart across the square. *He's new,* she thought. Then she continued on, passing the bodhi tree into St. Joseph's Road before pulling up in front of the school.

"Bye!" Vishal called as he hopped off, almost making Aditi lose balance of the scooter.

"Bye, monkey. Study hard, God will do the rest," Aditi replied.

When Vishal was out of sight, Aditi placed a purple shawl over her mouth and nose and headed back to Chimbai Road, driving south as she passed the small Hanuman temple and St. Andrew's Church until she stopped at the busy Hill Road crossing. The street was a whirl of vehicles, but she joined the heavy traffic with confidence. Past Mehboob studios, the beacon of iconic Indian films, she turned onto Mount Carmer Road, around Lilavati Hospital, and finally onto the Western Express Highway. The sprawling six-kilometer Bandra-Worli Bridge that crossed the murky sea from Bandra to Worli was on her right, but she veered left, driving twenty kilometers north to Malad.

In the basement of an old office building, she parked her scooter and took the lift to the third floor. Walking through the labyrinth of call center desks, she suddenly heard a voice from behind.

"Good morning, Aditi."

She turned to see Maya, the floor director standing outside her office. "Good morning, Maya," Aditi said.

"I have news to share. Let's sit in my office?" Maya gestured towards the room behind her.

"Yes, sure," Aditi responded eagerly, her heart pounding with anticipation.

This is much faster than expected, Aditi thought, following her. Apprehension crept in as she sat opposite the director. This was the moment she had been waiting for. *I really need this,* Aditi thought.

"Aditi, I'll get straight to the point. Unfortunately, it's not good news," Maya began.

Aditi felt a knot tighten in her stomach.

"You were not successfully considered for the team leader role," Maya said.

A rush of disappointment washed over Aditi, but she forced a nod and a smile. *I knew it,* she thought.

"I know you've applied a few times for this type of role, and you have made tremendous progress these past years. You're a high achiever and never troublesome." Maya smiled.

Never troublesome? What is that supposed to mean? Aditi wondered.

"It's just that someone else in the team was better suited this time. It happens," Maya concluded.

"Okay," Aditi replied, waiting for further explanation, but there was none. Feeling somewhat defeated, she said, "Maya, is there something I need to improve to increase my chances of being offered a managerial role? I've applied a few times now. Are there skills I need to develop further?"

"No, Aditi. You're doing fine," Maya answered. "Sometimes it is just that someone else is better suited. We will announce it soon, and you will understand. Chal, let's get back to work," the director said, standing up to end the conversation.

"Thank you, Maya," Aditi replied, smiling politely as she stood up and left. *I can't take these rejections any longer!* Aditi shouted to herself internally, now briskly walking across the call floor. *What do I need to do to get promoted after all these years? I've hit my targets and built relationships with the team leaders, and lately I've been sharing ideas on sales strategy, organizational structure, and productivity improvements to help the business.*

Back at her desk, she opened her laptop, fighting off a storm of discouragement and confusion. *Maybe I am just good at sales and don't have what it takes to lead,* she thought, staring at her screen.

"Aditi, did you hear?" her best friend voiced from behind, interrupting her thoughts.

"Hey, Maryam. Hear what?"

"You won't believe it," Maryam started, pity showing across her face.

"What? Tell me," Aditi urged her.

"It is Veda. Veda will be our new team leader," Maryam revealed.

Aditi's face flushed. "What?"

"I know, I know. I am so sorry, Aditi. Everyone knows it should have been you," Maryam said. "You should have been promoted years ago. Veda graduated only recently and lacks experience."

After shaking off her disappointment, Aditi said convincingly, "It's okay, Maryam."

"Honestly, Aditi, you should move elsewhere, to a place where they appreciate you," Maryam suggested.

Aditi felt grateful for the comments from her friend and nodded slightly, not wanting to reveal that she had been applying externally for a long time but without any luck.

"You know," Maryan continued, "this time you had one clear disadvantage. Maya and Veda's families know each other; they grew up in the same neighborhood. And you… well, you know how it is. They just don't want someone like you to rise in the ranks. And I can already predict that…"

Aditi stared ahead, no longer listening as she thought about her next steps.

Arjun

Back in Chimbai Square, a *pani puri* vendor passed the supermarket with his entire stall balancing on his shoulders. It was a large metal plate attached to wooden sticks that could swiftly transform into a high table. On the plate was a pyramid of hollow, crispy shells called *puri*, surrounded by many containers with potato mash, chickpeas, onions, and *masala*, a blend of ground spices, for filling the puri. Others contained dressings: tamarind, mint, coriander, chili, and masala-infused water, and another with *dahi*—yogurt enhanced with cumin powder and *chaat* masala. The man offered two types of chutneys: one sweet and tangy, primarily with tamarind, and the other spicy and aromatic, made from herbs, garlic, lemon juice, and roasted cumin seeds.

Two women in sarees passed him by, but their attention was captivated by the local produce laid out by the vegetable sellers: lady fingers, cucumbers, beetroot, cabbage, cauliflower, and more. He moved on, passing the chaiwallah's cart and the newspaper stand.

Several drivers in brown uniforms lounged in their parked rickshaws, chewing *tambaku* paan—betel leaves filled with areca nut, slaked lime, tobacco, rose syrup, and cardamom. In front of the white crucifix, a group of women in black veils, only showing their eyes, were laden with groceries. They chatted and laughed among themselves, paying no heed to the vendor who continued to the other side of the square.

As the pani puri vendor strolled to the opposite side of the square, Arjun yelled at him from underneath the bodhi tree. "Hey, give us some!" The man ignored him and quickened his pace. "Pass me the *tharra, bhai,*" Arjun muttered to Rohit, calling him brother.

Rohit handed him the transparent bottle of locally brewed coconut alcohol. Arjun took a big gulp, his bloodshot, weary eyes scanning the square. His thinning black hair, peppered with grey, mirrored the untended beard on his face. He wiped his mouth with the short-sleeve of his green business shirt. His jeans were cut in several places and his sandals were dull and cracked.

After another swig at the tharra, he tried to stand up but struggled, using the bodhi tree for support. Pushing himself off, he nearly collided with two passing women wearing colorful sarees, who hurriedly moved out of his way, their eyes filled with disdain. Arjun regained his balance and staggered to the fruit seller next to the other side of the bodhi tree, near the newspaperman.

"Bastard! You are always in our way," he bellowed drunkenly.

The short, fragile fruit seller looked up, startled and frightened.

"How about you give me and my friend an apple for our trouble?" Arjun demanded in a menacing tone.

The fruit seller glanced around, desperation etched on his face.

"Are you not hearing me?" Arjun snarled.

The vendor didn't budge, his eyes locked with Arjun's fiery red ones. "Come on, *dost,* I am just trying to make a living here," the fruit seller pleaded.

"Dost!?" Arjun mocked. "I am not your friend, you bastard! I was going to leave with two apples, but now it's three."

The fruit seller sighed in resignation. "Take them. Just leave me," he murmured.

Arjun grunted, took the apples, and trudged back to the tree.

"You are such a mean drunk. The alcohol turns you into me!" Rohit laughed.

Arjun sat back down sedated. He grabbed the bottle from Rohit and took another gulp. After a while, Arjun tried to rise again. *Shit! The square is spinning. I'm too drunk,* he thought. "I'm going home. We need to... must... discuss our next move," Arjun slurred.

"Tomorrow," Rohit replied.

"Really. We have to. You know I need the money," insisted Arjun.

"Don't worry. We will, bhai," Rohit assured him.

Arjun pushed himself off the tree, zigzagging towards the supermarket, and turned south onto Chimbai Road.

After stumbling for ten minutes down the road, with the Koliwadahs on his right, he turned into one of its alleys. He stopped to rest against a brick wall to relish the incoming sea breeze on his face. Continuing down the same alley for a few minutes, he reached the beach and sat on a large black rock partially submerged in the brown, murky sea.

Watching the sea, he lit a cigarette. After inhaling deeply, his mind started to race. Even after almost thirty years, he could vividly remember his time with his father. *The first time I saw the sea,* he reminisced, *was on Juhu Beach.* He thought about the four-hundred-kilometer bus ride they had taken together from their farm in Jalna for his father to secure better contracts for cotton, legumes, soybeans, and maize. *The roads were so bad back then.* His father suggested they should see Juhu Beach after spending most of their days in Navi Mumbai and Vashi wholesale markets. Arjun let out a wistful smile, remembering the samosas they ate together on the beach.

Taking a deep drag from his cigarette, he thought, *it has been more than twenty years since I ran away from Jalna. Damn this life!* He softly cursed his fate, flicking his cigarette into the surf. Winding back through several alleys, Arjun entered one of the ramshackle rooms, pulling a cord to light a bulb dangling in the middle of the cramped room. He poured a glass of water from an aluminum container, drank it quickly, and collapsed onto the old, moldy mattress.

Sumeet

A LUXURIOUS BLACK SEDAN entered Chimbai Square from St. Joseph's Street, turning right and passing the fruit seller and the rickshaw behind the newspaperman. It turned right again into a gated community located behind the bodhi tree. This was one of Bandra West's most posh, high-rise apartment buildings.

"Good night. Same time tomorrow, please," Sumeet told his driver, then stepped out and hastily grabbed his brown leather briefcase. He took the lift to his home on the top floor. When he entered, his wife Manisha immediately called him to join her in the living room. *One thing after another,* he thought, stressing. He dropped his briefcase in front of his home office opposite the front door.

"*Namaskar,*" he said, greeting his parents at the dining table. "Sorry, I was a little delayed," he added.

"No problem, baala. How are you?" his mother asked warmly.

He smiled at Manisha, thankful she had taken care of his parents in his absence.

He kissed his mother's forehead and patted his father on the shoulder, telling them he would freshen up and quickly come back. Entering his home office, he walked behind the desk and laid his dark navy blue suit jacket on the back of the leather office chair and left his blue and purple checkered silk tie and white business shirt on the seat of the chair. Catching sight of himself in the mirror, he stroked his black moustache and inspected the dark black circles underneath his eyes then touched his potbelly, declaring the daily walks weren't helping much. He opened one of the drawers of his polished teakwood desk and took out two paracetamol pills and swallowed them with water from his briefcase.

"What a feast," Sumeet said as he returned to the dining table and admired all the different dishes laid out. There were eggplants stuffed with peanuts, coconut, spices and jaggery in a gravy. Dal that was cooked overnight, creamy white mutton curry, and a variety of breads like *puran poli* and *bhakri*.

"How are you, *baba*?" he asked, sitting down opposite his father.

"Good, how is the new job?" his father asked with a hint of seriousness.

"We're making good improvements," Sumeet answered, trying to sound confident. "*Aai*, do you still have that *ginger rama tulsi tea* from your trip?" he quickly asked his mother, hoping to steer the conversation away from work.

"Yes, baala, lots of it," his mother answered. "Why? Are you feeling sick?" she immediately asked, concerned.

"Migraines… they keep coming back," he admitted somewhat sheepishly, avoiding eye contact.

"Are you sleeping well? Drinking enough water?" his mother inquired, worry etched on her face.

"It's just work stress," Sumeet said, glancing at his father.

"I didn't want to tell you, but the wrinkles around your eyes are deepening and darkening baala," his mother pointed out, concern growing in her voice. "I am worried about you."

Sumeet could see the feeling of responsibility show across

Manisha's face and quickly responded. "It's just a tough period at work. Lots of changes," he said, trying to calm her down.

"I will send a whole bunch to your secretary tomorrow morning," his mother said. "Do you still walk every morning?"

"Yes, every day before work," Sumeet responded, trying to reassure her.

"What kind of improvements at work are you seeing, Sumeet?" his father suddenly asked solemnly.

Sumeet wasn't surprised his father steered the conversation back to work. "Well," he answered, "I am a lot clearer now about the responsibilities of my new role and the priorities for the business. Recently, we filled up our most critical roles." His father nodded and he concluded with, "But our team still needs time to understand their roles and the new ways of working proposed by the new management. Overall, lots of changes, but we're making good progress."

"Are you happy in your new role?" his father asked, eyebrows raised.

"Yes, it's another step forward and very challenging. We'll get there." He sounded hopeful.

Manisha stepped in. "I always tell him he's too kind to his people."

Sumeet glanced at her, feeling the comment was somewhat condescending. *How would you know?* he thought.

"My job gives me energy," his father pointed out, studying his son's face closely. "But it doesn't seem like yours is providing that."

Sumeet paused to give himself a chance to answer calmly, but inwardly, he felt the familiar sting of his father's doubt about his career. "We are all just getting used to the changes in the office."

"Do we have dessert?" his mother asked, breaking the tension.

"Yes, aai," Manisha replied. "Would you like some *shrikhand*? Or *rasgulla*?"

"How can I resist?" she smiled. "A bit of both, please," she laughed.

Sumeet declined.

"The only man I know who doesn't like Bengali sweets," Manisha remarked.

As Manisha instructed the maid to prepare tea and dessert, Sumeet's mother asked about their daughter, Nandini. Sumeet felt pity seeing the question trigger sadness in Manisha's eyes, but she explained proudly that their daughter was happy in Canada, achieving good grades and enjoying a large social circle.

"It's perfectly normal to feel the empty nest syndrome, *soonbai*," Sumeet's mother stated.

Sumeet realized he too greatly missed Nandini's presence in their house.

After enjoying dessert, his mother stood up and said to Manisha, "Well, that was lovely."

Sumeet quickly moved to help her up and walked alongside her to the front door, his father following behind.

"You can expect that tea in the morning, baala," she said.

"I hope you have a good week, Sumeet," his father said, encouragement in his voice.

"Thanks, baba. I will do my best," Sumeet replied sincerely.

After closing the door, Manisha immediately turned to Sumeet. "You better go to bed early. I'm sure you have another big day tomorrow."

"Yes, back-to-back meetings all day." He sighed and turned to his office to change into his pajamas. Looking out the large window, he watched Chimbai Square for a while. It was quiet and dark, except for lights coming from the supermarket and a few stalls around the square, including the chaiwallah's.

*

THE NEXT MORNING, Sumeet stepped out of the elevator, happy to enjoy his daily moment of refuge. *No one can take my daily meditation away from me,* he mused, walking across the parking area. Outside the compound, he turned left onto Chimbai Square. A rickshaw was stationed beside the newspaperman, who sat next to his stack of papers observing the square's movements from his wooden board. Ahead of him, Sumeet observed the supermarket. The racks in front, where staff often sat atop, were now empty. Walking ahead, he looked for traffic that always came in unexpectedly, but there was none. On his left, he saw the bodhi tree standing tranquil and alone.

When he passed the newspaper man, a cheerful greeting stopped him in his tracks.

"Good morning, sir! How are you today?" said an old man, smiling warmly at him from behind his cart.

"Good morning," Sumeet responded politely, impressed by the neat look of the old man.

"Would you care for a cup of chai, my good sir?" the chaiwallah asked.

"Well," he started, unwilling to delay his walking, "how about when I come back," he promised.

"Wonderful," the chaiwallah replied, smiling broadly. "That gives me time to brew a fresh batch."

Sumeet walked on, turning right into the northwestern Chimbai Road, passing Jogger's Park, and finally reaching the Carter Road promenade beside the sea. The sea was restless, its waves crashing through the mangroves onto the large black rocks that lined the space ahead of the promenade. He walked along the footpath, passing the many empty beige colored stone benches that separated the road with plants and palm trees. The benches, usually deserted during the day, attracted local residents and city-wide youth at night who wanted to unwind from the vibrant chaos of Mumbai life.

After covering a little over one kilometer on the promenade, Sumeet reached his cue, the play-rack that was part of small park. He turned around, and when he was back at Chimbai Square, he went to the chaiwallah, who was without customers.

"How was your walk, sir? There's a wonderful cool breeze this morning," the chaiwallah said as Sumeet approached.

"Yes, there is," he replied, enjoying the old man's efforts to make conversation. Sumeet saw the chaiwallah pour his masala chai into one of the glasses, its fragrance making him wonder about the different spices involved.

"Are you new at Chimbai Square?" Sumeet asked.

"Yes, I am," the chaiwallah replied, drying the bottom of the glass. He handed Sumeet the cup and said, "You will not regret it, sir."

Sumeet felt amused by the chaiwallah's enthusiasm as he took a tentative whiff. "Very aromatic," he stated. Then he closed his eyes and took a sip.

After his first gulp, the old man asked, "To your liking, sir?"

"Oh, yes, it's the perfect blend of spice and sweetness." Sumeet took another sip. "Better than my usual at the office," he chuckled.

Sumeet turned his back toward the chaiwallah to take in the sights of the square and enjoy his tea. When the chaiwallah asked him about the day ahead, Sumeet replied he would be very busy attending meetings.

"I wish you a successful day, beta," the old man said, seeing Sumeet finish his glass of chai.

"Thank you, sir. This was a good way to start my day," Sumeet replied, appreciating the affectionate term given to him.

When Sumeet reached into his pocket, the chaiwallah said, "Your first one is on me, beta."

Sumeet insisted, surprised by the generosity. He presumed the old man needed the money, but the chaiwallah refused.

"What is your name, sir?" Sumeet asked.

"Daasa, but call me dada," the old man smiled, proposing to call him grandfather.

"Thank you, dada. My name is Sumeet," he responded, wondering about the old man's given name, meaning "servant" in Hindi. Sumeet waved goodbye, passed the newspaperman's stall, and picked up his pace. *The name does reflect his customer service, but it can't be his real name,* he thought, having enjoyed the interaction. *Rare nowadays to receive such unbridled friendliness and enthusiasm from a street vendor,* he thought happily.

Aditi

Y*ES!* A{DITI} {THOUGHT}, watching her office computer screen. Then she quickly scanned the area around her to ensure no one could read the email. *Finally, an external interview this week! That call center is well regarded,* she thought with a smile. She quickly replied to the email by stating her preferred date and time to meet and got up from her chair.

She navigated through the immensely crowded, noisy hall, passing the many desks with u-shaped walls that didn't help confine the countless conversations happening all at once. Despite all the air conditioners running, the air was warm and humid. Aditi eventually reached the director's office on the other side of the call room floor and saw Maya was on the phone, so she waited patiently at the door.

"Excuse me?" Aditi called after she saw Maya hang up her phone.

"Yes, Aditi?"

"This Thursday I will need to leave at three," she said, then quickly added, "I will make sure to hit my daily target in the evening hours. Is that okay?" She was sure it wouldn't be a problem.

"Sorry, Aditi, I really need everyone here as much as

possible this week. Especially you as senior member of the team. Normally, I would be okay with you leaving early, but not this week, Aditi."

"Okay," Aditi said in surprise.

"I am making the announcement now. That will clarify everything." Maya stood up.

"Okay, madam," Aditi replied, now realizing it was because of Veda's new role. Maya nodded and walked from behind her desk toward her office door. "Come," Maya said.

Aditi followed.

"Can I have your attention, everyone!" Maya shouted across the floor as she stepped out.

Aditi saw surprised faces pop up from the many cubicles.

"Please come closer, I would like to make an announcement," Maya said. Aditi could see people whisper as they walked up, wondering what this was about. "As you all know, we are making structural changes to improve results. And I'm thrilled to announce that Veda will be our new corporate team leader."

Everyone clapped as Veda smiled proudly.

"Veda has been a successful sales executive for some time. She will start in her new role immediately and will report directly to me. Please support her during this transition," Maya said.

Maryam shot Aditi a disapproving look from afar, but Aditi chose to ignore it.

"Veda, anything you want to add?" Maya asked.

"Thank you, Maya. I'm super excited and will give it my all. Everyone, I hope I can count on your support," Veda said.

What does she have that I don't? Aditi wondered with sadness as she looked at Veda.

"Thanks, Veda. That's it," Maya concluded, returning to her office.

Aditi quickly forced herself to overcome her self-pity and

walked up to Veda. "Congratulations, Veda," Aditi said. "I look forward to working together."

"Thank you, Aditi. I'm very excited to get started as our new team leader," Veda replied.

Seeing the pride on Veda's face as she announced her new title made Aditi swallow the disappointment again of missing out on the role.

"We'll get together with the entire team this afternoon," Veda added.

"Great," Aditi said. "Now that you are my new manager, Veda," Aditi continued, "I spoke to Maya about leaving a little early this Thursday as there is something urgent I need to do. Is that okay with you?"

Veda's face soured. "Right. Well, I asked Maya to have everyone in the team completely tuned in this week due to our poor performance. I hope this won't be a problem," she said, sounding like a teacher.

Aditi pursed her lips. "No. No problem," she conceded, sensing Veda's insecurity. "I look forward to the afternoon meeting." She then swiftly walked off to the other side of the floor, opened the emergency exit door leading to the building's humid stairwell, and took out her phone.

Aditi listened to the ongoing ringtone, nervously tapping her foot, until finally someone picked up.

"Swift Link Call Center, how can I help you?"

"Yes. Hello, this is Aditi Sawant. Could you please connect me to human resources," she said softly.

"Just a moment," the voice instructed.

Aditi waited anxiously, on the alert for colleagues walking up and down the stairs.

"This is Neha. How can I help?" a different voice asked.

"Hello. You are speaking with Aditi Sawant. I am calling regarding the interview for sales executive. About fifteen minutes ago, I replied to your email with my preferred day and time, but I just found out the only availability I have this week is late evenings or weekends."

"Give me a second, madam," the voice requested.

After some time, the voice said, "Aditi?"

"Yes?"

"I'm sorry to inform you that the hiring manager will only be able to take interviews with the options provided. They already have very strong candidates in hand and want to finish this week."

Aditi considered her options and potential repercussions. *If I go, I may not get the new job, and I might lose this one. I can't take that risk,* she thought. "I really can't make it. How about next Monday?" Aditi asked.

"Sorry, Aditi, there's nothing I can do."

Are macchi! she thought. "Right. Okay, I understand. In that case I will need to cancel."

"We will keep your resume on file as we may have another opportunity soon."

"Thank you. Yes, please do let me know. Goodbye." Frustrated, Aditi leaned against the warm concrete wall. *Who knows when something else will come up. I cannot believe this opportunity has slipped through my hands.*

*

THAT EVENING, ADITI turned her scooter from Hill Road's heavy traffic onto the tranquil Saint Paul's Road. The evening air was beginning to turn slightly chilly. Her thoughts drifted to the long and stressful day she just had. *If today was an example of what's to come, dealing with Veda will be challenging.*

Forced to stop beside the bodhi tree, she saw Chimbai Square bustling with activity. *Vishal will see the stress on my face,* she thought, waiting for cars to clear the road. Then her eyes landed on the chaiwallah's cart next to the newspaper stand. *Perhaps a cup of tea from that new chaiwallah will refresh,* she thought.

She maneuvered her scooter through the cars, rickshaws, and evening shoppers to park in front of the supermarket. Stepping off, she almost bumped into a dwarf-like, fragile-looking man. It was the neighborhood garbage collector who was stacking flattened cartons into his rudimentary trolley made of dissimilar-sized wooden planks held together by a metal frame. When traffic cleared, she walked across.

"Hello, dear!" The chaiwallah immediately greeted her warmly. "You look like you could use a good cup of chai."

"Is it that obvious?" she laughed, surprised by the old man's enthusiasm.

"Well, my dear, I meet a lot of people every day," he said, immediately pouring chai from his patila into a glass.

"Here you go, *beti*," he said, addressing her as daughter. "You live around here?" he asked smiling.

"Ah, yes, the Koliwadahs," Aditi answered.

"An important part of Mumbai's beginnings," he noted.

She took a sip, appreciating the recognition of her heritage.

"Could I ask you what work you do?" he followed up.

"Sales, in a call center."

"Oh, wonderful!" he exclaimed. "It's not easy for a young woman from the Koliwadahs to build such a career," he added. "Office politics, prejudice, traditions, and men," he explained.

"Ha! That's very true," she laughed, surprised by his insight. "It can be hard to get ahead, dada," Aditi admitted. "It hasn't really happened for me yet."

"Yet! That is the magic word, beti. It is darkest before the dawn, my dear. You just keep on going. Make sure you show up every day and put in the work. Your luck will come. And, if you ever need a word of advice from an old chaiwallah, you come see me."

"Thank you. I will do that," she said, feeling safe and uplifted by his words.

While enjoying the chai, she glanced at her watch. *Oh! Vishal will be waiting,* she thought.

"How much is it, dada? I need to go."

"This one is on me, beti. I'm happy we had a good talk," he said warmly.

"That's very generous. Thank you. I will be back again. Goodnight." She finished her glass and placed it back on his cart. *What a friendly old man,* Aditi thought as she walked back to her scooter.

When Aditi reached her aunt's home in the Koliwadahs, she called out, "Vishal?" before opening the aluminum door. The room was filled with the aroma of their local Koli spices, their masala.

"Aai!" Vishal shouted at Aditi from behind the table.

"Hello, *bhachi,*" her auntie greeted her niece warmly, stepping out from the kitchen. "Your boy is full and ready to go," she added.

"Thank you so much, *kaku,*" Aditi replied with gratitude. "Chal, Vishal," she said, telling him to hurry.

After their familiar short walk through the pitch-dark alleys, they were home. Aditi and Vishal both dropped their bags next to the small dining table.

"What were you working on tonight, baala?" she asked him, curiosity sparkling in her eyes. "Let's quickly review it together."

Vishal pulled out one of his books and slumped onto the seat. "Sure," he said, his voice hinting reluctance. "I was just going through some math questions," he explained, flipping open the book.

"Show me!" Aditi said enthusiastically. She scanned the page as he pointed to the first question. "Interesting," she murmured, reading through.

"It's four and a half," Vishal noted with pride in his voice.

"How did you get to that answer?" she asked excitedly.

"Well," his eyes lit up, "he travels at sixty kilometers per hour for one hundred and twenty kilometers. That is two hours. Then he's driving forty kilometers per hour for sixty kilometers. That is one and a half hours. And then twenty kilometers per hour for twenty kilometers. That's another hour. In total, it's four and a half hours," he concluded, a proud smirk spreading across his face.

"Very good!" Aditi praised, her pride in him shining through. "You see! It is just like what Swami Sivananda said on reflecting on yourself to improve weaknesses. Previously, you had difficulty with math, and you didn't focus on it much. Now that you are putting in more effort, you can see the results." She smiled proudly.

He nodded. She enveloped him in a warm hug, her affection palpable. "Let's go through the rest, and then we'll watch that animation movie you wanted to see."

Arjun

Mumbai experienced heavy downfalls during this year's monsoon. As usual, the rainy season brought its challenges, like city-wide power cuts, heavy traffic jams, and waterlogging. The results included wastewater flooding in many homes on the ground floor. During the last few months, the Mumbaikers had shown their resilience, as always, continuing on with their daily lives and finding creative ways to overcome the obstacles the annual monsoon brought. Now that the rains had stopped, this new season brought much needed relief with cooler air in the mornings and evenings, although the afternoons remained hot and humid as the residual moisture from the monsoon lingered.

Arjun and Rohit sat beneath the branches of the ancient bodhi tree at Chimbai Square. It was mostly deserted, except for all the fruit and vegetable stall owners who were half asleep, right before the usual late afternoon shopping rush. Arjun grimaced as he took a sip from the bottle in his hand.

"Where did you get this poison, bhai? Even paracetamol can't get rid of the headaches this tharra gives me," he muttered.

Rohit shrugged, his eyes shadowed and weary. "I know, but

I still have a few bottles left. We need to finish it," he replied, determined.

Arjun leaned closer, urgency flashing in his eyes. "Let's talk about our next move. You know I am in big trouble." His voice broke with anxiety.

Rohit placed a reassuring hand on Arjun's shoulder. "I know very well. Don't worry, I've got something lined up for both of us. My friend knows this guy..." His sentence trailed off as they were interrupted.

"*Namaste, kaise ho?*" The chaiwallah greeted them warmly in Hindi, instead of local Marathi, face creased into a genial smile as he held out two glasses of chai.

That new guy, Arjun thought.

"What do you want, old man?" Rohit snapped, irritation flaring in his eyes.

"I just made a fresh batch of chai, and you two look like you could use a refreshment," the chaiwallah said, extending the glasses towards them with a gesture of kindness.

"You think we're going to pay you for this?" Rohit laughed bitterly.

"Oh no," the chaiwallah laughed softly. "This is on me."

Arjun and Rohit exchanged a puzzled look. After some hesitation, they reluctantly accepted the glasses, feeling awkward about the undeserving generosity. "What do you want?" Rohit asked, suspicion lacing his words.

The chaiwallah smiled, patient and unoffended. "I come in peace," he replied softly, his eyes twinkling with sincerity.

Arjun lifted the glass. The sweet, spicy aroma of the chai engulfed him. He took a tentative sip then another, feeling warmth spread through him. He nodded at Rohit in approval.

"Where are you from?" Arjun inquired. "South India?"

"Yes, a long time ago," the old man said. "Now I move around. I enjoy selling chai and meeting new people."

When they finished their tea and returned the glasses,

Rohit's demeanor hardened. "Your chai is good, old man, but don't think we will treat you any differently around here," he said sternly.

Arjun stared at the chaiwallah, sensing a profound kindness that both comforted and unnerved him.

"Enjoy the rest of your day," the old man said, his voice gentle as he walked back to his cart.

"Weird old guy," Rohit muttered as they watched him go.

Arjun didn't respond. The kindness made him feel uneasy.

"Come," Rohit urged. "I feel refreshed. Let's talk about our next move."

They stood up, strolled across the square, and turned into the northwestern Chimbai Road, passing the different vegetable stalls. On Perry Cross Road, the speakers of the local masjid went off: "*Allahu akbar! Allahu akbar!*" which translated to, "God is the greatest, God is the greatest." Arjun and Rohit continued straight ahead toward the main road as some local residents entered the mosque. The speakers continued, "*Ashhadu an la ilaha illallah!*" I bear witness that there is no God but Allah. "*Ashhadu anna Muhammadan Rasulullah!*" I bear witness that Muhammed is the messenger of Allah. "*Hayya 'ala-s-Salah!*" Hasten to prayer. *Hayya 'ala-l-Falah!*" Hasten to success. "*Allahu akbar! Allahu akbar!*" God is the greatest, God is the greatest. "*La ilaha illallah!*" There is no God but Allah.

Reaching the Master Vinayak Road, they turned left and eventually reached the Carter Road promenade. They found a shady bench to sit on beneath the swaying palm trees separating the main road crowded by cars and rickshaws and the now quiet pedestrian promenade.

"Wait here, I need to piss," Rohit said brusquely, leaping over the low stone wall in between the promenade and the sea to walk across the rocks toward a bunch of mangrove trees.

As Arjun saw Rohit disappear among the mangrove trees, his gaze turned to the turbulent waves crashing against the shore, his mind suddenly a whirlpool of anxiety. *How will I ever pay off my debt? Eight lakh rupees,* he thought, letting out a big sigh.

Arjun felt his foot get hit by something hard, and his dark emotions instantly subsided. Looking down, he saw the familiar brown-reddish leather ball in front of him. He smiled, bent forward to pick it up, and spotted a group of children in the distance staring at him. He got up, shouting; "Which one of you is Sachin Tendulkar?"

"That's me!" a young girl in brown shorts and white t-shirt yelled confidently. Arjun threw the ball skillfully onto the promenade bricks with a slight spin towards her. She waited until the ball hit the ground to react to its spinning direction and caught it comfortably with both hands.

Arjun nodded, satisfied with her catch.

"Listen, bhai," Rohit said, suddenly standing before him.

Arjun turned back to Rohit, his demeanor serious once again and sat back down, the joyful moment vanishing as quickly as it had come.

"My friend reached out to me," Rohit continued. "He knows a guard that works at a house on Pali Hill. The family just left for Goa. There's easy access from the back garden. We'll go tonight. Are you with me?"

Arjun's expression hardened. "Yes," he replied, determined.

Sumeet

A T THAT MOMENT, Sumeet stood in front of a U-shaped form of connected desks in the main conference room. On his left, across the hall, was the automotive factory, and on his right, the company garden. He glanced at his watch. *Five minutes left,* he thought. His footsteps echoed softly as he wandered around the room, absorbed in his thoughts. *I hope they show some positive energy and optimism today. It's been tough on everyone, but we've come a long way,* he convinced himself. He stared out the window at the gardener meticulously trimming boxwood. With a twinge of envy, he contemplated the man's tranquil existence, harmoniously engaged with nature all day. Sumeet noticed the pink-rose ringed parakeets flitting among the mango trees and recollected he had once read that more than half of Mumbai's trees were non-native.

"Hello, boss."

The voice behind him snapped him out of his daydream. Sumeet turned to see Prashant, the newest member of their team. "How's your day been?" he inquired, trying to infuse warmth into his tone.

"Good," Prashant replied.

Sumeet noticed his leadership team and their most senior

members trailing behind him, chatting animatedly, holding laptops, teacups, and notebooks. *They're very sociable together, but this energy drains every time they see me,* he thought, watching them enter the room.

"Hello, Vikas." Sumeet greeted the well-dressed man of equal seniority whom his boss Radhika had assigned to his department to help implement the re-structure and operational changes. "Thanks for joining us."

"Sumeet." Vikas nodded and responded in a lackluster tone.

"Okay, everyone," Sumeet said, "please sit so we can get started." He positioned himself at the head of the table and looked around the room wearing a smile, but few met his gaze. Most were entranced by their screens.

"Thanks for joining. I hope everyone has had a good day so far," he began, but silence greeted him. "Let me start by acknowledging that the last few months have been tough on everyone." He paused but didn't get any reactions. "However," he continued, "we have made tremendous progress in many areas, wouldn't you agree?" He scanned the room for agreement, but instead caught Shanthi's sarcastic smile directed at Prashant. *Continuing to sow her seeds of dissent,* he thought, frustrated.

"We have taken input from all your teams and implemented actions for more than 80 percent of the key issues we identified together." He pointed to the slide on the large screen. "We will track progress and continue to work on that last 20 percent in the coming weeks." He paused again; the silence in the room was deafening.

"Team, could I please ask you to close your laptops and pay attention? This is important," he urged. Sumeet noticed Vikas ignored his request. "This is not just for your information," he continued. "These are actions we need to take as the leadership team, and they will greatly help our people."

Priya, one of his department managers, nodded, but the room's energy remained flat.

"Look," he began emphatically, "I know directions from the top were confusing at times, but we have now clarified many things. Don't you agree?" He searched for affirmation, but found blank faces instead. "If there are questions or concerns, please let me know now or after this meeting if that's more comfortable. We have simplified ways of working with each other and the region, reduced the number of meetings, filled critical roles, and set up an active social program. We are making good progress!" he said, trying to excite his team.

"Shanthi? Priya? Prashant? Any feedback to share?" he asked his direct leadership team, hoping to spark engagement.

Sumeet saw Shanthi glance skeptically at Vikas, and pressed, "Shanthi?"

"Nothing to share," she scoffed, seemingly irritated by being chosen to respond.

"Team, this is our business. We are the leadership team. I expect you to propose ideas for us to improve," Sumeet appealed, feeling frustrated.

Prashant, the newcomer, voiced a suggestion to include certain updates in monthly instead of weekly reports to save the team time. The idea gave Sumeet much needed relief. He complimented him on the proposal and agreed to take it up with the head office.

When silence kicked in once again, Sumeet focused on Vikas at the back of the room. "Vikas? Anything you want to share?"

"No, nothing from me," he answered firmly.

As expected, Sumeet thought, annoyed.

Wrapping up the meeting, Sumeet thanked everyone for their hard work and asked them to hit targets this month. Some nodded, but his words felt mostly hollow as the team dispersed. He walked back to the window and sighed deeply. *How can I make this team thrive? It has been six months, but they are still not on my side.* Sadness crept in. *Shanthi and Vikas's negative influence remain palpable.* His gaze fell back on the gardener. *Can I really turn this around?*

He looked at his watch and panicked. *My next call starts in five minutes. Again, back-to-back meetings until evening,* he thought.

*

THE NEXT MORNING, Sumeet stood in front of the chaiwallah's cart after his walk.

"Don't drink too fast, beta," the chaiwallah commented, watching him. "You need to give the aroma and spices a little time to create that moment of serenity."

"Yes, sorry, I'm in a hurry this morning," Sumeet replied, quickly sipping the rich, velvety liquid. After the last gulp, he placed the glass back on the man's cart. "How much, dada? This time I am paying."

"If you insist," the chaiwallah smiled. "Twenty rupees, please."

Sumeet paid and left waving.

"Good luck, beta. Don't let them get to you!" the chaiwallah called after him.

Sumeet turned and smiled, then headed home. As he walked through the door and removed his shoes, he nodded to the maid mopping the hallway. In the kitchen, he drank some water.

Manisha called out from the couch, "How was your walk? I think you will be late for your meeting."

"Yes, yes, I need to hurry," he replied, feeling slightly annoyed by her usual concern about his work, but not his well-being.

In the car, feeling refreshed and fully suited, he received a message from his boss Radhika. She said she was disappointed with the factory's cost-saving progress so far this month and wanted to see improvement immediately. Nausea hit him, knowing he had to confront Shanthi and Vikas, which had been difficult since he took on this role. Radhika ended the message by telling him she expected him to get the results required and reminded him he was hired based on the many recommendations she had received.

That's very motivating, he thought. Sumeet sighed, frustrated with Radhika's condescending and whip-cracking leadership style, doing nothing to unlock things for him. He replied with an affirmation of his commitment but immediately began to worry how he would approach Vikas and Shanthi; he knew they would push back.

Arjun

THE COLORFUL, LOUD, and fragrant Pali Market in Bandra West during the day was now transformed into a haunted quiet deep into the night. Arjun and Rohit, wearing backpacks, moved like shadows along the Pali Mala Road, only a fifteen-minute walk from Chimbai Square. They then turned left into the hilly, leafy Nargis Dutt Road. After a few minutes, Rohit stopped.

"You see that white house on the left?" he pointed out, whispering.

"Yes," Arjun confirmed.

"Wait here. Let me check it out first." Rohit disappeared into the narrow dark alley beside the house, leaving Arjun alone.

The loneliness increased Arjun's anxiety. He leaned on one of the large tamarind trees beside the road. *Aaicha gho! I look suspicious standing here alone,* he cursed nervously under his breath.

A few minutes later, Arjun was relieved to see Rohit's face poke out from the alley and signal him. He quickly crept across the road and dove into the alley.

"The garden is on the other side of this wall," Rohit whispered. "First, you lift me up then I pull you onto the wall."

With his back against the wall and knees bent, Arjun intertwined his fingers and held them against his stomach for stability. Rohit held onto Arjun's shoulders and placed his left foot in Arjun's hand to push himself up. With his right foot on Arjun's shoulder, he waited.

"Glass shards!" Rohit whispered sharply from atop.

Arjun watched Rohit balance himself on the wall, move further down, and squat with his arms out.

"Pull yourself up here. Fewer shards on this side. Hurry up!"

Arjun used a small indentation in the wall as a launchpad to push himself up with ease and scale the wall with Rohit's help. *Muscle memory from all the training during my youth, I guess,* Arjun thought proudly.

They landed like cats in the grass on the other side. "This way," Rohit urged, tiptoeing through the garden toward a door beside several large windows. "This must be the maid's room!" Rohit smiled broadly at Arjun as the knob turned to open the door.

Arjun's heart started to pound like a bass drum as he followed Rohit into the small dark maid's room, their flashlight beams barely cutting through the pitch black.

"Come!" Rohit said, exiting the room and turning left.

Trailing behind Rohit, Arjun got distracted when he saw a small round table with shiny statues. *These must be brass, copper, or even gold,* he thought, picking up a glittering statue of a peacock. Then his beam shone across the wall revealing a family photo. *Rich, lucky bastard,* Arjun thought, watching a man in a suit pictured beside a woman and two children.

"Come!" Rohit said in a stage whisper behind him as he beamed his light on a room roadside of the house. "This guy has two!" Rohit laughed, holding up laptops.

"Shh!" Arjun replied.

"Check the drawers of the desk," Rohit instructed him.

"Keep your light down! This room can be seen from the road," Arjun urged, shifting through stationary from one drawer to the next. "Look!" Arjun said shining light on his discovery beneath some magazines then holding up his treasure toward Rohit.

"All thousand-rupee bills?" Rohit asked excitedly.

"I think so," Arjun confirmed, shifting through.

"The bastard tried to hide it from his wife!" Rohit laughed out loud.

"Quiet!" Arjun hissed, wiping away beads of sweat from his forehead. "This isn't a game!"

"Take it easy, bhai," Rohit replied.

After putting the cash into his bag, Arjun continued his search through the other drawers but found nothing valuable. When he turned, shining his light around the room, he could no longer see Rohit. "Rohit?" he whispered sharply. He waited, but there was no answer. Flustered, he walked out of the room and scanned the living area. *Where the hell did he go?* Now Arjun was more nervous than ever.

Arjun froze at a sudden loud noise from the front of the house . *What is that?* he thought, listening carefully. *Someone coming home?*

"Turn off the light!" Arjun suddenly heard from the stairway. He tiptoed to the front door where filtered light from the street revealed Rohit's shadow on the steps above.

"Rohit?" Arjun whispered. Sweat streamed down his face.

"Don't move!" Rohit replied.

Arjun stood in breathless silence, every creak and rustle amplifying his fear. He saw Rohit carefully gliding down the stairs.

"We need to go now," Arjun whispered, pushing Rohit back toward the living room.

"I think it was just a dog," Rohit noted.

Back in the hallway near the maid's room, Arjun turned around to see Rohit coming toward him carrying a luxurious flatscreen television.

"Jackpot," Rohit said, leaning heavily to one side and wobbling with every step.

"No!" Arjun snarl-whispered. "We can't carry that!" After waiting for a moment, Arjun's ears were again drawn to the front door. "Stop! I hear footsteps on the pathway outside."

Rohit quietly lowered the screen, dropping it onto the couch, then scurried toward the hallway.

Arjun followed him back through the maid's room, and they slipped into the darkness of the back garden.

"Okay, let's go. Don't panic!" Rohit urged.

When Rohit stood on top of the wall, Arjun grabbed his arm in desperation.

"Argh! Help me up!" Arjun hissed. Adrenaline helped him swing up atop the wall. After jumping back down into the alley, Arjun noticed his sandal was painted red from the blood gushing out of the bottom of his foot. "Damn shards," he whispered, gritting his teeth.

"Put your arm around me," Rohit said.

Leaning heavily on Rohit's shoulder, Arjun hobbled to the end of the alley. Sporadic rain drops started to fall as they peeked out the alley, scanning for danger.

"I told you it was just a dog," Rohit said, carrying Arjun down Nargis Dutt Road. "We can't take you to a hospital now. We'd get caught," Rohit said.

They reached the intersection down the hill on Pali Mala Road and sat down on the sidewalk.

"Bastard, you left a trail of blood," Rohit said. Suddenly he stood up. "We're lucky," he said, trying to flag down a rickshaw heading toward them.

The rickshaw stopped and Rohit lifted him into the

backseat. Resting his head, Arjun felt his dopamine levels crash down, intensifying his pain. Rohit ripped off his sleeve and hastily bandaged Arjun's foot. "Keep the pressure on. It's not too bad."

Rohit saw the rickshaw driver evaluating the situation of the two men. "What are you looking at?" Rohit snarled. He leaned close to Arjun and whispered, "I will take your backpack and meet my guy first thing in the morning. Then we'll meet later, and we'll see what to do about your foot. First, take a rest."

Arjun nodded weakly, handing over his bag. Stabbing pain shot through his foot, but he felt relieved that they got away.

"Chimbai Road. Chal!" Rohit instructed the driver.

The rickshaw sped off into the dark as heavy rain started to fall.

Aditi

AFTER DROPPING VISHAL at school in the morning, Aditi turned back on her scooter toward Chimbai Square and stopped at a mobile sugarcane juice cart. After Aditi ordered, the vendor ran two sugarcane sticks through his two heavy rollers that were quickly crushed, squeezing the fragrant yellow-green drink into a transparent tall glass. The man added a little chaat masala and a small piece of lime before handing it over.

As she drank the sweet and slightly spiced liquid, she spotted a group of dark-toned women with children. The women wore faded, frayed sarees with different types of tattoos across their arms. Aditi knew these were not Kolis. Rather, they were women from the Matang tribe who lived in shacks on land behind the apartment blocks facing Chimbai Square. The Matang originated from the Narmada Valley in Madhya Pradesh in central India and were known for rope making, non-surgical cattle castration, leather curing, and arts.

Aditi watched them as the group sat down on the bricks of Chimbai. One of the women started setting up two sturdy wooden poles with metal footplates. Her rough hands deftly tied a coarse rope between the poles, creating a makeshift tightrope. To secure the poles, the woman used heavy bricks and arranged them carefully to ensure stability. A young boy in a singlet and shorts stood patiently nearby, watching his mother put up the structure. When the rope was tight, the boy picked up his balancing stick, placed one bare foot onto the rope and outstretched his arms for stability. The woman placed a piece of cloth in front of the rope for donations. With much care, and trying to capture attention from any of the housewives shopping, the boy slowly placed one foot in front of the other. When he reached the middle of the rope, he stood still, his body suddenly shaking from side to side to make the audience believe he was about to fall, but then regained his composure and continued on until the end. Mother and son looked around to see who was watching their performance, but no one was. The boy then re-started the routine from the other side.

Aditi shifted her glance toward three women in front of the supermarket, believing they were of a similar age to her. Their makeup was light and natural, and they wore dark business skirts of colorful silk, white blouses, and thick black sunglasses, and they carried leather designer handbags. They chatted away, paying no attention to the Matang performance happening right next to them.

Two completely different worlds, Aditi thought. *They cannot even slightly imagine each other's lives.* Continuing to observe the well-dressed women, she sighed. *Even with my university degree and work experience, can I really move up the corporate ladder and join their world? Maybe that's what scared off Vishal's father.* She placed the empty glass back on the vendor's aluminum counter, handed over forty rupees, and walked back to her scooter.

From across the square, Aditi saw the chaiwallah wave, signaling her to come see him. She hesitated for a moment as it was time to drive to work but decided that the old man's kindness and warm velvety masala chai would do her well.

"Good morning, beti! How are you this morning?" The old man smiled broadly, his eyes twinkling.

"I'm well, dada. You are starting early," Aditi noted.

"Oh, I'm here before the sun rises and late after the sun sets," he replied happily, stroking his white beard. "Old men don't need much sleep," he added with a chuckle. "Chai?" he asked.

Aditi nodded, immediately feeling invigorated by the chaiwallah's energy.

As Aditi watched the old man pour his concoction, she suddenly asked, "Dada, do you ever worry about people not liking your chai?"

The old man's face lit up, deepening his wrinkles. "Oh yes, sometimes, dear." He smiled. After a pause he added, "But then I remind myself that it's based on personal preference. Something I cannot change."

Aditi smiled at his answer.

"Our mind is a wonderful tool, isn't it?" he noted. "We must take great care it. We need to feed it the right information. We need to clean it, or weeds can grow, and we need to decide which thoughts are true and helpful."

"Right." Aditi nodded in between sips.

"We cannot just let the mind lazily wander around like that," he smirked, pointing at a street dog passing by.

Aditi let out a laugh. But after a moment, she turned serious. "Sometimes it can be difficult to fight off fear and self-doubt."

"Oh yes, beti," he agreed immediately, "but we also must remember that our fears and doubts are mostly based on the past or future. We should try to focus on the present," he said.

Aditi nodded.

"With time and consistency, we can teach our mind to see the world the way we want to see it, my dear. That's one of the beautiful things in life. It's all an illusion." He smiled kindly.

Aditi let the old man's surprising knowledge sink in. She

reflected on the doubt creeping into her own mind while observing the three women in front of the supermarket. *Be careful with your self-talk, Diti,* she warned herself.

"And," the chaiwallah continued, "over time, I have come to believe that my chai is just marvelous!" he exclaimed.

Aditi laughed out loud. "I agree with that, dada. But, speaking of the present, I need to get to work."

Arjun

ARJUN WOKE UP on his mattress with sharp pains in his foot. He winced as he lifted his head to inspect it. *Those damn shards,* he thought. The fabric wrapped around his foot was completely red, but no blood had spilled onto his mattress. *Rohit did a good job,* Arjun thought, feeling some gratitude. He sighed deeply. *Let me get up and see how I feel.* He put his hand down to push himself up and leaned onto the wall to stand on his legs. "Aaicha gho!" He cursed aloud. The pain shot through him like a dagger. For a moment, he considered lying back down, but he clenched his teeth and forced himself to move. He stumbled toward the kitchen sink to get a cup of water. "Walk it off, you bastard," he barked out loud, trying to motivate himself.

Unwashed and wearing the same clothes as last night, he stumbled out the door. *The cuts are too deep,* he thought. *I need help.* Every step felt like it could be the one to send him crashing to the ground. It took much longer than normal for him to reach Chimbai Square. Before he could see if Rohit was there, he noticed the chaiwallah swiftly walking toward him from across the square.

"It looks like you need help, my friend," the old man said, showing genuine concern.

"Not now, old man," Arjun said, trying to forge ahead.

"Come, beta," the chaiwallah insisted kindly. "You can hardly walk. You need help now. Let me take you."

"Take me where?" Arjun said defensively.

"I know someone who can help you," the chaiwallah replied. Arjun hesitated, weighing his options. Taking a few steps forward, he caught a glimpse of the bodhi tree and saw Rohit wasn't there. *Put your pride aside, Arjun,* he thought reluctantly.

Arjun allowed the chaiwallah to guide him forward with an arm around his shoulder. After passing the supermarket, hardware store, and pharmacy, they stopped in front of the general practitioner's office beside the liquor store.

"Wait! I can't afford this. This is for rich people," Arjun said and lifted his arm off the old man's shoulder. But the chaiwallah held on with surprising strength.

"Don't worry about that," the chaiwallah reassured.

"No, really. I can't afford this doctor," Arjun said desperately.

"The doctor is a friend of mine. No need to worry," the old man replied, his eyes radiating kindness. "Let's take care of your foot now, before it gets worse."

The chaiwallah's words and body language defeated Arjun's doubts. *Maybe this old man can get me a steep discount.* Before he knew it, the chaiwallah had helped him through the door, and they stood inside the bright white practice.

The chaiwallah sat him down and said, "I will be right back."

Arjun's anxiety dropped, seeing he was alone in the waiting room. *Why is he helping me?* Arjun wondered as the chaiwallah talked with the woman behind the counter.

"Come, beta. The doctor can see you now," the old man

said. "He has already become a loyal customer of mine," he added with a smile.

Arjun had a last spurt of hesitation but got up and hobbled alongside the chaiwallah. He noticed the receptionist staring at him with contempt.

"Good afternoon, dada," the young doctor greeted the chaiwallah kindly.

"Hello, Doctor. Thank you for seeing us so quickly. My good friend here hurt his foot, and I hope you can help."

"This is your good friend?" the doctor asked, eyeing Arjun curiously.

"Yes," the chaiwallah said confidently.

The old man's reply made Arjun look at the chaiwallah with suspicion. *What does he want from me?* All of a sudden Arjun panicked, realizing he had given all the stolen money to Rohit, but it was too late to walk out.

"Okay," the doctor said, "let me see how I can help your friend." He carefully started unwrapping the blood-soaked bandage. "The cuts are deep," the doctor declared. "Does this hurt?" he asked, touching Arjun's foot.

"Only the bottom of my foot," Arjun answered. *If I can't pay, I won't be able to walk around Chimbai,* Arjun thought, feeling anxious as the doctor continued to inspect his wounds.

"You will be better in no time," the doctor affirmed. With the help of the doctor and the chaiwallah, Arjun moved onto the examination table. After his treatment, Arjun walked out from the doctor's office into the reception area by himself, with little trouble.

"These are for you," the receptionist said, handing over strips of pills and ointment. As she explained what to take and when, Arjun didn't listen, only worrying about the bill she would quote.

"How much is it? Can I pay in installments?" he asked hesitantly, wanting clarity.

"Everything has been paid," she replied with disdain.

"What do you mean?" Arjun immediately said, thinking she must be mistaken.

"Well, I don't know why, but that friendly new chaiwallah paid your bill," she explained.

Arjun smiled in confusion and picked up his medicine.

Standing outside, he put some weight onto his freshly bandaged foot. It felt much better. Across the road, he stared at the chaiwallah back at his cart serving customers. *This old man paid? He doesn't even know me.* Scanning across the square, he saw Rohit sitting beneath the bodhi tree and started walking toward him.

"Looking good, beta!" he heard the chaiwallah shout from his left.

"Ah, yes! Yes, it feels much better!" Arjun smiled hesitantly, unsure how to respond after the enormous gesture. "Thank you, sir," he added. He saw Rohit waving at him to come over and was happy to have an excuse to move along.

"That looks professional bhai," Rohit said, pointing at his foot. "You went to that practice? We could have gone somewhere cheaper."

"Never mind," Arjun said not wanting to get into it.

"Stupid. I told you to watch those shards." Arjun sat down. "Have a drink. It will help with the pain."

Arjun took a long, familiar gulp while gazing at the busy chaiwallah.

"Easy, bhai, we have all day!" Rohit laughed. "As promised, I got it all organized this morning." Rohit opened his backpack and explained that the guard tipping them got one-third of the loot, leaving them thirteen thousand each. Arjun nodded, accepting the money, but knowing this was nowhere near enough to get rid of his troubles.

"Don't worry, I am lining up other opportunities, and I

am working on something really big," Rohit said, trying to put Arjun's mind at ease.

With money in hand, Arjun suddenly got up.

"Where are you going?" Rohit called out, but Arjun didn't respond.

"How much do I owe you, old man?" Arjun said in front of the chaiwallah's cart.

"What for?" the chaiwallah smiled.

"The medical bill," he stated.

"You don't owe me anything. Just be more careful next time," the chaiwallah requested.

Arjun's suspicion rose, and he decided to hand over two thousand rupees, but the old man rejected his offer.

"Why do you help me and don't want anything in return?" Arjun asked.

"Why not?" the chaiwallah smiled.

Because I don't deserve it, Arjun thought, but answered, "Up to you, old man."

"What is your name?" the chaiwallah asked before he could walk off.

"Arjun."

"It is really nice to meet you, Arjun," the chaiwallah said kindly.

Arjun nodded, feeling the old man meant it, and started to walk south down Chimbai Road.

The street was deserted this afternoon, with most residents at work or hiding from the hot sun. After a while, a woman's bright yellow saree fluttered in the wind against the dull surroundings, like a burst of sunlight on a dark, cloudy day. But Arjun was oblivious to the world around him, mulling over the undeserving kindness he had received. After a few minutes, he veered right into his narrow alleyway in the Koliwadahs.

As he turned the corner, a man in sunglasses, a black leather jacket, and black jeans stood in front of him. *Aaicha gho!* His internal alarm rang out before the wind was violently knocked from him by a thunderous punch to the stomach. The pain forced him to drop to his knees. He braced for another blow, but nothing came. *They will kill me!* his thoughts screamed as he noticed the gleaming black leather shoes before him.

"You bastard!" a voice roared. When Arjun raised his head to meet the man's eyes, another attack came from behind the man in black—a knee to his head that jerked his body back and slammed his skull against the dirt road. Blood oozed from his nose across his face. *This time they are going to kill me.*

Before he could beg for his life, the second assailant mounted him, unleashing a nasty ground and pound onto his face. His vision blurred, seeing only fists as his head bounced from side to side. "Don't dirty my shirt, you bastard!" the man yelled, hitting him.

"Enough!" commanded the man in black. The assault halted. Rolling to his right side, Arjun gasped for air as he took out the stack of bills from his pocket, before slowly inching himself upward.

"Look!" he yelled out, desperately holding up the money. "Here is thirteen thousand. I got more in my house. Really!" He could feel shattered fragments of his teeth, gritty between his tongue and cheeks.

"That's what you said last time," the man mocked.

"No! I swear! I have more!" The man in the black leather jacket yanked Arjun up.

"If you make us walk for nothing, you are dead," he threatened, shoving him forward.

Arjun stumbled, cradling his aching stomach with one hand and touching his bleeding nose with the other. After a brief walk, they reached his front door. Arjun entered first, quickly bending over in front of his mattress. With trembling hands, he unearthed a stack of bills. "Here, that's five more," he offered.

The man in black snatched the money, his face etched with disdain. Arjun scrambled toward his simple chair, using it to reach the top of his closet. His hand emerged with more cash. "Here. Here," he pleaded, handing over the bills.

"Thirteen thousand. Plus, five. Plus, six. That's twenty-four," Arjun stuttered, looking down. "Wait!" he quickly cried, anticipating another brutal beating. He pointed to a statue atop the closet. "I also have that brass Ganesha statue. It will be another five or six thousand."

"We're not taking a statue, you bastard. Cash only," the man in all black sneered, looking around the room. "Ahh." He smiled. "But I will take this for my son," the man said picking up the cricket bat that stood on a small side table leaning against the wall.

"No! Come on, please don't take the bat!" Arjun pleaded, stretching out his arm.

"Oh, this is valuable to you? Good, that will teach you!" the man laughed, stepping back with bat in hand.

Without warning, Arjun got shoved against the closet. "When will you get all?" the other thug demanded.

"It is coming soon. Really! I got a big job lined up."

"I'm counting this as interest. The next time we come back, we need all of it. The whole eight lakh rupees." The man in black clamped his hand around Arjun's throat, squeezing just enough to steal his breath. "We will be back in a few weeks," he declared coldly, his eyes boring into Arjun's soul. "If you don't cough up all of it next time, you know what will happen."

He pushed Arjun's head against the wall before releasing him. Both men exited the room.

Arjun slumped against the wall, tears running down his cheeks as he stared at the now empty side table.

Aditi

Aditi hung up the phone inside her cubicle at MumbaiKonnect and started scrolling through her emails. Suddenly, her eyes lit up at the subject line of an email. *Oh my!* she thought. Miraculously, it was another invitation for an interview at a different call center. *Maybe that chaiwallah was right about my luck!* she thought, reading through the message. Aditi realized that all available interview slots were during the workdays this week, similar to last time. *The role is the same, but it has a direct report, which will help develop my people management skills,* she thought, hopeful at the prospect.

She got more and more nervous as she walked to Veda's desk thinking, *Last time she rejected my request, but now that I just acquired Cotton Bazaar as our new client, she should be more lenient.*

"Aditi," Veda said enthusiastically as Aditi approached. "Congratulations on getting us that big new client. Well done. Reviewing these last few months, you have been getting good results. Now I need some others in the team to do the same," she smirked.

"Thank you, Veda," Aditi replied, thinking now would be a good time to make her request. "I came to see you to ask if

I could leave a little early on any of the evenings this week. Wednesday, Thursday, or Friday? Is there a day that suits best?" Aditi requested.

Aditi saw Veda's expression suddenly harden upon her request. "No, Aditi, not this week. I've planned workshops every day, and I need you there," Veda answered.

"I see. Unfortunately, it has to be during a weekday. How about next Monday then?" Aditi asked kindly, considering that was the last interview option provided in the email.

"Monday afternoon is our final workshop session. And while having these workshops, we still need to achieve daily targets. We are behind on our key performance indicators. Whatever you need to do, do it before or after work," Veda said and turned her attention back to her screen.

"Okay, will do," Aditi said, feeling déjà vu as she walked visibly distressed toward the quiet staircase behind the emergency exit.

"Gupshup Kendra. How can I help?" a voice answered.

"Hello, this is Aditi Sawant. I received an email for an interview."

"Let me check," the voice replied. "Ah yes, your interview with Krish Sir," she confirmed.

"Unfortunately, I won't be available this week or next Monday. Do you have any evening or weekend slots?" Aditi requested.

"No, madam, you must choose one of the options in the email."

Aditi reflected on the very few interview invitations she had received these last years, the interview that slipped away last week, and Veda's comment about the Monday afternoon workshop. *I can't let this one get away.*

"Madam?" the voice asked.

It hasn't happened for me at MumbaiKonnect, so I need to

move on, to move up, Aditi thought determined. "Book me in for Monday morning please," she confirmed.

"Done. See you then."

Arjun

ARJUN WOKE UP with a wince. *First my foot, and now this. I feel like I got hit by a bus.*

Carefully, his hands touched across his face and midriff. *Ribs are sore, face is bruised, but nothing is broken.* He entered his bathroom to get a better look in the mirror. A hematoma bulged in the middle of his forehead from the knee strike he received, large black circles shadowed his eyes, and his cheeks were swollen from the ground and pound he received. He rinsed his mouth and inspected the damage. *No teeth missing, just small cracks in my molars. I still got off okay,* he thought with some relief. *Next time I won't be so lucky.*

With his hands, he washed away the dried blood from his face, undressed, and sat on his plastic stool in the corner of the small bathroom. As he poured water over his head and neck with a small plastic mug, he noticed the water turning red. Running his fingers across his scalp, he felt the wound at the back of his head from his fall backwards after getting hit by the man's knee.

He decided to rest against the tiles. *What have I achieved in the last twenty years in Mumbai?* he thought. Unable to give himself a satisfying answer, his thoughts raced back to the reason he left Jalna. With his head in his hands, he reminded himself he'd gone through this a million times. *I cannot stay, and I can't go back.*

He forced himself to snap out of his thoughts. Fighting nostalgia as he dried off.

Giving in, he closed his eyes for a moment and was instantly transported back, remembering the smell of freshly tilled soil, the hibiscus and jasmine, seeing a peacock strutting in the field, and taking in the sunset behind the rows of sunflowers every August. His eyes started to tear, reminiscing about that day his father taught him how to use the plough with patience, and how they had walked across the land together to plant cotton or sorghum.

Suddenly, the broad proud smile of his father appeared before him. His father cheering from the tribunes of the Narendra Modi stadium at his first ever inter-state match in Vadodara, Gujarat, as part of the regional West Zone Under-19 Cricket Tournament. Then the visual of that pivotal moment appeared. The spinning bowler looked menacing right before he threw the ball. Due to his focus and preparation, Arjun somehow saw the ball move in slow-motion, giving him ample time to switch his stance and sweep the ball with an aggressive swing into the tribunes on his right to give his team the win. Everyone cheered, with Arjun spotting his father's immense pride in the tribunes amidst the crowd.

Still standing in front of the mirror, Arjun squeezed his eyes tight to relive the happiness of that moment. *Where would it all have led to?* he wondered, as a tear ran down his cheek.

"Look at this shithole!" he suddenly shouted, opening his eyes. "Look at me!" his voice echoed with anger and regret. "The only thing I had in Mumbai was Savitri, but I couldn't keep her," he muttered. The memory of her leaving him soon after marriage hurt as much as the bruises on his face. *Useless bastard,* he thought, knowing the deep-seated simmering emotions were still impacting him decades after the horrible things that had happened in that house in Jalna.

To snap himself out of his dark thoughts, he quickly dressed himself in old grey corduroy pants and a long-sleeve shirt and slipped into his sandals. Before heading out, he glanced once more at the now empty side table.

When he got to Chimbai Square, he spotted the chaiwallah serving customers. Seeing the friendly old man gave him anxiety, hoping the man wouldn't see him and comment on his bruises. When the traffic and crowd dissipated, he noticed the bodhi tree was abandoned. *Where is Rohit? I need him.*

Determined, he maneuvered himself straight ahead through the shoppers toward the liquor store to seek salvation, when someone suddenly grabbed his arm. *That old man again!* he thought instantly, but then turned to see it was the doctor.

"What happened to your face? It looks like someone beat you," the doctor said, concerned.

"Oh, it's nothing," Arjun smiled, hiding the truth.

"Let me just quickly address those bruises and cuts at no cost; it will speed up the healing process," he offered. "A friend of the chaiwallah is a friend of mine."

"Ah, no, that's okay. Thank you. Really." Arjun said, trying to move along to end the conversation.

When Arjun finally sat down underneath the tree, he took a big gulp from the flask he just bought, providing him comfort. And then another, and another, helping to overcome his frustration and drown out his earlier thoughts.

"Starting early today, you bastard!" Rohit laughed from behind. When Arjun showed his face, Rohit's laughter was abruptly cut short by a gasp.

After Arjun explained what happened, Rohit said, "You made a deal with the devil, bhai. That gang is responsible for many murders across the country. There is no other way than to pay them off."

Arjun nodded fearfully, the alcohol no longer soothing him as he realized his predicament.

"Come, I will get you something to eat, and we can discuss our next move," Rohit suggested.

Just as they turned into the northwestern part of Chimbai Road near the doctor's office, someone touched Arjun's shoulder.

"Doctor, I told you," Arjun said in agitation, but then he saw the old man's smile.

"What happened to your face, beta?" the chaiwallah asked kindly.

Arjun pushed the hand off his shoulder. "Leave me alone!" he said, storming off ahead. "What's wrong with that old man?" Arjun said to Rohit further up the road, but Rohit didn't respond.

Aditi

"KAKU, I FORGOT one of my books," Vishal said, walking into the home in the Koliwadahs, affectionally calling his grandfather's sister 'aunt'.

Aditi followed, but then stood still for a moment, admiring the picture on the wall that showed the entire Sawant family in front of their boats during Narali Purnima years ago. Her father, with his distinct, thick, flamboyant grey moustache with curled edges, wore a green *dhoti* loincloth and grey *kurta* shirt. Her mother stood beside him in an eight-meter-long maroon saree with the golden necklace and bangles her father had gifted her from his visit to Kolhapur in the east of Maharashtra.

Nostalgia washed over Aditi. She remembered that day clearly, waving their lights in front of the ocean god Varuna, offering coconuts, and praying with many other Koli families for calm waters and prosperity at the end of the monsoon, which marked the start of the fishing season. *Life for a Koli fishing family is tough,* she thought, reflecting on the fear that had grabbed hold of her every time her father headed out to sea.

"Missing your parents, bhachi?" her auntie asked, suddenly standing beside her.

"Always." Aditi sighed.

"They will be back in a few weeks," her auntie reassured her.

Aditi shifted on her feet. "Baba and aai sacrificed so much to get me into university, and into this unique position. I hoped I would have achieved more by now," she said with a deep sigh.

"More?" Her auntie laughed heartily. "You were a little Koli girl who became a wonderful mother with a thriving office career. What more? Your parents couldn't have wished for more! You're showing other Koli girls the way and the possibilities. Everyone is proud of you, bhachi."

Proud of what? Aditi thought, but replied, "Thank you, kaku. I just feel that I could do more than just sales at a call center."

"Well, if that's what you feel, you just keep chipping away," her auntie said, walking back to the kitchen.

Come on, Diti, watch your thoughts. It just hasn't happened yet... not yet, she thought, remembering the chaiwallah's comments about the mind as she watched her auntie walk off. Her eyes turned back to the picture of her parents. *My upcoming interview is for a similar role at another call center, but maybe something else will come out of that,* she thought, trying to encourage herself.

Aditi's facial expression quickly softened seeing Vishal join her. "Ready to go?" she asked.

"Why were you staring at this picture?" Vishal asked, munching on a deep-fried snack made from flour, coconut, poppy, and sesame seeds. "Auntie's *bakarwadi* is delicious as always. You want some?"

Aditi shook her head. "Don't you remember this day, baala?"

"Narali Purnima, right?" Vishal guessed.

"You helped paint your grandfather's boat that day. He still believes that your painting job made him sell his boat faster, before moving to Mahabaleshwar. But," she continued, her expression now turning cheeky, "the rest of the Kolis remember you for something else that day," she laughed.

Vishal thought for a second then suddenly turned around. "Let me get my bag."

"Oh, come on, baala, you know what I'm talking about. You gave them quite a show!" she teased.

With his bag on his shoulder, Vishal stormed out the door. "I'm out of here."

"Your dance moves made you famous! Don't suddenly get shy! Everyone loved it," she shouted, following him outside.

Sumeet

As usual, Sumeet was working in his home office this weekend. Reviewing the update from Vikas and Shanthi on the cost savings, he muttered unsurprised, "This month is well out of reach." As he remembered Radhika's message, he thought about all the interactions they'd had these last six months. *We're doing so many things well, but she continues to focus only on the gaps.* He closed his laptop, deciding he would tackle the rest on Sunday.

"Sumeet?" Manisha called from the kitchen as he wandered towards the living room.

"Yes?" he responded.

"Tomorrow, we have lunch with your parents," she reminded him, while adding different cuts of fruit into the juicer. "And knowing you, you'll work until late evening afterward. Therefore, we should have high tea with the Pandeys at Land's End this afternoon. It is well overdue," she proposed.

Sumeet came into the kitchen and exhaled in exhaustion. "Every weekend these social commitments," he complained. "Yes, tomorrow I'll be working most of the day, so let me take my walk this afternoon."

In response, she turned on the loud juicer. When finished,

she turned to face him, annoyance in her eyes. "Where will you go? You walk every day!"

"Just quick walks up and down Carter Road. But on weekends, I want to explore other parts of the city. It helps me clear my mind and prepare for the week ahead," he reasoned.

Her disapproval was evident as she got her glass of juice and walked off.

"It's important to me," he added, following her, trying to soften the moment.

"Where will you go?" Her voice revealed irritation.

"Around Dadar. Maybe Dharavi. I haven't been there in ages. There's a lot happening nowadays."

Manisha offered no response.

"You want to come along?" he asked sincerely, knowing they never spent much time together.

"No, Sumeet. I do not. Who wants to walk around Dadar and Dharavi for fun? Fine, I will have high tea with the Pandeys by myself," she said curtly.

"Maybe we can meet the Pandeys during the week one evening?" he suggested, but she didn't reply.

*

A LITTLE LATER, Sumeet exited his apartment building compound, his feet moving with purpose across the square. When he passed the newspaperman's stand, the chaiwallah greeted him as usual, but the conflict with Manisha made him want to walk on with speed. When the chaiwallah called again, insisting, his guilt didn't allow him to continue. *Maybe the man needs someone to talk to,* he thought, and turned back.

"How was work this week?" the chaiwallah asked.

Sumeet winced slightly. "Challenging."

"How so?" the old man inquired, his tone genuinely curious.

Sumeet pondered briefly about what to reveal, believing the vendor's world was alien to his. He noticed the chaiwallah's friendly dark eyes waiting thoughtfully.

"Lots of meetings with many different people, dada," he offered vaguely, sipping quickly.

The chaiwallah nodded. "For someone in your position, I guess it's about setting clear priorities, having the right people in the right jobs, good time management, and effective delegation."

Sumeet blinked in surprise. "Um, that is very true," he said looking curiously at the chaiwallah, wondering how the old man could know this.

The chaiwallah nodded confidently. "One other thing can make a big difference for someone in your position," the chaiwallah said, intriguing Sumeet. "A strong right-hand man or woman who supports you in the team."

"Right, right," Sumeet said, his fingers tapping the cart softly, thinking about Vikas or Shanthi, but realizing he had no one. After a moment, he nodded and continued on.

Walking off high-paced into the south of Chimbai Road, he thought about the old man's comments and suggestion. *How can a chaiwallah on the side of the street give such advice?* He chuckled to himself. On Hill Road, he crossed the road and gained a yellow and black taxi. "Siddhi Vinayak," he instructed the driver.

The stuffy air inside pressed on him, but he had no choice since rickshaws weren't allowed in the south, also called "The Town." The driver wove through the familiar route towards the Bandra reclamation area, then right onto the Worli Bandra Sea Link Bridge, stretching six kilometers across Mahim Bay. Thoughts about work continued to linger. *Every day this feeling of pressure and overwhelm... it can't be right.* He pondered his work situation while looking out of the window. In front of him, on the other side of the water, high-rise buildings pierced the sky in Worli, and on his right was the vast Arabian Sea. Reaching the other side, the Worli Fort stood amidst the many fishing boats belonging to Worli's Koli community.

The route snaked through various roads until he got sight of the two-century-old nagara style tiered pyramid with its golden *kalasha*, atop the *shikhara*. While seemingly beige from a distance, the majestic temple was colored with hues of red and yellow that were only visible up close. At the entrance, Sumeet bought some marigold flowers and *boondi ladoo*, Lord Ganesha's favorite sweet. The weekend crowd was thick as usual. Stepping into the complex, Sumeet felt the weight of the week's burdens lift with each step toward the great mandir to give him the respite he desperately sought.

After waiting in line for some time, Sumeet finally reached the reason why he was here: the bright orange idol of Ganesha, glowing amidst gold decorations. He stood before the deity, a moment of *darshan*, an intense spiritual connection, and wished for blessings.

"O Lord Ganesha, remover of obstacles, grant me the strength to overcome my challenges. May your divine presence guide me through life's trials with grace. Om Gan Ganapataye Namo Namah." Opening his eyes, Sumeet felt serene and hopeful. As he walked off, he suddenly fondly remembered that one year, the Bandra West mandal, his neighborhood committee, had recreated the famous and majestic "Lalbaugcha Raja" Ganesha idol for the ten-day Ganesh Chaturthi Festival.

Once outside, Sumeet turned into a side street towards Dadar Beach, west from Worli's Koliwadahs. The beach was littered with plastic bags and bottles, the warm air heavy with the smell of dead fish and sewage. He strolled to the Chowpatty and turned right until he reached the enormous Chhatrapati Shivaji Park, the same name as Mumbai's beautiful international airport, in respect to India's ruler who played a significant part in the country's modern history.

Cricket matches spanned the ground. Sitting on the shaded wooden bench, he thought about visiting Dharavi nearby, as he recently read the world's largest slum became a billion-dollar economy with more than five thousand businesses and fifteen thousand factories. *They must have some good food,* he thought, his stomach growling.

The air was thick with exhaust fumes, smoke from food carts, and a mixture of horns and shouts on the main road, the Ninety Foot Road in Dharavi. A constant stream of rickshaws, hand-pulled carts, cars, and pedestrians filled the dusty road. Both sides of the street were cluttered with vendors selling fruits, vegetables and snacks, and behind Sumeet were shops with hardware, groceries, clothing, and recycled materials. Sumeet turned into one of the narrow alleys to enter the enormous maze, which led him to an open space with children playing cricket with a handmade bat and ball. Sumeet stood still for a moment admiring a large mural behind the bowler. The painting showed a ballerina smiling up to the sky in an arabesque pose wearing a classic tutu and pointe shoes decorated with Indian patterns. Her body was adorned with *maang tikka*, a forehead pendant, *jhumkas*, bell-like shaped earrings, and *ghungroos*, ankle bells. Several stray dogs seemed to be watching the game from the sidelines.

Sumeet strolled ahead and entered another narrow lane, passing recycling shops, leather and garment producers, and a pottery factory, until he came into another open space with a *paav bhaji* stall getting his attention. Seeing the calorie-rich gravy in front of him made him hesitant.

Then a voice interrupted his decision-making.

"You will feel guilty but happy," a woman at one of the plastic tables behind him remarked. She was wearing a simple purple saree.

Sumeet turned and laughed. "Well, in that case, count me in," he replied, and ordered one portion with chopped onion, lime, and bread plus *dhahi balla*—deep-fried lentils with yogurt and chutney.

"Do you live around here?" he asked, sitting down at the next table.

"I teach at a nearby school," the woman replied.

"Wonderful. I am in the automotive industry," he said, wanting to return her openness.

"You look like a senior businessman," she pointed out.

"Do I?" He laughed, touching his belly, worrying that stress had started to make him look older than his age.

"I taught in international schools and university for some time, but then a one-off experience made me realize my calling. And now I teach these underprivileged kids—most of them young adults who already work simple jobs."

"That's inspiring," Sumeet replied, observing her, thinking she was from Northeast India.

"Now I am the sole teacher with almost forty students," she continued. "I teach them mostly about sales, marketing, and management. It is tough but very fulfilling," she said.

Sumeet noticed her almond-shaped eyes sparkle as she spoke. "Well, despite the big pay cut you probably had to accept, I imagine you are creating real change," he stated with admiration. "So, what exactly drove you to make that change?" he asked, dragging another piece of bread through the fragrant reddish gravy.

"It's the feeling that these kids give you, compared to other schools."

Sumeet nodded, trying to imagine.

"What do you do exactly in the automotive industry?" she asked.

"I'm a general manager for car, van, and truck factories in

Central and South India," he replied, his title always instilling pride at how far he had come.

"Wow, that's great," she replied. Sumeet saw another thought come to her mind and a moment later she said, "Sorry to be so straightforward, but would you like to guest lecture one day?" she asked. "You can experience that feeling for yourself." She smiled.

Sumeet instantly felt humbled and thrilled, but realized his calendar wouldn't allow it. Still, he said, "Yes, absolutely. I would be honored. Let me give you my number. My name is Sumeet."

"I'm Ananya," she said, watching him insert his number in her phone.

"My class starts now, and your paav bhaji is finished. How about a quick look before you commit?" she proposed.

She led Sumeet through various narrow lanes with makeshift homes to the front of a large, worn-down apartment building with its ground floor turned into a classroom.

"*Aat chal!*" she told a group of youngsters standing outside to join class.

Sumeet peeked inside the classroom and saw a raw concrete floor with several wet patches and concrete walls painted bright blue. More than thirty children sat scattered around the floor. There was no furniture or school supplies. In the left corner, a yellow bucket sitting on the floor caught water dripping from the ceiling. The children watched him curiously as he stood beside the door; they seemed eager for class to start.

"Hello, uncle," a young man in the front row greeted him kindly. Outside, Ananya was gathering the last of the students.

Just before she entered the classroom, Sumeet said, "Thank you so much for inviting me." He instantly felt drawn to the possible teaching opportunity.

"You can join my class now if you have time," she proposed, turning to him.

On the smooth, coffee-colored skin on the left side of her jaw, Sumeet noticed a birthmark. "Ah, sorry, not today." He remembered Manisha's high tea request.

"I will message you," she confirmed.

"Yes, yes. Please do," he urged. Sumeet observed Ananya for a moment as she stood in front of her students, thinking, *Such passion. She is changing lives.* Finding his way back to the main road, his mind raced with ideas for his lecture.

Aditi

ON MONDAY MORNING, Aditi and Vishal sat at their dining table. She smiled, seeing Vishal enjoy the *upma* she cooked with onions, tomatoes, peas, and seasoned with mustard seeds, curry leaves, and green chilies. *Gupshup Kendra. I am ready for the interview,* she thought, energized, after preparing all Sunday afternoon.

"Please finish your breakfast, Vishal. I'll be right back. I just need to make a call, and we will go."

Aditi placed her own bowl in the sink and stepped onto the dirt road outside her studio. Taking out her phone, she pondered. *I feel bad, but Veda left me no choice.* Then she convinced herself by thinking, *I will easily hit my targets this week anyway, and I will be on time to attend the workshop this afternoon.*

"Hello?" came the voice on the other end.

"Hello, Veda. It's Aditi."

"Yes?" The response was rather cold.

"I'm so sorry, Veda. My son is ill this morning, and I can't drop him at my aunt's house until ten. I can work on my administrative tasks and be in the office around ten-forty to join the workshop at…"

"Well, the time has changed," Veda jumped in. "The workshop is now at nine this morning."

"I see," Aditi replied, in limbo.

"Look, Aditi, I've got a lot on my plate in my new role. I'm not going to create a separate dial-in just for you. I will note your absence and will see you later this morning. Bye." Veda hung up abruptly.

Aditi stared at her phone in shock. *Really? Just like that?*

She quickly forced herself to snap out of it and walked back into the house. "Baala, are you ready? I'm not sure how long it will take to get to this office in Goregaon, so we need to leave a bit early." Waiting for Vishal, she couldn't help thinking about Veda's response. *So unnecessary. Veda clearly doesn't like me, despite my results.* Starting the engine of her scooter, she instructed herself to focus. *I need to ace this interview.*

*

One hour later, Aditi sat nervously in the lobby at call center Gupshup Kendra in Goregaon West. *It's good I left early. Mumbai traffic is so unpredictable,* she thought looking around the lobby, comparing the office environment to MumbaiKonnect.

"Aditi?" the receptionist called.

"Yes," Aditi said and instantly stood up.

"This way, please," the woman said pointing toward the hallway.

Aditi followed confidently. The receptionist opened the door to one of the meeting rooms. "Good luck," the receptionist said with a smile. Aditi saw a man and woman seated next to each other across a large table.

"Welcome, Aditi, please sit," the man said.

"Thank you." Aditi smiled and placed her bag next to her seat.

"My name is Krish. I lead our sales department, and this is Tanvee. She's one of the high performers in my department. This interview is part of her professional development," he said.

Aditi felt hopeful hearing about career development.

Krish pulled his chair closer to the table and continued in a more serious tone. "Our immense growth enables us to hire new people, and you have lots of experience in similar roles," he said, scanning the resume in front of him. "Please tell us a bit about yourself," he asked.

"Yes," Aditi said enthusiastically. "Thank you for inviting me." She started by telling them about her MBA degree, and then she explained her various customer service and sales roles in call centers and emphasized her responsibilities, results, and growth in each role. On top, she mentioned how she recently proposed a new sales strategy and team structure to improve efficiency and results, knowing this was far above the expectation for this role.

Krish asked Aditi to explain how she planned her day and workweek and to provide examples of handling high-pressure situations and conflicts at work. Aditi answered confidently and in detail. Afterward, Aditi inquired about the Gupshup Kendra organizational structure, ways of working, and company culture.

After answering Aditi's questions, Krish concluded the interview. "Any last question for us?"

"Yes," she smiled. "I'm excited about this role because I can improve my people management skills and hope to grow within the organization. If I perform well, how long would it take for me to be promoted from sales executive to department manager?" she asked.

"If you do well, I'd say two to three years," Krish answered. "We want our people to grow and take on more responsibility."

Aditi thanked Krish for the answers given, thinking she could forget about any promotions at MumbaiKonnect with

Veda at the helm. Krish told Aditi he would get back to her in the next few days and got up, leaving Aditi and Tanvee behind.

"Where are you from, Aditi?" Tanvee suddenly asked. She had not said a word during the interview.

"Bandra," Aditi smiled, happy to get to know her.

Tanvee looked curious. "Oh, where?"

"Chimbai," Aditi replied somewhat softly.

Tanvee raised her eyebrows, leaving Aditi with a dismissive gaze before walking off.

The reaction made Aditi sigh and cast her eyes downward, but then she quickly picked up her bag from the chair to walk back to the lobby.

She had experienced similar reactions before in her career when someone discovered she was from the Koliwadahs. Even Aditi herself never met another Koli woman in any of the companies she worked at. While mulling over Krish's answers from the interview, she walked to the lift and waited with mixed feelings. *The role has a direct report, and I may get promoted faster than at MumbaiKonnect, but hopefully I don't have to work closely with Tanvee.*

As she stepped inside the lift, she thought about the chaiwallah's comments about the inability to please everyone, which led to him deciding his tea was marvelous. She smiled and thought, *Diti, overall, this could be a good chance.*

Unlocking her phone, she noticed with surprise she had two missed calls and three messages from her colleague and friend Maryam at MumbaiKonnect. She clicked on the last message and read, "Diti, I tried to call you. You need to hear this from me first. Veda announced structural changes. Shockingly, you will be reporting to me. Ridiculous, I know! Call me the soonest."

What the hell!? Aditi thought.

*

ADITI IMMEDIATELY RACED back to the MumbaiKonnect office, enduring a constant wave of nausea during her drive. Walking briskly through the parking area and up the stairs, she reached the third floor of the call center breathless.

"Aditi," Veda called as Aditi reached her desk. "Good, you are finally here. We need to talk."

"Yes, yes, I believe we do," Aditi replied, masking her frustration and catching her breath.

"Come." Veda directed her into the meeting room behind her desk, laptop in hand.

"Let me take you through some changes we're making in our team to ramp up our productivity," Veda began, opening her presentation. Aditi sat down next to her, a tightness gripping her stomach. Veda showed her the slide with a new organizational chart. Aditi leaned in, scrutinizing the names and reporting lines while thinking, *This is the exact structure I proposed to Maya months ago.*

"You seem a bit concerned," Veda noted.

"Well, this just seems like the same organizational structure I proposed to Maya a while back, except for my role reporting to Maryam, which creates an unnecessary reporting layer," Aditi stated, frustration simmering within.

"Not unnecessary," Veda quickly noted, somewhat flustered. "Maryam excelled these last few quarters. Now that my role encompasses more direct reports, I am giving Maryam the opportunity to practice her people management skills," Veda explained. "I thought you would be happy to see your friend do well?" she added.

Aditi struggled to find the right response.

"Come on, Aditi," Veda said. "Don't view this as a demotion. We recognize your outstanding results and want you to continue to deliver." She smiled, as if attempting to soften the blow. "I really need your full support on these changes. Everyone will have to adjust."

"Honestly, I'm taken aback, Veda. I have consistently achieved my targets these last few years and expressed my desire for greater responsibility for some time now," Aditi said, trying to stay composed. "But this new structure obviously doesn't reflect that," she added.

"Don't take it personally, Aditi. We are doing what's best for the organization," Veda retorted. "Your time will come. Just keep delivering."

Aditi exited the room and navigated the maze of cubicles toward Maryam's desk, frustration flooding her mind. *How could Veda do this to me? I need to leave this company as soon as possible.* "Hey Maryam, thanks for the heads up," Aditi said, immediately sensing Maryam's guilt. "I'm happy for you," Aditi quickly added, meaning it. "You will do great."

"I am so sorry, Aditi," Maryam said hesitatingly. "I can still learn so much from you, and you're my best friend here. Please don't see me differently," she pleaded.

"No. You are my boss, and you need to step it up!" Aditi laughed enthusiastically, masking her emotions, knowing everything had changed.

"Okay," Maryam replied, a hesitant smile creeping onto her face.

"I will be leaving a bit earlier this evening," Aditi informed her.

Sumeet

AT THE SAME time, Sumeet was in a small meeting room, excited for one of his monthly skip-level meetings with junior staff for him to get knowledge from the work floor and give them guidance. His mind drifted off for a moment, reflecting on meeting Ananya in Dharavi, but then a young woman entered the room, mildly flustered. Fatima apologized for being late and thanked Sumeet for meeting with her. She shared that she never had the opportunity to meet top management in any of her previous jobs.

Sumeet smiled and asked about her experience in her new role so far, keen on understanding her perspective. Fatima explained that she was still learning, that Shanthi was very supportive, and that she was improving her data analysis and reporting skills. Sumeet nodded, satisfied with her answer, but he wanted to dig deeper to discover root causes for the disconnect he found within the production department.

"How do you feel about the collaboration between the departments—production, quality control, and engineering?" Sumeet probed, searching for more insight.

Fatima thought for a moment. "I think it's okay," she replied somewhat hesitantly. Sumeet paused, waiting for her to add more thoughts. "I guess everyone is still getting used to the new ways of working," she added.

Sumeet felt she was holding back. "Fatima, you know this talk is confidential, right?" he encouraged. "Are some things not yet working well? That knowledge could really help me."

She smiled at him. "Well," she continued somewhat shyly, "the operational directions don't always seem consistent."

Sumeet nodded, wanting details.

"Especially between the updates and directions you present in monthly updates to the entire team, compared to what we hear on the factory floor," she clarified.

Again, Vikas and Shanthi, Sumeet declared to himself, an intense frustration taking hold of him, knowing they had continued to dismiss any of his requests, suggestions, or directions these past months.

Fatima detailed specific examples. Sumeet responded by asking her ideas for improvement, but he knew that the only solution was for him to get Vikas and Shanthi on his side, which he had been trying to do since he started.

After they finished chatting, Sumeet immediately walked over to the water cooler to swallow paracetamol. Fatima's comments roamed around his head. *I must address this right now,* he thought and took out his phone.

"Vikas. It's Sumeet. How are you?"

"Fine," Vikas answered dryly.

"Vikas, I'd like us to catch up. When can we talk?"

"About what?"

"About ways of working," Sumeet said, not wanting to reveal much.

Sumeet got another call. It was Radhika, his boss.

"I can't see my calendar right now. I will get back to you," Vikas answered.

"Okay, please let me know; it's important," Sumeet requested in a hurry then answered Radhika's call.

"Sumeet? I hear your team is not happy," Radhika immediately stated.

"Excuse me?" Sumeet said in shock.

"Yes, Vikas told me. What is going on?" she questioned.

"When you say team, who are you talking about?" Sumeet asked, internally raged by the backstabbing.

"Shanthi and others," Radhika said.

"Right," he replied without surprise. "It's a work in progress. I have been taking all the steps we discussed before. I will pick this up with Shanthi directly." Before she could answer, he quickly added, "Radhika, I need your help," thinking she could help, because Vikas had the same seniority as him and reported directly to her. "The production team mentioned that Vikas's directions on the floor often differ from the ones I give to the team."

"Well, Vikas has a wealth of experience, Sumeet, that's why I asked him to help you during this transition period," Radhika explained.

"I understand, but he's not helping when his directions to the team differ from mine," Sumeet argued. "I have spoken to him about this before, but he continues on his own path. Could you pick this up with him?"

"No, Sumeet. I'm counting on your leadership here. You're lucky to have Vikas with you, and I don't want to hear about unhappy teams again."

Sumeet sighed quietly, feeling disappointed but reassured her. "Okay, leave it with me."

Aditi

I N THE EARLY evening, having left the office earlier than usual, Aditi opened her aunt's front door. The scent of freshly made *kolambi kalvan* wafted through the air, the coconut-based curry with pomfret made with her own masala.

Vishal was at the table, his books spread out like a fortress of learning, instantly excited at seeing his mother come home early so they could watch Chimbai's annual talent show together. He asked her about the job interview, and Aditi replied that it went very well and that she would hear more soon.

Strolling toward Chimbai Square, they saw the neighborhood committee had set up a small stage adorned with bright streamers, and a few rows of blue plastic chairs were arranged neatly in front and around the sides of the square. The hum of chatter among the residents filled the air.

"Only a few years ago, it was you on that stage with your magic tricks," Aditi reminisced, her voice tinged with nostalgia.

"I was pretty nervous," he laughed.

"Time has flown by, baala," she said softly. "Look at you now, almost as tall as I am!"

The announcer stepped onto the stage, and a muted wave of anticipation rippled through the crowd. Aditi's eyes roamed around the square and landed on the chaiwallah. They exchanged a friendly wave. *I'll go talk to him after this,* she thought happily.

"And now!" the announcer's voice boomed. "We have our first brave soul at this year's Chimbai Talent Festival. Please welcome Natasha!"

A young girl walked up to the microphone, her presence commanding immediate attention. The audience clapped in encouragement.

"Namaste," the young girl greeted her neighbors with her palms together and a slight bow. "Today I would like to share a short story. It's a story about Job, the shepherd," she began, her voice confident.

"Job was a hard-working, dedicated, and faithful father and husband, just like many of our fathers in Chimbai," she said, scanning the audience. "But," she paused, "Satan was watching the shepherd closely from afar." She attempted a scary face. "Look at him, Satan thought. I can change this man's faith in a heartbeat. I will challenge God and have some fun." The young girl gave the audience an evil smile. "And so, Satan said to God, 'Do you see this man?' 'Yes,' God answered. Satan said, 'The only reason this man's faith is strong is because life has been kind to him.'"

The girl paused to make the captivated audience wait, then continued. "Satan said, 'If I bring hardship to this man, you will see his faith crumble!'" she shouted. "'Test the man!' God said confidently. But," she paused again. "'Do not harm him physically.' Satan agreed." The girl's voice took on a somber tone that spoke of danger. "Satan started by killing off all Job's livestock! Stripping away all his income. Yet Job's faith did not waver. He found another way to earn money," she said proudly. "But that was only the beginning of his test."

She scanned the audience. "Satan laughed and then took away his wife!" she shouted. "Of course, Job was heartbroken, but he remained faithful and continued to work hard to provide for his children." The residents looked visibly impressed by the girl's storytelling skills. "Lastly," she continued, "Satan took his children. Job was down on his knees, struggling to carry on. But after some time he said, 'Naked I came from my mother's womb, and naked shall I return. The Lord gave, and the Lord has taken away; blessed be the name of the Lord.' His faith stood firm," the girl said and paused once more, receiving some smiles from the audience. "Satan watched in awe. He had failed. And God began to restore Job's fortunes, blessing him with—"

"Why do we believe in multiple gods?" Vishal suddenly asked Aditi.

She collected her thoughts. "Well, baala, we were brought up as Hindu Marathi Koli. The girl on stage speaks of the one God that Christians believe in. Different people in India have diverse ways of thinking about God or gods. Your mother prays to different deities or gods but also believes that God is part of every person, every living thing, and everything in the universe." Aditi gestured to the stage. "Like the girl on stage." She turned, pointing. "Part of that bodhi tree over there, and even the pigeons perched on that apartment building."

Vishal's gaze shifted to Arjun beneath the tree. "How about that drunk guy? Is that God too?" he asked skeptically.

"Yes, Vishal, I believe so. God doesn't judge. We don't know what that man has been through or what he is experiencing. I also believe that God is within our senses—a thought, a taste, a touch, a smell, a sound. God is infinite, unidentifiable, and universal," she added.

"So, God is everything?" Vishal questioned, still pondering.

"That is what I believe, but you can grow up believing whatever you want, as long as you are a good person." Aditi smiled.

Vishal turned his attention back to the performance, seemingly unimpressed with his mother's explanation.

Aditi's gaze drifted back to the building where she spotted the pigeons. In one of the large windows of an apartment block, a poster read, *Apartment for Rent.*

That would be a dream come true, she thought, staring in awe. After a moment, she snapped herself out of her daydream, thinking, *Come on, Diti, even Maya the call center director doesn't live like that.*

Arjun

WHEN IT WAS deep in the night, Arjun walked south by himself from the end of Chimbai Road. The streetlights barely illuminated the bricks. After passing Mehboob Studios, he turned left onto Mount Harmel Road. At the end of his ten-minute walk, just before he reached the now-closed public toilets, a car passed, and he pulled his cap low, looking around anxiously for Rohit. A hushed yet sharp call pierced the silence up ahead, and there, next to the statue of the legendary Telugu cinema director, at the intersection of Hill Road and Mount Camel Road, stood Rohit.

Just when he crossed the street, a rickshaw sped from behind out of nowhere, almost hitting him. "Aaicha gho!" Arjun exhaled, his heartbeat quickening.

"Chal!" Rohit called, motioning for him to move.

Arjun followed him into one of the side streets, the Dr. Peter Dias Road. They strolled ahead for a while until Rohit suddenly whispered, "It's this block, but just keep going."

They slowed down their pace, both scanning the area for any sign of onlookers. "It's the ground-floor apartment, which we can enter from the back of the building. There is no security," he smirked, as they passed the five-story ocher yellow building. Arjun noticed the windows were not barred, which was unusual in the area. Pondering how to enter from the back, Arjun listened as Rohit explained their next move.

"We jump the gate quickly, duck, and bear crawl to the rear of the building," he instructed.

The deserted street bore no sign of life—not even street dogs. "Okay, go," Rohit commanded, walking back and leaping over the rusty gate in one swift motion. Arjun mimicked his move. Now both crouched low behind the gate. Rohit stuck up his head one final time to check for movement and instructed Arjun, "Now!" Creeping down low, Rohit moved through the parking area to the rear. Arjun lifted his head once to make sure they were alone before following.

At the rear, Rohit pulled out his phone to light the wall. "Here's the back door. I can break the small lock."

From his jacket, he took out a hammer and, in one powerful stroke, shattered the lock. The sound echoed distressingly. *My God! Too loud,* Arjun thought, hurrying back to peer around the corner to see if anyone noticed.

"Quick!" Rohit insisted, the door wide open.

They slipped inside, immediately landing in the living room, their phone lights cutting through the darkness.

"Stick together this time," Arjun urged him.

Arjun quickly started to rifle through a wooden cabinet, but found nothing valuable. He looked around and saw Rohit had disappeared once again. He cursed silently and shone his light on a nearby table to grab some items.

"Don't move, bastard, or you're dead," a threatening voice commanded from behind Arjun. He froze instantly, his heart pounding wildly, realizing the voice wasn't Rohit's. "Turn around," the voice demanded. Arjun hesitated momentarily, but then turned to see the barrel of a gun pointed at his forehead.

"Drop everything," the voice said. Arjun's objects clattered to the floor. He squinted his eyes to see the man, but he remained a shadow in the darkness. "Lay down, face flat, arms behind you," the voice ordered.

Putting his hands up, Arjun lowered himself slowly, his mind panicking.

The voice added, "You either die here or go to prison for a long time. Your choice, bastard."

As Arjun quickly fell to his knees, he saw a flicker of movement behind the gunman. Then there was a loud cracking sound and the gun fell to the floor.

"Who the hell is this guy!?" Rohit shouted, standing atop the man, hammer in hand. Rising slowly, Arjun stared at the body and the profusely bleeding head. He started to hyperventilate. "Calm down!" Rohit snapped, picking up the gun. "Nothing valuable here, except this bastard's gun. Let's get the hell out of here," Rohit said. Arjun stared at the man, in shock and unable to move.

"Snap out of it, Arjun!" Rohit yelled, his voice breaking Arjun's trance. "Come on!" Rohit urged. Arjun hunched over and followed Rohit out the same door they entered until they reached the corner of the building.

Rohit crawled back to the gate, still urging him. "Chal!"

Arjun dropped to the floor, but the shock of seeing the bloodied body kept him from pushing his body forward. "Hurry up!" Rohit hissed, irritated. When Arjun finally crunched beside him, Rohit was frantically eyeing the street left and right, and instructed him, "I'll go down south. You go home via Rebello and Veronica. Walk slowly, like nothing happened tonight."

"This is the last time. I am not doing this anymore," Arjun said, his hands shaking.

Rohit didn't respond. He just disappeared into the night.

Arjun, now alone, waited a moment, but then jumped the gate. A sudden overwhelming angst made him sprint into a side street then run into Rebello Road. He urged himself to calm down to avoid looking suspicious and started to speedwalk until he reached St. Sebastian Road. *Enough! Don't panic!* he yelled internally, trying to regain composure.

After passing Mount Carmel Road, he continued northward on Hill Road and turned onto Chimbai Road when a street dog jumped out of the shadows, causing his heart to skip a beat. He shut his eyes briefly to calm his nerves, but the sudden visual of the gun and blood caused him to quickly open them again. *That was too close,* he thought anxiously, nearing his home.

Aditi

LATER THAT WEEK, Aditi watched Vishal enter the school building. Instead of immediately driving off to work, she hesitated, the stress of dealing with Veda throughout the week had sapped all her motivation. After a moment, she slowly approached Chimbai Square and saw a short queue at the chaiwallah's cart. The thought of chai and the old man's friendly demeanor comforted her. *He's becoming popular,* she thought, feeling vindicated. She decided to park her scooter and wait in line.

A familiar voice broke through her reverie. "Good morning, Aditi."

She turned around, surprised. "Oh, hello, Mr. Daruwalla. Good morning. How are you?"

"Good, Aditi," Sumeet lied. "Working hard as usual."

"And the family?" Aditi asked.

"Nandini is studying in Canada and seems very happy," he remarked. "How about you? And your father? I haven't seen him for a long time," Sumeet admitted.

"My parents retired and moved to the hill stations," she explained. "Enjoying the tranquility of the hills after a lifetime of sea views."

"They've done well!" Sumeet replied with admiration. "Your father worked hard enough, being a fisherman and Chimbai's most skilled handyman. The Kolis have it tough nowadays with increasing pollution, fewer fish, and climate change," Sumeet added, his tone turning somewhat somber.

"Yes, difficult times for our people," Aditi nodded in agreement.

"How about you, Aditi?" Sumeet asked. "You were in sales, right?"

"Yes. I've been good, sir," she lied. "Always exceeding my targets," she added excitedly, feeling a little intimidated by discussing her work with such an established businessman.

"Your father always spoke so highly of you," Sumeet said. "I remember him saying you were a logical thinker, a hard worker, and more intelligent than him." Sumeet detailed the many times her father came over to his parents' home nearby to fix things around the house. Aditi immediately felt a pang of longing for her father. "He said more than a few times that you were destined for greatness." He smiled broadly at the memories.

Aditi blushed. "It's extremely competitive to move up the ladder, sir."

Sumeet nodded and asked, "What are you looking for?"

"A move to management," she said. "But," she quickly added, "I am confident my breakthrough will happen soon." She tried to sound hopeful and exude confidence.

"That's the right attitude, Aditi," Sumeet replied approvingly. "It's a combination of consistent results, ongoing learning, being ready, and, of course, some luck."

"Namaste!" the chaiwallah interrupted. "How wonderful to see you both at the same time," the old man greeted them warmly.

Sumeet looked sideways at Aditi. "You've met the new chaiwallah?" he asked.

"Yes, yes." She laughed. "Namaste dada," Aditi smiled, pressing her palms together with a slight bow in a gesture of respect.

Sumeet noticed the old man's face light up.

"You are absolutely right, beta," the chaiwallah suddenly pointed out to Sumeet, who looked puzzled in response. "About luck," the old man said. "But our luck usually comes through others," the chaiwallah stated wisely.

"True," Sumeet conceded, still unsure where the conversation was headed.

"Just a simple recommendation or introduction is often the only luck needed to change someone's life," the old man said locking eyes with Sumeet.

"I guess you are right," Sumeet said, wondering why the chaiwallah was fixated on him.

"Yes, when we join hands together, we can create luck and prosperity for others." The chaiwallah smiled, handing over glasses to both of them.

Sumeet glanced sideways at Aditi, who raised her eyebrows in intrigue. They both turned around to face the square, sipping their hot masala chai.

"Interesting chaiwallah, don't you think?" Aditi whispered to Sumeet.

"Most definitely." Sumeet smiled, checking his watch before taking another sip.

"How is business?" Aditi asked, eager to keep the conversation going to learn more.

"Good. We have just gone through lots of change in the organization, so it has been very busy," he replied, finishing his glass. "Let me get this chai for you," he said, handing over forty rupees to the chaiwallah. "Sorry, Aditi, I need to get to the office," he said apologetically and left.

When Aditi walked back to her scooter, she felt energized by the chai and conversation. Just before she turned the key, her phone rang with an unsolicited number. She hesitated for a moment but picked up anyway.

"Hello?" she answered, thinking it may be a sales pitch.

"Hello, Aditi?" a man's voice asked at the other end.

"Yes?" she replied, her pulse quickening, the voice sounded familiar.

"This is Krish from Gupshup Kendra."

"What a surprise to get your call," she said, her heart pounding.

"Aditi, I wanted to tell you personally that we want to offer you the position you applied for. Are you interested?" Krish's voice rang with excitement.

Her heart leapt. "Yes, definitely," she said, trying to keep her voice somewhat steady despite the elation.

"Wonderful, Aditi. About the one-month notice period, do you think this can be shortened?" he queried.

"I'm headed to office now and can let you know later today," she promised. Then she added earnestly, "Krish Sir, thank you so much for this opportunity. I'm truly grateful."

After hanging up, Aditi smiled in the direction of the chaiwallah, but he was serving customers. Then she let herself glance up at the luxurious apartment for rent, which she spotted during the Talent Festival, thinking happily, *Yes! Finally! Who knows where this could lead.* With renewed determination, she sped off on her scooter.

*

WHEN ADITI ENTERED the office, she marched straight to Veda's desk.

"Good morning, Veda. Do you have a moment?" she asked, her voice firm.

Veda turned her chair to face her. "Yes, Aditi. Are you

feeling a bit better about all the changes?" Veda inquired. Aditi detected a hint of irony in her tone.

"Actually, Veda, I've accepted a position at another company," Aditi declared.

Aditi saw Veda's eyes widen for a split second, but she quickly changed back to her usual stony expression and said, "Good for you, Aditi. Perhaps it's best you move on." Her face was devoid of emotion.

That's right, Aditi thought. "We have a one-month notice period. Is there any way to shorten it?" she asked directly.

"Today can be your last day. I didn't promote Maryam for no reason," Veda stated.

Aditi was taken aback by the crude comment but reminded herself to stay professional. "Thank you. In that case, today will be my last day. I'll confirm by email to you and HR," Aditi replied, maintaining her composure. "I will make sure to hand over all my work to Maryam."

"Yes, do that, and hand in your laptop and office pass," Veda instructed her curtly. "All the best," Veda added coldly, already turning her eyes back to her screen.

"Thanks, you too," Aditi said. With great relief, she walked off excitedly into the maze of desks.

"Maryam, I was looking for you!" Aditi exclaimed from a distance.

"What has you so energized?" Maryam said, turning a curious eye to Aditi as she approached.

Aditi moved closer and whispered, "I've got a new job."

"No way! Congratulations! Where?" Maryam asked, eyes wide.

Aditi appreciated her excitement, knowing that Maryam would now feel stressed about finding her replacement. She explained about the new role and possible growth opportunities ahead of her.

"Brilliant! You deserve it," Maryam said, genuinely happy.

"Sorry, Maryam, today is my last day," Aditi revealed, feeling apologetic.

"What? You're leaving me so soon?" Maryam said, her eyes glistening. "It is okay, Diti! Go and conquer!" she added with a grin while holding back tears.

"Thanks, Maryam. You've always been a great friend." Aditi's smile was full of emotion.

Sumeet

Sumeet hurried out of one of the meeting rooms, walked downstairs, and turned right towards the company canteen to meet his visitor. At one of the large steel tables, he spotted his childhood friend and tapped him on the shoulder. "*Kasa ahes tu?*" Sumeet said enthusiastically, asking him about his wellbeing.

"Bhai! So good to see you," Anish said, quickly getting up to hug Sumeet.

"So sorry, I just got out of a call," Sumeet explained, wrapping his arms around his friend.

"No problem, I know how it is," Anish replied as they sat down.

"Oh man, it is so good to see you again," Sumeet said with a big sigh, feeling he could let his guard down.

"Last time was Dahi Handi?" Anish asked, referring to the annual celebration for Krishna's birth.

"Yes, it's been too long," Sumeet said. "I remember watching your cousins with the Bandra's Govinda Pathaks."

"Those guys were exactly like Krishna as kids," Anish smirked.

"It was quite the sight," Sumeet said." I forgot your cousin's name—the shortest of the two who climbed up fearlessly, almost losing his balance at the top, and then got the pot."

Anish laughed. "His mother almost had a heart attack."

Sumeet asked Anish about Bhavishya Sankalp Ventures, his consulting business. After updating Sumeet on the start-ups they had been working with, he paused and scanned Sumeet's face. "Speaking as your friend, you don't look so good." Sumeet nodded in acknowledgement. "Your skin is dry, you've got big dark circles around your eyes, and you have gained weight," Anish said, observing him. "Are you still walking in the morning?"

Sumeet stared ahead and admitted, "Actually, I am not doing well. It's this new job."

"I can tell, Sumeet," Anish replied, his voice full of concern.

Sumeet nodded, feeling ashamed, but then confessed somberly, "It is funny, you know. I am supposed to be at the pinnacle of my career, but I feel hopeless. Absolutely nothing has worked out, and I am battling constant migraines."

"Come on, hopeless?" Anish inquired, apprehensively. "What do you mean?"

Sumeet explained that his new role required him to implement all the changes the company wanted to make across the business, but that the corporate culture had turned aggressive, political, and uncollaborative. He told Anish that the new leaders he reported to continue to challenge him instead of helping him. "I just can't get along with my new boss, and my newly appointed team seems hostile and unresponsive after having to let some people go."

Anish nodded, listening as a friend. Sumeet told him about the progress he had made filling up critical roles, clarifying the constant changing directions from the top, and implementing feedback from the team to improve ways of working. But after six months of working tirelessly, team culture remained poor and results were average.

"It feels like the world has slowly turned against me," Sumeet admitted.

Anish was taken aback by the gloomy revelation. "That is a bit worrisome," he replied concerned. "You better take a holiday before you burn out," he suggested. "You've taken one promotion after another. Refresh and focus for another six months. As for your boss, I suggest you enforce a weekly one-on-one to get her alignment and accountability. If things don't change after six months, your resume will ensure you get another job anywhere you like."

Sumeet sighed. "Thanks, it's so good to see you again, Anish."

On their way out of the canteen, they grabbed a handful of sweetened and regular fennel seeds. Anish told Sumeet to drink a good glass of whiskey in the evening and take the job a little less seriously.

"Call me anytime if you need to talk. I'm here for you," Anish said with some concern.

"Thank you, bhai. I really appreciate it," Sumeet said, hugging Anish, grateful for his advice and friendship but knowing he couldn't take a holiday right now.

Aditi

THE FOLLOWING DAY was Aditi's first day at Gupshup Kendra. She dressed well, wearing a dark green kurti, white leggings, and white low-heeled leather glittery sandals she had bought the night before. During her interview, she had seen the reception area and the corridor with meeting rooms. Now, she found herself navigating the expansive call center floor. *It's much bigger and more modern than MumbaiKonnect,* she thought excitedly. The floor was still relatively quiet this early in the morning.

"Good morning, sir," she said, seeing her new manager Krish in the hallway.

"Hi, Aditi. I was so surprised that you could start today. Amazing! You see that corner?" Krish pointed out to the far right. "That is Rukma's office from human resources. Please go there and she will run you through the company introduction, hand over your laptop, and answer any questions you have." Aditi nodded in agreement. "Afterward, please come back to my office here behind me, and I will take you through our strategy, performance metrics, and targets," he said.

Walking toward the corner, Aditi saw Tanvee from the interview behind one of the desks, remembering her reaction as she found out about her Koli heritage. Aditi smiled politely but got only a short nod back.

"Hello, Rukma?" Aditi said peeking her head into the office.

"Welcome, Aditi. Please sit." Rukma waved her inside from a black leather chair.

Aditi settled down as Rukma opened a folder and began talking her through her contract, company policies, benefits, and safety protocols.

"Rukma," Aditi's curiosity peaked as she examined the organizational chart. "I am not seeing the direct report to my role?"

"It will come when we implement that change," replied Rukma.

Aditi hesitated, smiling weakly. "We haven't hired or chosen someone for that role yet?"

"No. The role is part of our growth vision," Rukma said.

Growth vision? Aditi thought, her face paling somewhat. "I am sorry, Rukma," she interrupted. "Krish sir mentioned in the interview that my role would have a direct report to help achieve sales volume and manage administrative tasks," Aditi explained.

"Yes, it will. You can discuss this with him," Rukma said to reassure her.

Aditi turned in her chair. *Beside the small salary bump and higher possibility of getting promoted, having a direct report was the other key reason I wanted this role,* she thought. "Okay, will do," she replied. *Don't panic, Diti. Talk to Krish. Maybe there's a misunderstanding.*

Rukma handed her the induction folder, a laptop, a bag, and an office pass. "I think that's it!" she said. "If any issues arise, don't hesitate to come see me," Rukma said kindly.

"Thank you." Aditi packed everything into the black company-branded backpack and quickly made her way to

Krish's office on the other side of the floor. The floor was now noisy with conversations from the many cubicles filling the air. At Krish's office, she knocked on the open door.

"Yes, Aditi. Come in. Let's quickly run through a few things, and then you can start. With your experience, you will pick this up in no time."

Aditi nodded. "One question before we start. Rukma mentioned that my role doesn't have a direct report right now, and it's part of the vision?"

"Yes, but don't worry. That will happen soon," Krish smiled.

"From the interview, I was under the impression the role would have a direct report right now," Aditi said in a friendly manner, fighting off the feeling she had been misled.

"Yes, not straight away, but soon," Krish explained.

"What is the expected timeframe?" Aditi inquired.

"Definitely within eighteen months, if we continue to grow at this rate."

Aditi screamed inside. *Eighteen months?* "Then who will help with all the administrative work until then? I didn't see that clearly in Rukma's chart and thought my direct report would assist with that."

"Right now, that is part of your job, Aditi. I am sure you can handle it," Krish said smiling confidently. "Come, let me quickly introduce you to the team." Krish got up and walked out of the office, announcing, "Everyone! Please gather for a moment!"

Even at MumbaiKonnect, I had administrative support, Aditi thought, her mind panicking as she followed. After a moment, four women, one of them Tanvee, and a man joined them. Krish introduced her to the team, conveying her rich experience in similar roles and that the team shouldn't hesitate to ask her questions.

Aditi smiled after the introduction. The women nodded, scanning her from head to toe.

As Krish returned to his office, Aditi asked, "Ladies, when is chai time around here?"

"There is no set time," Tanvee stated dismissively, her eyes gleaming with malice as she smirked to the other women.

Aditi saw the women giggle as they turned back to their desks.

*

In the evening, Aditi stood in front of her auntie's door in the Koliwadahs. She grabbed the door handle but pulled back her hand, tuned left, and started walking down the narrow dark lane until she reached the sea. In front of the black water, she stood still for a moment taking in the warm salty air. *What did I get myself into?* she thought angrily, reflecting on her first day at Gupshup Kendra. *After all the years of diligence, this career move will give me nothing.* She sighed.

She watched as the large moon lit up different parts of the choppy water when the low heavy clouds allowed. Taking off her sandals, she stepped into the water with her bare feet, submerging her ankles, hoping Varuna Dev, the Vedic god of water, rain and the oceans, would calm her, but her thoughts continued. *No direct report, too much admin work, and no promotion in sight as I must first prove myself and work my way up. But that's what I did at MumbaiKonnect all those years, and it got me nowhere.* She spotted some tiny green lights across the water, fishing boats on the move.

Do I deserve this? she suddenly thought angrily. She picked up a small rock from the now pitch-black sand and threw it far ahead of her into the water. Her eyes started to well up and she quickly used the long sleeves from her kurti to wipe away the tears trying to roll down her cheeks. After a moment, she strolled toward one of the beached boats and touched the port side.

Looking down, the moon revealed the boat painted orange, white, and green like the colors of India's national flag. Her shoulders drooped. *Diti,* she wondered, *are you setting the bar too high? I really wanted to climb up the corporate ladder, but it's just not happening. And I'm not getting any younger. Do I need to be more realistic about my and Vishal's future to avoid disappointment? Well, at least I'm a Koli girl with an office job,* she thought, but she was unconvinced that was where she wanted to be.

She sighed deeply and tuned around to walk back up the slightly hilly alley towards her auntie's home. Pushing open the flimsy door, she said from the door opening, "Thank you, kaku. Chal, Vishal." She didn't feel like entering the house.

A short time after, Aditi and Vishal stood in front of the supermarket on Chimbai Square. Aditi saw that the chaiwallah was without customers and suggested to Vishal they walk across the square. "Good evening, dada," she greeted him.

"Namaste, beti! How is your luck going?" the chaiwallah said, referring to the conversation they had with Sumeet.

"Not yet there," she admitted with pursed lips, the disappointment of her first day in the new job resurfacing.

"Yet," he smiled, emphasizing the word. "The mind, my dear," he reminded her, pointing his right index finger to his temple.

His response quickly forced Aditi to stop feeling sorry for herself as she smiled at Vishal.

"Is this your boy?" the chaiwallah asked, grabbing one of his glasses.

"Yes," she said proudly, running her fingers through her son's thick black hair.

"He looks like you," the old man observed. Aditi nodded but suddenly felt alarmed about the possibility of the curious chaiwallah asking about the father. He didn't and simply handed over the chai.

She continued to play with Vishal's hair, sipping her tea. *It's been so many years,* she thought. *Poor baba. He thought he picked the right man for me. The wedding was beautiful. Everything went well until Vishal came into this world. He just couldn't accept that I wanted to continue my career. And then one day he wasn't there anymore.* She took another sip, the chai comforting her. *That's why I need to make it count,* she thought, looking at Vishal.

"Are you okay, beti?" the chaiwallah asked, detecting her nostalgia. "The eyes, dear. It's our window," he added.

Aditi smirked, feeling caught, and noticed the chaiwallah's warm, caring stare, similar to her father's.

"The road to success is never a straight line up, beti," he suddenly said.

"I guess that's true," she replied, feeling that her own line had been flat for a long time.

After another sip, the old man's comment made her remember the time her father's boat was destroyed by a storm when she was eight years old. The following day, she overheard her parents talk about the years of savings they had to spend to get the boat repaired ahead of the upcoming fishing season. *That was a big setback they overcame,* she thought, finishing her chai.

"Patience is key, my dear," he added. "Sometimes, when the world seems to be against you, when you least expect it, luck suddenly comes your way." He smiled warmly.

The comment comforted her. "Don't worry, dada. We will keep going, won't we, Vishal?" she answered, wrapping her arm around his shoulder. Vishal looked confused as the chaiwallah nodded confidently.

As Aditi and Vishal left the dimly lit square, Chimbai started to rest, now entertaining only a few late-night shoppers. Aside from the supermarket and liquor store, all the other shops underneath the apartment block were closed. Three rickshaws were parked near the newspaperman, the drivers all sitting in one of them chatting and smoking. Along Chimbai Road, some light bulbs lit up a few fruit and vegetable stalls with their owners in the shadows, hoping for one more sale before closing up.

Arjun

The following afternoon, Arjun finally got ahold of Rohit.

"Where have you been?" Arjun yelled from across the square, storming over to the bodhi tree.

"Quiet down!" Rohit urged, his expression a mask of caution. "We don't want to attract attention." As Arjun sat down, Rohit explained he was gambling in Navi Mumbai for a few days. His voice exuded an unsettling calm.

"For all the risk we took, we got nothing that night!" Arjun's voice trembled with frustration. Every word he spoke felt like a release of the pent-up tension gnawing at his insides.

"Don't worry, the opportunities are unlimited, bhai!" Rohit laughed, seemingly unbothered.

Arjun stared at him, feeling a sudden coldness grip his heart. "Really? Are we not going to talk about what happened?" His voice was tense, remembering their last robbery attempt.

"What do you mean? We went in, didn't get anything, and now we need to find the next one," Rohit responded, his tone chillingly indifferent.

"You may have killed him," Arjun whispered, the horror of that night flashing in his eyes.

"Shh!" Rohit hissed. "He pointed a gun at you. What could I do?" His eyes bore into Arjun's, unflinching and remorseless.

Arjun stared at Rohit, his mind struggling to comprehend the sheer lack of guilt in his friend's eyes. *What is wrong with this guy? Zero remorse,* he thought, feeling a shiver run down his spine. *Ever since I met Rohit, I've gotten into all sorts of trouble.*

"He would have shot you or called the police!" Rohit pointed out, angry now. "Which one would you have preferred? I think I gave you a better outcome."

Arjun sighed as the truth of Rohit's words weighed on him. "Yes, you did, bhai. Thank you," he said, considering the alternative. *I need him,* Arjun thought.

"But you are right," Rohit said. "The problem is that we left empty-handed, and those bastards will be coming for you soon. Next time they will kill you!" he urged. "I am also running low."

"They will," Arjun muttered, feeling the walls closing in.

"Maybe you can ask your old friend for some money," Rohit smirked, pointing at the chaiwallah.

"Funny," Arjun replied, his tone sarcastic.

Rohit suddenly got up from underneath the tree, determination in his eyes. "Okay, follow me. This will be quick and profitable." Arjun followed without questioning him. Rohit woke up the rickshaw driver parked behind the newspaperman.

Twenty minutes later, they stepped out of the rickshaw at the large intersection near the Bandra train station, with Rohit immediately marching into the bustling Hill Road.

"Where are we going?" Arjun called, trailing behind.

"Look around," Rohit said, stopping on the footpath. "This place is crowded. There are numerous jewelry stores, multiple escape routes, and no CCTV. Am I right?" he asked.

"I guess," Arjun agreed, looking around the area.

Rohit pointed to the bus stop, which allowed them to oversee customer traffic for three different shops at the same time, and instructed that they should target older, middle-aged couples exiting one of the stores.

Arjun listened, his brows furrowed and lips pressed together.

"Couples without children," Rohit added, trying to put Arjun's mind at ease. "Do you have a better idea?" His voice was aggressive, not wanting an answer. "You said you didn't want to rob houses anymore after that gun in your face, but when those bastards show up next time, you need something to give them."

"*Theek ahe*," Arjun conceded, hesitantly.

Standing at the bus stop, Arjun lit up a cigarette. He was so nervous, his hands were shaking. *He's always so convincing,* Arjun thought, irritated for letting himself get pulled into this. He watched Rohit scan the footpath traffic on both sides of the road.

After a while, Arjun turned around to ease his nerves and saw the restaurant behind him was showing a cricket match between the Mumbai Indians and Kolkata Knight Riders. Arjun watched as Ambati Rayudu hit the ball towards the fielders and ran ferociously toward the wickets in front of him. *Got it,* Arjun thought. *Oh, what I wouldn't give,* he thought. *I was good. My style was a combination of Virat Kohli's and Sachin Tendulkar's, my two all-time favorites. Would I have made it to the IPL?* he wondered, imagining his life as a professional as he watched Ambati get ready for another hit.

"Hey!" Rohit shouted, snapping Arjun out of his daydream. "Are you paying attention? There!" Rohit added, pointing to the other side of the road.

"Yes, yes I am," Arjun replied swiftly, acting like he was focused.

A luxury sedan stopped in front of a jewelry store. After a moment, a couple got out of the car and swiftly entered the shop. "Go!" Rohit urged. Arjun walked quickly across, parking himself next to the window shop to see inside. The couple sat down for a few minutes, and Arjun saw the shopkeeper come back with a large purple velvet box. When he opened it for the couple, Arjun caught a glimpse of the yellow gold pendant necklace. His eyes widened as he realized it was worth more than one lakh rupees. The thought of what he was going to do sent his heart rate through the roof. Turning back, he evaluated his escape route through the sea of people into a side street a short run away.

In front of the shop window, he waited for the couple to step out. After a few minutes, his impatience made him look inside once more, and he saw the couple standing right behind the glass in front of the door. Before they exited, Arjun saw they were holding hands, their fingers intertwined as they stared into each other's eyes. Observing them, he felt their strong sense of intimacy and love. Arjun sighed and his shoulders drooped. *I can't do this,* he thought as the couple exited the store. Arjun saw Rohit throw his arms up, urging him to take action. Arjun shook his head and crossed the road.

Aditi

A WEEK INTO THE new job at Gupshup Kendra, Aditi was seated behind her desk when Krish, her manager, called her into his office.

"Aditi, with your skills and experience, I see you are picking up the work well," he observed.

"I do my best, sir," she said.

"I need you to help Tanvee with some client support because she is overloaded. Could you please see her after our talk?" he requested.

Oh, that tough cookie, she thought. "Yes, sir, of course. I will do that," she responded.

The work itself is not challenging, but I already have quite a lot to do, she mused, walking toward Tanvee's desk. *But maybe by helping others in the team, it will give me an edge with Krish,* she thought, pushing herself to be optimistic. Tanvee's desk was now straight ahead. *The women in the team feel threatened by me, and I need to ease their minds. Maybe by helping Tanvee, I will get accepted into their circle.*

"Hi, Tanvee. How are you?" Aditi greeted kindly.

"Hello," Tanvee replied somewhat apathetically.

"Krish asked me to help you out with email support."

"Oh, yes, yes," Tanvee said, instantly changing her demeanor.

Now I have her attention, Aditi thought. "How long have you worked here?"

"About four years. Here, let me show you where I need help," Tanvee said, cutting off the conversation.

Going through her work, Aditi noticed Tanvee's list of clients was shorter and less demanding than hers.

Tanvee pointed at the screen. "These are the clients I need help with so I can focus on the rest of the list."

"How much do they bring in every month?" Aditi queried, but Tanvee avoided giving a direct answer. *In my first week, I delivered one and a half lakhs including all admin, which is probably already half her monthly target,* Aditi thought scanning the list. *She is offloading quite a bit of work. Didn't Krish mention in the interview that she was one of his high performers?* she questioned internally.

"Managing all the different tasks can be quite stressful," Aditi pointed out.

"Well, it's more that I need to focus on the big clients," Tanvee responded. "Anyway, thanks, Aditi. I will send an introductory email and forward all prior communication. Let me know if anything is unclear."

"Will do," Aditi replied and started to walk back.

"Hey," Aditi heard Tanvee call from behind her and she turned back around.

"We're having chai in about thirty minutes. Join us?" Tanvee proposed.

"Yes, sure, thanks," Aditi said enthusiastically, happy about the little breakthrough as she walked back to her desk.

Strolling through the many desks, she thought about the additional customers and administrative work she had to take on. *This will probably add at least one or two more hours of work every day.*

Passing Krish's office, Aditi stopped at his door. "Sir?"

"Yes, Aditi?"

"I just caught up with Tanvee. No problem. I will start on this right away. How long do you think she will need my help?"

"I think it will be for a while, Aditi. Let's see."

"Right," she replied.

"We all have to be flexible, Aditi. Maybe you have to stay a bit longer in the evening, but that's what high performers like you do, isn't it?" he added.

Aditi smiled, nodding in agreement.

A few hours later, Aditi looked around her desk, noticing she was now alone. Outside was pitch dark, and the office lights in the office were dimmed. Feeling stiffness, she started to massage the back of her neck. After a moment of continuing to extract and transfer Tanvee's data from the enormous worksheet, she pulled her shoulders up and straightened her back to correct her posture. *I will need at least another hour,* she thought, sighing. She took out her phone from her handbag to message her aunt that she would be delayed.

*

THE FOLLOWING MORNING, fatigued by last night's work, Aditi stepped into the supermarket on Chimbai Square after dropping Vishal at school. She immediately turned left into the narrow aisle toward the fridges at the far end. *Is that Mr. Daruwalla?* she thought, squinting her eyes at the man in sneakers, shorts, and a t-shirt standing before her.

"Mr. Daruwalla?" she called from behind him.

Sumeet turned around, holding an orange earthen pot of curd. His dark, tense eyes immediately relaxed upon seeing Aditi.

"Oh, hey Aditi. What a coincidence!" he said excitedly. "I didn't see you for a long time, and now twice in a week."

His jovial response took her by surprise.

"You know, I was thinking about you!" he smiled.

The comment made Aditi feel slightly uncomfortable. Noticing this, Sumeet quickly added, "I mean, I thought about the chaiwallah's comments from the other day, and that made me think about you," he explained.

"Oh, okay," Aditi replied, still unsure of his intentions. She turned sideways to let someone pass by.

"I asked Manisha for your number, but she didn't have it."

"What for, Mr. Daruwalla?" she queried.

"Do you remember our new chaiwallah speaking about luck and joining hands?"

"Yes."

"This came to mind when my friend Anish mentioned he was looking for a new assistant consultant. He leads Bhavishya Sankalp Ventures, a consulting business that invests in start-ups. I thought this could be you."

Me? Assistant consultant? she thought, feeling intimidated by the title, but quickly responded, "That would be amazing. I would love that."

"Wonderful!" Sumeet said. "Honestly, I do think it may be a big jump for you, but I am happy to introduce you based on your experience in sales, customer service, your enthusiasm, and your father's high hopes."

Aditi nodded excitedly.

"I remember you telling me you needed a shot," he smiled.

Aditi's eyes sparkled with an eager intensity. "I'm a hard worker and a fast learner, Mr. Daruwalla. I can do it," she declared. "And yes, I really need that shot," she said passionately.

After exchanging phone numbers, Sumeet said, "Great! Let's see what happens," and he walked toward the counter.

Aditi froze in the aisle as she watched Sumeet leave and

tried to process the highly unexpected, enormous opportunity. *I can't believe it!* she thought. *Keep calm, Diti, chill. Maybe, just maybe you get an interview. Don't get too excited yet.* She picked up the dal she was looking for and headed toward the counter. *What an incredibly kind gesture from Mr. Daruwalla,* she thought while waiting in line. *I need to immediately go home to research the industry, company, and role.* As she considered the opportunity, she remembered the way she looked at those women in front of the supermarket before. *Ha! Me? The girl from the Koliwadahs an assistant consultant at an investment firm?* She dreamed of what that might mean, what work she might do, as she repeated the title to herself.

She shifted forward as it was almost her turn. *And, unbelievably, I owe this opportunity to the chaiwallah!* she thought and laughed out loud, surprising the customer and cashier in front of her.

*

REINVIGORATED BY SUMEET'S surprising suggestion, Aditi walked across the call center floor at Gupshup Kendra. As she passed her manager's office, she saw Krish quickly get up from his chair. "Aditi, could you step into my office for a moment?" he called.

"Yes, of course," she said, wondering what this was about.

Just as she was about to sit in the chair in front of his desk, Krish said, "Come to my side, Aditi, I want to show you something." She walked around his desk and bent forward to look at his computer screen. "I'm missing the data from Tanvee's customers you started to manage," he said, pointing at the empty cells.

Aditi's eyes widened with surprise. Bending forward

further, she saw last night's hours of work missing. *Are macchi!* she yelled to herself.

"I also checked your profile, but it's not been saved there either," he explained.

"Oh," she said. "I am so sorry, sir," she added, reflecting on her tiredness last night. "I must have forgotten to save my work last night," she said, sighing deeply.

Krish gave her a friendly nod. "It's not a problem. I just wanted to let you know."

"I will make sure it's in the system within the next three hours," she stated confidently.

"Sure, anytime today is fine," Krish said.

Rushing to her desk, she thought, *Diti, how could you make that mistake!* Sitting down, she immediately turned on her computer to get started. *Too many hours of mundane admin work, yes, but you can't let this has happen again,* she urged herself. *Krish can't see me making any small error or mistake.*

Sumeet

As Sumeet sat behind his desk in the early afternoon, the subject of a new email instantly made him stand up. "Really?" he said aloud. Clicking on the email, the message read: *Congratulations Mr. Daruwalla. We are excited to announce that you and your team won this quarter's sustainability award. The CEO will share the news in next month's global results call.* Relief washed over him. "Finally, some good news!" An enormous sense of excitement filled his chest. *We really needed this. It will definitely lift team morale,* he thought.

Sumeet leaped into the meeting room where everyone was already seated, thrilled to make his announcement. "Hello, everyone!" he said, injecting enthusiasm into his voice. The room remained quiet, except for the sound of clicking keys on laptops. Sumeet scanned the room and noticed Vikas's absence. He thought, *Damn, he should be here, but this can't wait.*

"Team, I have wonderful news to share!" he started with pride. "We have won this quarter's national sustainability award for all our hard work these last few months! This will be shared by the CEO himself. Really well-done, guys!"

Expecting a burst of celebration, there was an odd silence instead, until finally Prashant responded, "Great!"

Sumeet looked around the room, wanting more. Priya gave him a slight smile, but Shanthi continued to stare coldly at her screen. "Come on, everyone, you should feel proud!" he added, masking his disappointment from their reactions. "Please share this great news with all your team members." He paused to give the team another moment to respond, but there was none. Frustration absorbed him, but he forced himself to continue. "Okay then, let's move to today's agenda." Sumeet sat back down while someone from Prashant's team rose to present slides.

When the meeting finished, Sumeet walked to the bathroom, his steps heavy with thoughts. Sitting in a stall, he overheard voices. "How's it been, dost?" one said. "Okay, I guess." Sumeet thought he recognized the voices to be senior members working in Priya and Shanthi's teams. "I've been looking outside the company for opportunities," one of them said. "Yeah, me too. Sumeet doesn't know what he is doing," the voice laughed. The words cut through Sumeet and his heart sank. *What!?* he thought. The voices continued, "I expect many to leave soon. Yes. Let's go, we start in five minutes." Sumeet listened to their footsteps leaving, feeling the weight of their words and questioning himself.

In the late afternoon, Sumeet decided to take leave early. Now he sat in his car, mulling over thoughts on how he had reached such a low point with the team. He messaged Manisha telling her he would not come home for dinner, and then instructed his driver to take him to the Hilltop Grill restaurant on Hill Road. There, he decided to spoil himself by ordering risotto with black truffles and sangria, which he would never order with Manisha. While emptying the pitcher of wine, he couldn't figure out the specific causes that led to his alienation and the lackluster vibe across his team.

Outside the restaurant, he told his driver to head home and slowly strolled straight ahead along Hill Road. After turning right with the bending road, he read the message on St. Andrew's Church billboard. "Life begins the moment you decide to be yourself." *What does that even mean?* he thought, feeling tipsy. Then his gaze fell on a hole-in-the-wall bar on the corner. Taking off his jacket, he loosened his tie and unbuttoned the top two buttons of his shirt and told the boy, "Old Monk, ice, soda, water, chaat masala peanuts." The order would give him some comfort. He focused on the cricket match on the screen, hoping it would diminish his troubled thoughts.

After two glasses, he decided to head home and turned right behind the bodhi tree on Chimbai Square. From the dimly lit square, a voice pierced the evening air.

"Sumeet?" It was the chaiwallah. "How are you this evening?" Sumeet turned his head lethargically toward the man, the veins in his eyes showing red. "Come," the chaiwallah insisted gently. Sumeet hesitated but breathed deeply and made his way to the chai stand. As he sat down, his bright white business shirt and tailor-made suit contrasted awkwardly against the cheap plastic stool.

"I only drink chai in the mornings," Sumeet remarked, but he accepted the glass. He felt a warmth, a comforting kindness from the old man's eyes.

"Tough day at the office?" the chaiwallah asked.

The question made Sumeet's bitterness and frustration reemerge. "Tough days, dada," he said, sighing heavily.

The chaiwallah leaned in. "I will close up my cart, so we can talk."

Sumeet felt a wave of vulnerability. The alcohol, the chaiwallah's kindness, and the dark, quiet square made him feel safe. When the old man sat down next to him, he said, "I have always been successful in my career. Everything went as I planned until I got this new job six months ago that made everyone proud. Since then, everything has gone wrong."

"What do you think caused such change?" the chaiwallah asked.

Sumeet hesitated to answer, but then admitted, "I am actually not sure." After a moment, he sighed deeply and said, "I have never felt like this before. I feel like I am swimming against a powerful current. With every stroke, the current carries me back even further."

The alcohol, disappointments, and fatigue turned Sumeet emotional.

"It's not just a few things. It is everything!" he bellowed. "For the first time in my career, I really dislike the people I work with. I'm experiencing a company culture I do not condone, and despite working harder than ever, the results are not showing."

He looked at the chaiwallah who nodded in understanding. Sumeet felt embarrassed sharing his feelings to a street vendor he barely knew, but the flood gates were open.

"It feels like a perfect storm hitting me," Sumeet said, almost desperately.

"Maybe it's not a storm, beta. Maybe they are messages from the gods," the chaiwallah replied calmly, touching his white beard.

"What kind of messages?" Sumeet demanded.

"Messages instructing you to change your path. Sometimes we believe our path is right because it is familiar or we tell ourselves or loved ones tell us that we should just power through. But the universe sends us messages. Most people ignore them, fearing change, until the messages become undeniable."

Sumeet pondered this, feeling somewhat skeptical, still believing he needed to fight through challenges.

"Sumeet?" the old man nudged him gently. "Besides work, how are things?"

He laughed off the question, telling the old man there was no life besides work. The chaiwallah then asked about his family. Surprisingly, the question stung. Sumeet decided the conversation was becoming too personal and mentioned that a change in work would be the answer, almost convincing himself.

"Well, in my experience, a feeling of a perfect storm is often about more than just work, beta," the chaiwallah suggested, looking into Sumeet's eyes.

The old man's suggestion and look made Sumeet's pride creep in, and he thought, *I'm a general manager at one of India's largest companies. How could this street vendor understand my world?*

"No. It's either push through the challenges or change jobs," Sumeet said firmly, standing up to end the conversation. He fished for his wallet, but the chaiwallah stopped him.

As Sumeet undressed back in his home office, he stared down through his window to see the chaiwallah push his cart onto Chimbai Road. *Where does he live?* Sumeet wondered. When the old man turned the corner, Sumeet watched the moonlight glitter across the dark sea water.

Aditi

I N THE MORNING, Aditi padded from her bathroom to the kitchen to prepare breakfast.

She had stayed up another few hours after getting home late from finishing her data entries to learn about the consulting industry. Vishal was still asleep. As the pomfret started sizzling, her phone on the kitchen bench rang, and she picked it up.

"Hello, Aditi, this is Lakshmi. I'm calling on behalf of Anish Chopra…"

Aditi's heart immediately skipped a beat. *Anish? That is Mr. Daruwalla's friend!*

"…from Bhavishya Sankalp Ventures," Lakshmi continued. "I appreciate this is very last minute, but we would like you to come in tomorrow at three for an interview."

"Thank you. Yes, I will be there," Aditi said immediately, trying to keep her voice steady, unsure how she would make it.

"Great," she said and spelled out her email address. "Please send me your updated resume before this evening, and we will see you tomorrow," the women said cheerfully and hung up.

"What? This is unbelievable!" Aditi yelled out. She jumped onto the bed and hugged Vishal, who woke up when she yelled.

"What happened?" he asked wiping the sleep from his eyes.

"Huge news, baala!" she announced.

"But you just started a new job," he responded, puzzled after hearing she had another interview.

"Oh, but this is different, baala. This would be a dream come true for your aai. Something I could never even have imagined!"

After dropping off Vishal, she quickly stopped her scooter in front of the chaiwallah's cart on Chimbai Square.

"Well, well!" she announced.

"You are glowing, beti!" the chaiwallah swiftly responded.

"Guess what? I just got offered an interview for a job far beyond my wildest dreams!"

"That is wonderful news!" the old man smiled broadly.

"Yes, and interestingly, Mr. Daruwalla is the one who set this up."

The chaiwallah raised his eyebrows in response, the wrinkles on his forehead deepening even further.

"Mr. Daruwalla did that because you told him the other day that he could create luck for others!" she explained. "Do you believe it?"

"Ha!" the old man laughed aloud. "It really worked?"

"It was intentional?" she inquired. The old man smiled broadly, affirming Aditi's hypothesis.

"You are an interesting man, dada," she said, intrigued. "I must go to work now. I wish you a wonderful day."

"Perhaps you can find someone who works at the company to get insider information," he proposed as she was about to drive off.

"How do you come up with these things?" Aditi laughed. "That's a great idea. I will do that. Bye!"

Arjun

Diagonal across from the chaiwallah's cart, Arjun and Rohit drank in silence underneath the bodhi tree.

Arjun recollected the failed robbery attempt in front of the jewelry store, remembering the hesitation he felt seeing love in the couple's eyes. *I can't harm anyone,* he thought.

"That gun incident was a million-to-one chance. That will never happen again," Rohit said, breaking the silence, worried the incident haunted Arjun. "I suggest we roam around Pali Market again. You need to do something. There is no other way for you to pay off that eight lakhs. Or," he paused, "we plan for that one big heist I mentioned to you some time ago. My friend's wife works in that building and knows the guards. That would change your situation in one single night."

Arjun turned to Rohit. "We are petty thieves; that heist is for big-time criminals. And it is too risky."

Rohit took another sip from his tharra. "We can do it, bhai. We just need to plan carefully."

Arjun scoffed and outright dismissed the idea, thinking, *He is right about one thing… that debt isn't going anywhere.*

Sumeet

That evening, Sumeet's car got stuck in the middle of a frustrating traffic jam. *It's only ten kilometers, and it's taking me almost forty-five minutes,* he sighed, looking at the sea of red taillights ahead. When he finally ran into the hotel, the prominent sign in the lobby caught his eye: *Banking Industry Awards.* Beneath it: *Grand Salon Ballroom, 2nd floor.* His heart quickened, knowing the significance of the event.

In the lift, Sumeet tried to shake off the frustration and guilt for being delayed. *I am here now,* he thought, adjusting his immaculate jacket for the black-tie event. As the doors opened, an usher took him to the grand ballroom.

Sumeet scanned the elegantly appointed room, noting the beige, silk-covered tables, each adorned with silverware and a centerpiece of white lilies and red roses. His family was already seated—his mother, father, wife, and sister.

"Why are you so late?" Manisha whispered loudly.

"My last call went over and traffic was horrible," he muttered, slipping into his seat.

He quickly apologized to his parents with his mother returning a nervous smile and his father giving him a cool nod, both gawking at the podium.

"This is such a big moment for him, yet he seems so composed," Sumeet thought, watching his father. A waiter interrupted his reverie. Sumeet ordered a glass of Black Dog Black Reserve with one ice cube, soda, and still water mixed and chaat masala peanuts.

The speaker in a black tuxedo announced, "And now, the main award of the evening. India's most prestigious award in the banking industry." A pause followed as tension built. "Bank CEO of the Year!" Anticipation electrified the room. "Thousands cast their votes this year, and our winner led the tally by far! A true pioneer in the industry! Drumroll please… please congratulate Mr. Nitin Daruwalla!"

Applause erupted and everyone stood up. Sumeet's father smiled broadly and exuded a calm confidence. Sumeet's eyes followed his father's every movement. *Look at him,* Sumeet thought happily, with some envy. *Always that calm confidence, managing pressure with ease, and naturally belonging in the corporate world.*

His father ascended the stage, commanding attention with a humble "Namaste" and a slight bow while pressing his palms together in front of his chest. "Thank you. I am truly honored," he began, first acknowledging his team and partners. "This year, our industry has made great strides," he continued, listing advancements in digital lending, open banking APIs, and more. "But there is still much to do." He went on to mention artificial intelligence, machine learning, and digital identity solutions. "We will break down barriers and make our fellow Indians proud!" he shouted, raising his fist in the air.

He gestured toward his family and concluded, "I could not have achieved this without my wonderful wife and my two wonderful kids." Sumeet saw his mother shyly glowing with pride. "I am proud of you both," he said, looking at Sumeet and his sister. The comment made Sumeet skeptical, and he couldn't help but think, *Proud of me? Really?* He forced a smile as those around him applauded. He lifted his glass in an awkward salute before taking a gulp.

"Join us on stage," the speaker said. After posing for photos with his father, they moved as a family from table to table.

Sumeet followed his father, shaking hands, when he suddenly got distracted by a text message. It was Ananya, the schoolteacher in Dharavi. Sumeet stopped to read her message and checked his calendar. *I will make time for it,* he thought and confirmed his availability.

"Sumeet!" Manisha's voice jolted him back. "Follow your father closely," she urged him.

Sumeet nodded, trying to focus on the momentous evening. "Who was that?" she asked.

"It was that schoolteacher I met in Dharavi the other day. I'm going to lecture next week," he explained.

"For work?" she asked stiffly.

"No, just for fun." His voice reflected his excitement and the gratitude he felt for this rare sense of enthusiasm coming over him. A blank expression washed over his wife's face. While continuing to greet the strangers around the room, Sumeet's mind filled with ideas for his lecture.

Aditi

"THIS IS HOW you dress for the dentist?" Aditi's colleagues joked during lunch the next day, observing her saree and accessories. "Are you already running off?" Tanvee said. Aditi laughed off the comments.

She had sent her resume and worked again all night to collect more information on Bhavishya Sankalp Ventures, the consultancy industry, and all the ins and outs of being a consultant, which felt somewhat relatable to her sales and customer service experience. Following the chaiwallah's advice and with enormous luck, a former classmate had called back in the early evening with insights she would have never found online.

Aditi had driven from Goregaon all the way south to Lower Parel downtown, and was now confronted by the enormous and modern glass office building. The area was congested with traffic jams, dust, and noise from all the new buildings being constructed in town, a testament to India's continued economic boom that turned the country into one of the world's top ten economies.

She entered the immense lobby with her eyes wide open, looking for the reception desk and feeling somewhat intimidated by the luxurious surroundings. After taking time to get through the different security controls, she finally entered the lift feeling nervous. Her visitor pass let her go up to the eighteenth floor. In the glass lift, she scanned the meticulously dressed men and women moving in and out. Waiting patiently, she fought a feeling of not belonging and decided to turn around to admire the breathtaking city views instead of others moving in and out of the lift. *I'm early, so I will let them know I am here and head off for coffee and a final review,* she thought, feeling pumped up.

When the doors opened on the eighteenth floor, the reception of the consultancy was right in front of her.

"Good afternoon," she said. "My name is Aditi Sawant, and I am here for…"

"Yes, Aditi. Great that you are early; they can see you right away," the receptionist cut in.

"Wonderful," Aditi responded, her heart racing. "Let me quickly stop by the washroom."

"That way," the woman pointed.

After checking to see she was alone in the bathroom, she sighed deeply, looked into her own eyes in the mirror, balled up her fists, and whispered sharply, "Diti, this is your moment!" She took another deep breath. "I am an assistant consultant. I belong here!" She ended her motivational speech with, "Do your best, Diti, the rest is up to God," which was something she told Vishal every morning.

"Hello, I am Anish. You must be Aditi," the man walking into the meeting room said. Aditi quickly stood up and reached out her hand.

"Yes, it's nice to meet you Mister Chopra," she answered.

"Please, just call me Anish. And, also no 'sir', please." he said smiling, the informality pleasantly surprising Aditi.

The woman beside Anish said, "Hi, Aditi, my name is Lakshmi. We spoke on the phone."

"Thank you for coming on such short notice… and early,"

Anish said. "Your profile came in last minute through Sumeet Daruwalla. We have some candidates in hand, but we wanted to talk to you before making a decision."

Aditi smiled, thanking them for the opportunity.

"Could you tell us what we do here at Bhavishya Sankalp Ventures?" Anish asked as his first question.

Aditi confidently explained the company's mission and values, impressing them with her thorough research.

"You clearly did your homework on the company and our work," Anish responded. Aditi saw in his eyes that her answer evoked pride and passion. "You are right. Our slogan *Aage Badho*, to forge ahead, describes both our investment model and our culture."

"Please tell us a bit about yourself Aditi," Lakshmi said.

The question triggered Aditi to reflect on how she had answered this question in interviews before, her struggle to forge ahead in her career, and the self-doubt she felt upon entering the building and in the lift. Suddenly, the chaiwallah's comment crossed her mind about his decision to believe his tea was marvelous, which gave her comfort. She answered, "I am proudly the only woman from Bandra's Koliwadahs to graduate with an MBA and build a corporate career."

She noticed her answer immediately put smiles on the interviewers' faces.

After talking them through her roles, achievements, and personality traits that would make her a successful assistant consultant, Aditi asked some questions. The answers got her even more intrigued and excited about the company and the position.

Finally, Anish asked, "Aditi, one last question from me before we finish. What do you think is the reason your career has not progressed faster? You have a wealth of experience in sales and customer service, but you've never been promoted to managerial roles."

Aditi felt a surge of emotion, recollecting all her examples of unfair treatment, exclusion and denial of opportunities, but stayed composed and explained, "I believe the key reason is simply that I just have not yet come across someone willing to take a bet on me." She smiled with sincerity.

"Everyone needs a little luck, sir," she added, thinking how the comments from Chimbai's chaiwallah led her to this interview. "But I cannot wait to show you, Lakshmi, and the BSV team what I am made of."

"It was a pleasure," Anish responded, his gaze friendly but professional. "We will get back to you on whether you will pass through to a second interview."

Waiting for the lift, Aditi smiled, feeling satisfied. *It's unlikely I will get through. I can't compete with candidates having real consultancy experience and skills, but I gave it my all.*

Sumeet

A WEEK LATER, BEFORE heading back to Chimbai Square, Sumeet walked along the Carter Road promenade and took a moment to sit down on one of the benches to watch the murky brown waves crash onto the rocks that protected the coastline. *I really do not feel like attending today's hectic meeting schedule,* he thought, walking passed Jogger's Park where many local residents ran and walked along the oval-shaped course.

Reaching the chaiwallah's cart, Sumeet greeted the old man and settled onto one of the plastic stools.

"Sitting down this morning?" the old man said happily. "Usually, you're in such a rush."

"Do you have children, dada?" Sumeet sighed, accepting the chaiwallah's glass while reflecting on his father.

"No, one of my great regrets," the old man admitted. Sumeet was surprised at his answer. "But now I see my customers like my children," the chaiwallah added in a grateful tone, resting both hands on his chest.

"I have one child," Sumeet said. "My wonderful daughter, Nandini. I cannot be sure, but I've always thought the relationship between father and son is more difficult, like the relationship between my father and me."

The old man nodded thoughtfully. "Sometimes fathers pressure their sons," he said.

"My father is an important man in India," Sumeet began. "Growing up I always thought he wanted me to be like him, some type of executive in the business world. But as my career progressed, I never felt it gave him the satisfaction I expected. He loves me, but I feel something has been amiss for many years. I just don't know what that is."

"Different expectations perhaps," the old man suggested.

"Perhaps," Sumeet replied, reflecting on his own career and the lingering urge for his father's approval and pride. "My father doesn't really share his feelings, so it's difficult to know."

The chaiwallah's voice softened, "Maybe the truth is inside you, beta, without worrying too much about others."

Sumeet thought about that for a while.

The chaiwallah said, "When I was younger, I also climbed an endless mountain peak, but later in life realized the right path should not be an endless battle or, like you mentioned last time, a powerful current. I believe if it feels that way, it's time to pivot."

Sumeet nodded, reflecting on his career, the endless pressure to achieve and hit the next goal post.

"There's often fear, beta," the chaiwallah said. "People fear following their dreams—they fear the opinions and expectations of other people, especially loved ones. They fear failure and even their own capabilities. Once they are set on their path, they tend to create an identity matching their path, but that's nothing but an illusion."

Sumeet thanked the chaiwallah for their talk, already realizing mid-way through the conversation he would be late for work but decided the conversation was important to him.

*

LATER IN THE day, Vikas made Sumeet wait for thirty minutes, forcing Sumeet to re-schedule his next appointment in his usual jampacked calendar. As Vikas walked into the meeting room, Sumeet decided not to mention it and thanked him for making time.

"What do you want to discuss?" Vikas asked coldly, taking a seat.

Sumeet forced a kind smile, remembering the backstabbing, with Vikas telling his boss Radhika that Sumeet's team wasn't happy. "Firstly, I want to thank you for helping the production team." Sumeet paused, sensing Vikas's distrust. "Radhika placed you in this advisory role for your experience, and it has been very helpful."

"What are you getting at, Sumeet?" Vikas asked defensively.

The comment triggered Sumeet, but he remained calm and professional. "I have been hearing some discrepancies in the directions given to the team by you and me," Sumeet explained.

"Like what?" Vikas asked with barely contained irritation.

"For example, production priorities, ordering, and factory floor movements," he said, using Fatima's insight. "I think it would be useful if we have weekly meetings to ensure alignment, especially with the current target pressures," Sumeet suggested.

"You can check my calendar," Vikas replied curtly.

"Great, let's do that," Sumeet replied, smiling. "Now that we are talking, do you have any suggestions for us to help improve the business?" Sumeet asked, annoyed that Vikas seemed to constantly talk to people in his team, except him.

"Actually, yes," Vikas replied, taking Sumeet aback. "I think you should try to understand your engineering team better," Vikas said.

"Could you be more specific?" Sumeet asked, feeling insulted.

"You don't understand what they do very well," Vikas accused.

"I agree, it is one of my learning areas," Sumeet admitted, thinking his admittance could help build rapport. "That is one of the reasons why I sit with Shanthi every week and spend more time with her team compared to any others."

Vikas scoffed, his face showing impertinence. "Anything else?" he said, standing up to end the conversation.

"No, that's it. Thanks, Vikas," Sumeet said hastily, surprised by the abrupt ending. "I will make sure those weekly catch-ups are in your calendar."

Aditi

I N THE EVENING, Aditi was absorbed in finishing the day's data entries into the online customer relationship management program for Tanvee. Then a caller ID on her phone popped up, showing "Lakshmi BSV." Aditi's heart immediately jumped. She hastily answered, trying to keep her composure.

"Hello?" she said, her voice tinged with anticipation and her nerves making her stand up behind the desk.

"Aditi, this is Lakshmi from BSV."

"Hi, Lakshmi, nice to hear from you again," Aditi replied, hoping her tone conveyed the right mix of professionalism and eagerness.

"I'm calling because we want to invite you for a second-round interview."

Aditi's face paled. *Really!? Next round!?* she thought. "That is fantastic news. Thank you so much!" she exclaimed, then felt somewhat embarrassed by her enthusiasm. *How could I have beaten some of the others?* she pondered.

"Yes, well done, Aditi," Lakshmi continued. "And I apologize for the rush, but could you come in tomorrow morning at eight?"

Aditi's heart skipped another beat. *Calm yourself,* she

thought. "Yes, of course," she said confidently, masking any hint of anxiety. "I will be there."

"Great," Lakshmi said. "This second round involves a real-life case study. We'll provide information about a business, and seek your analysis and proposed solutions to help them succeed. You'll have time to read the case study on the spot, so there's no preparation needed. Just bring your problem-solving skills."

Case study!? She thought, her mind a whirlwind of shock and doubt. "Yes, great!" she said, putting on an enthusiastic front.

"The aim is for you to run through the assessment. Identify challenges and opportunities, explain your steps, predict outcomes, and suggest a possible exit strategy if applicable. Everything will be explained during the interview, so don't worry. You'll do fine," Lakshmi reassured her.

"I look forward to it," Aditi said, her nerves tightening into a knot as they hung up.

Standing behind her desk, she scanned her area. Krish and others had already left some time back. In a panic, she thought, *I need to go home now to practice.* But then forced herself to consider her experience and that her father had always shared his ideas and thoughts on people and business growing up. *There is almost no time to prepare, so just think on your feet. Be yourself... that's how you got through the first round,* she coached herself.

Sumeet

IN DHARAVI, SUMEET stepped out of the taxi in the dimly lit street. He wove through the crowd trying to find the right alley. He spotted the pitch-dark narrow lane next to the hardware store. Once he reached the end of the dark alley, he entered another, which was bright, lively, smoke-filled, and pungent with vendors selling deep fried pakoras, grilled fish, chicken tikkas, and chutneys. Remembering the way, he turned a few more times in the darkness, when finally, the rhythmic chanting of children from a well-lit room ahead of him confirmed his arrival.

Ananya saw him at the door and greeted him enthusiastically. "Come inside. You can begin," she told him.

Sumeet stepped into the classroom, looking smart in his suit, and put down his leather briefcase. Standing in front of the classroom, the young adults on the floor instantly called out in harmony, "Good evening, Mister Daruwalla!" A surge of love and inspiration washed over him.

"Good evening, everyone! And thank you, Madam Ananya, for the invitation," he said, glancing at the teacher. "My name is Sumeet Daruwalla. I work as general manager at an automotive company, and I am responsible for production in Central and South India. Looking across the factory floor this week, I thought long and hard about what I wanted to share with you today." He paused. "One thing that stood out to me were the large number of female leaders in our factory, which is not common in India. So, rather than talk about our engineering capabilities or production processes, I wanted to talk to you about our Indian women in leadership, and give you real-life examples about the challenges and solutions they face in the workforce." Sumeet saw the eyes of different young women in the room light up in approval at this topic.

He highlighted that the number of women in key decision-making bodies like government and corporate boardrooms was rising but remained limited. He then explained that women often face glass ceilings and biases that impact their opportunities, promotions, and salaries, and that work-life balance is a challenge for women with children who lack access to flexible work arrangements, affordable childcare, and parental leave options.

"There are many ways to help women thrive in business. Practices such as promoting gender diversity, setting targets for recruitment, and implementing policies for promotions and equal compensation can have enormous impact. Today, through real-life stories, I will explain why it is important for society and for business performance to promote more Indian women into decision-making positions."

Sumeet paused to let his words sink in. "Please raise your hand at any time if you have a question," he urged the students. "I will start by telling you Priya's story, who is our head of …" he began.

After answering some questions throughout the lecture, Sumeet saw more hands go up at the end. "Do I have time for a few more questions?" he asked Ananya.

She nodded, clearly excited.

A young woman raised her hand. "Mister Daruwalla,

please excuse me for being direct, but the women you speak about seem to come from wealthy families with degrees from reputable schools. The women in this classroom come from poor households and have no formal education. How can women like us get office jobs and thrive like the women in your stories?"

The question visibly touched Sumeet. "What is your name, young lady?" he asked.

"Anjali," she responded.

"That's a very valid question, Anjali," he said, thinking for a moment. "I wish I could give you a definitive answer, but honestly, I do not know," he admitted humbly. "Let me think about your question and come back to you."

"Thank you, sir," Anjali replied.

After the last question, Sumeet walked up to Ananya. "I felt very touched today," he told her. "It was humbling to teach and hear their stories."

"It was great for them to hear real office stories rather than theory," Ananya said.

"How can we help people like Anjali effectively?" Sumeet asked passionately.

"The answer is simple, but the implementation is difficult. Funding to create a structured program, get more teachers, access to computers with internet, and ability to earn a recognized degree," Ananya suggested.

"Right," Sumeet agreed, thanking her for the eye-opening experience.

Arjun

ARJUN KNEW THERE was no other way around it. He had to pay off his debt or face the consequences. With apprehension, he now padded beside Rohit in the dead of the night, turning from the Pali Mala Road into the quiet expanse of Nargis Dutt Road once again. The oppressive silence was only disturbed by their cautious footsteps. Arjun glanced up at the imposing walls that loomed above them.

"No more walls," Arjun told Rohit.

They passed by a handful of houses and then some apartment blocks that had Rohit's eyes sparkling with determination. "Let me have a look here," Rohit whispered, peering through one of the iron gates. "This is much easier to climb." Arjun's eyes scanned their surroundings. The street was deserted, wrapped in an eerie silence.

"That window on the ground floor doesn't have iron bars. I can get us in," Rohit said, pointing at the house, his voice barely a whisper. Before Arjun could protest, Rohit already had one leg over the gate, then the other, and landed softly in the garden. Arjun followed, full of trepidation.

They crept to the front of the house, street lights exposing them for anyone driving by. *This is stupidity,* Arjun thought, feeling his pulse quicken.

"You are on lookout," Rohit instructed him, pulling out a stiff putty knife from underneath his shirt. Arjun saw Rohit work the blade into the window sash, prying it open just enough to slip a small metal hook through. His fingers danced with precision as he manipulated the latch. Arjun watched nervously between the front gate, the first-floor windows, and the street, anxiety gnawing at his insides. "Got it," Rohit whispered, pride flickering in his voice. Rohit slithered through the window, vanishing into the darkness beyond. With a sigh and initial hesitation, Arjun quickly followed.

The outside streetlights pierced the darkness, casting ghostly beams from the window across the room. "In and out!" Arjun whispered sharply, trying to instruct Rohit, his heartbeat thunderous.

"Theek ahe," Rohit replied in agreement.

Arjun flicked on his phone's light. A large, somber painting of men staring blankly at Arjun loomed on the wall. *Who would hang this in their home?* Arjun wondered, the unsettling gazes from the painting made his skin crawl. Carelessly, Rohit sped ahead into the living area. Arjun stepped gingerly onto a rug, hoping it would muffle his footsteps as he inched toward the furniture facing the garden in a sunken area of the living room. His light showed Rohit rummaging through drawers beneath the bookshelves. Coming down the few steps, Arjun approached an enormous plush sofa, his breath shallow and quick. He opened his backpack then unplugged a smartphone charging on a wooden coffee table and slipped it into his bag. The small vase on the table looked expensive so he added it to his bag. His phone's light swept across a massive television screen and paused at the sight of framed calligraphy above it reading, *Karma Hi Puja Hai,* meaning "your purpose is revealed through your actions." A chill ran down Arjun's spine. He glanced back at Rohit, who remained engrossed at the shelves.

On the other side of the couch was another side table, but with drawers. Arjun searched through them but found nothing of value. On top stood a luxurious golden photo frame. He glanced at it, seeing an entire family in traditional Maharashtrian attire, and put it back down.

Suddenly, his heart skipped a beat and panic clawed at his throat. He picked up the frame again and shone his light on the picture, peering closer. *No! This can't be!* he thought, squinting in disbelief. *That man… it's the doctor from Chimbai!*

Fear surged through his veins, making his hands tremble. *I am cursed!* his mind screamed, putting down the frame with shaky hands and casting a frantic glance behind him. Rohit remained oblivious, deeply immersed in his search. Arjun's eyes darted back to the same window they entered. Without a word, he bolted, lifting himself up with superhuman strength. He landed face first, his palms scraping against the rough brick path. Panic-fueled adrenaline propelled him to his feet. He glanced around wildly, his breath coming in ragged gasps. The street was still eerily silent. He ran to the gate and hoisted himself up, scanning the street for any sign of danger. *How is this possible!?* His thoughts raced and terror consumed his mind. Finding the street empty, he jumped down and ran, heedless of the noise he made, desperate to get home.

Aditi

M ORE PREPARATION TIME *would have helped, but I will just go with the flow,* Aditi thought, trying to calm herself down as she waited in the meeting room at Bhavishya Sankalp Ventures for the interviewees to enter and start the case study for the second interview. *It's already amazing that I made it through the first round,* she thought happily.

"Aditi, welcome back," Anish said cheerfully as he stepped into the meeting room followed by Lakshmi and another person.

Aditi immediately stood up and greeted Anish and Lakhsmi, thanking them for the opportunity. She then introduced herself to the third person, a new face.

"My name is Kunal," the man said.

"This is our CFO," Anish announced, putting down some paper in front of her before he sat down.

"Aditi, this is the case study," Anish said, pointing at the table. "We would like you to deconstruct the business, explain your views on the challenges they face, what solutions you would propose, the results you expect, and outline an exit strategy that would optimize our return on investment."

Aditi nodded, listening intently to the instructions.

"You have thirty minutes to read through and prepare your thoughts. Of course, you will have limited information, so you will need to make assumptions. Then we'll have another thirty minutes to discuss your thoughts. You can present your analysis in any way you prefer—using the big screen, the whiteboard, or just written notes," Anish explained.

"You won't have all the information behind the financials, but estimates will do fine," Kunal jumped in, increasing Aditi's nervousness.

They left the room and Aditi thought, *Well, here goes nothing.* She didn't know what to expect when she picked up the first page and saw the title, *Green Steaks.* She read that the company was founded three years ago by two friends who invented, produced, and sold plant-based meat products made from soy, lentils, and peas. Their products were produced by a third-party and a separate distributor who sold their products across specialty businesses in Mumbai. The key challenges they faced were low sales and high operating costs, which prevented them from expanding.

Aditi instantly thought about some of her baba's wisdom, including lessons from his fishing trips, economics in the fishing industry, handyman experiences, and the entrepreneurship he noticed around him. He was always very perceptive, and said about business, "Everyone thinks about what they want to make or what they want to do, but you unlock success by giving others what they want, and that is easy to know, because you can tell by observing people around you."

Aditi read further, feeling intimidated seeing the extensive financial overview showing 1.25 crore, a gross margin of 19 percent, and a net margin of 5 percent. She reminded herself to read the entire document first before diving into sections. The back of the page included charts that showed retail market overviews, growth statistics, market share, and other details about Green Steaks' financials.

The last paragraph, in bold, stated that Green Steaks had growth potential with the right strategy and funding. Aditi needed to recommend strategies to help the company grow to a five-crore business in three years and improve net margins.

The first thing Aditi thought was, *I have never seen these products anywhere. Mothers like me wouldn't understand and trust what these products are made of, how to use them, and how they would taste. Mothers don't like to take risks, because we want our children to enjoy our food and eat well.*

She also thought about the brand and product names. *Most people don't buy "steaks," and "green meat" doesn't mean anything. I buy boneless chicken for kombdi rassa or goat shoulder for kolhapuri curry. With these names, I'm unclear which products to use for which dishes. And no one is going to buy them at these prices.*

Aditi recalled her mother's strategy when selling fish—allowing customers to taste the product with her home-made masala. *Green Steaks should do something similar at scale in familiar, relevant dishes*, she thought. Reading the entire case study once more, she remembered her father's teachings on competing with others and the actions he took to keep the costs low for his fish and part-time handyman services to build his network.

Finally, she wrote down all her key headlines before jotting down the details: Integrate production and distribution to lower costs. Brand and product specificity needed. Ramp up marketing funds. Educate consumers. Partner with large restaurant chains to get brand and products on menus. Pivot from premium outlets to supermarket chains. Accept an initial loss on profitability with lower prices to increase reach and volumes.

"Okay, Aditi, time is up," Anish said walking in after half an hour. "Ready to take us through?"

"Yes!" *Here it goes,* she thought, walking up to the whiteboard.

"Just a reminder, it's more important we understand your thinking and rationale rather than correct answers," Anish pointed out, before she began.

Aditi nodded and started writing on the board. After Aditi finished her presentation and answered their questions, Anish concluded with a smile, "Wonderful insights from on-the-ground experience, Aditi. I really liked how you approached the thinking from your role as mother and your examples from your parents' businesses.

Aditi blushed slightly, feeling invigorated, thinking, *I'm so out of my comfort zone and loving it.*

"Any questions for us before we close?" Anish asked.

"Yes, when will you let me know the final result?" she smiled.

"Well, our slogan is *Aage Badho*, so we will be quick," he answered.

Sumeet

Another late-night call, Sumeet thought standing before the U-shaped table in the conference room. He scanned the blank faces around him, a smile of forced enthusiasm stretched across his own face.

"How is everyone?" he asked, his voice bright and inviting a connection, hiding his mortification after overhearing the washroom comments the other day. A chorus of non-committal replies greeted him: "Not bad," "Okay." He apologized for the sudden, unexpected meeting, attempting to maintain his upbeat tone as he explained that the boss, Radhika, needed to urgently speak to the team and he needed each one of them to answer questions if required. At the back of the room, Vikas slouched in his chair, typing away, clearly disengaged from the situation. Sumeet connected his laptop to the conference station to enable everyone in the room to listen and respond.

"Hello? It's Sumeet," he announced.

"Hi, Sumeet," came the authoritative voice through the speaker.

Sumeet glanced around the table. "Radhika, I'm here with Vikas, Shanthi, Prashant, and Priya and their senior team members," he explained. "Can you see the slides?"

"Yes, I can. The entire head office team is on the call as well to listen in," the voice responded.

Sumeet's brow furrowed. *Why would she invite everyone including junior staff?* he thought.

"How is everyone?" she asked, her tone energized.

Vikas snapped to attention, suddenly leaning forward. "Hi, Radhika, Vikas here. We're good."

"Hi, Vikas, thanks for joining the call. The team could use the help," she said appreciatively, irritating Sumeet.

"Hi, Radhika," Shanthi chimed in.

Ah, now that Radhika is on the line, they are suddenly engaged, Sumeet thought.

"Sumeet, let's get started" she said, shifting gears. "I'll get straight to the point," she said sternly, tension rippling through the room. "It's looking like you won't achieve most of the targets again this month, and we need to understand the reasons and solutions."

Sumeet swallowed hard, shifting through the slides on the screen, feeling embarrassed by the harsh call-out in front of his team and the entire head office on the line. "Yes," he said, "it's been challenging. Let me..."

"Right, let me just jump in immediately," Sita, the finance director, interrupted mid-sentence. "Sumeet, I do not understand the slides you sent through at all. Start by taking me through slide three," the director demanded.

Sumeet's demeanor changed. His face darkened, and he clenched his jaw as he felt the eyes of the team bore into him. *Why does she have to be so rude all the time?* he thought bitterly, scrolling down.

"Okay. This is the one," he replied, showing slide three. "A week ago, we experienced a mechanical failure in our truck line. We ordered the components immediately, but were unable to recover 100 percent of the output lost."

"Sumeet, you cannot just blame this on a mechanical failure," Sita added sternly.

Radhika pressed on, "Where was the contingency?"

Sumeet took a deep breath, feeling apologetic toward his team for the unnecessary onslaught, which could have been solved by a simple three-way call between Radhika, Sita, and himself.

"The contingency kicked in immediately, with the team working throughout the night to get the line up and running. That's why you can see on the next slide," he said, scrolling down further, "we only lost partial output for two days. The latest numbers are on slide five."

"Hold on! Stay on this page," Sita urged. "Two days of output? That doesn't make sense to me!"

"It's not two full days of output," Sumeet countered, trying to keep his frustration in check. "The team had to…"

Sita interrupted again. "Sumeet, stop. I need you to let me finish. Where were the spare parts? That should have been part of inventory."

Damn it, how can she embarrass me like this? he thought, now finding great difficulty in controlling his frustration. "I was trying to explain," he continued, "that these specific parts are not part of regular inventory. The team had to inspect the line, identify the parts, make amendments, conduct a trial run on another station, and move parts around to ensure minimal disruption. Thanks to their hard work, we were still able to run parts of the line. The critical components will arrive Monday due to the good relationship we've built with our supplier."

The room fell silent, the tension palpable. Sumeet could see embarrassment and discomfort on most faces around the table. He felt humiliated, his anger boiling beneath the surface.

"Okay," Radhika said tersely, breaking the silence. "Well, honestly, Sumeet, our Delhi factory also faced a mechanical failure last quarter and didn't lose any output. Make sure you get back on track by Monday."

Finally, Sita concluded, "This is not an excuse to miss the numbers, Sumeet!"

Sumeet scanned the room again, weighing his response. He caught sight of Vikas and Shanthi smirking, clearly reveling in his predicament. His head started pounding and frustration etched across his face. "Sure. We'll work around the clock," he said, his voice a strained whisper.

Radhika thanked everyone and the line went dead.

This is a punch in the face. Radhika knows how difficult it has been to build rapport with this team and quell hallway chatter, Sumeet thought, watching the team avoid eye contact with him, their faces reflecting their disappointment.

"Team, please do not let these comments affect you. I know your hard work has been paying dividends," he quickly announced, as some stood up to leave. As the team walked out sluggishly, he overheard someone in the hallway mutter, "That was the worst meeting I have ever attended. How can he take it?"

After everyone left, Sumeet stood in front of the now empty conference table, feeling defeated.

Arjun

"How many messages did the gods send for me to turn my life around?" Arjun muttered, strolling from his favorite *vada paav* street vendor on the busy Hill Road. He reflected on his wounded foot, the chaiwallah's undeserving kindness, the barrel of the gun, the lifeless body, and the bizarre coincidence of breaking into the doctor's house. *They can't all just be mere coincidences.* His thoughts raced, consumed by fear and guilt.

He turned right into the more tranquil one-way St. Andrews Road on his way to the liquor store in Chimbai Square. After a few minutes, he glanced to his right and saw a group of teenagers playing cricket on the artificial grass of the football field. He stopped for a moment then decided to walk up close to watch them. Arjun saw they were playing maidan cricket, and that both teams were wearing customized professional-looking shirts with their names on the back. *Let's see how good they are,* he thought.

The boy holding the bat was fixated on the bowler, who was waiting and smirking at him confidently. "*Tu mala out nahi karu shakat or dam asel tar out karun dakhav!*" the batsman shouted at him in Marathi, arrogantly telling the bowler that he couldn't get him out even if he tried.

The bowler smirked, shouting back, "*Tula baghun radayla yeta!*" telling him he felt pitiful just seeing the batsman standing there.

Arjun chuckled at the banter.

The bowler took a few steps forward and threw a strong spinner that landed right in front of the batsman then twisted sharply up high to his left. The batsman took an aggressive shoulder-height swing and missed as the bowl span outwards. "That is what I will do!" the bowler laughed.

The batsman's face soured and he scoffed. "Lucky," he said softly, putting himself back into position. The bowler readied himself. The ball again dropped low ahead of him, and the batsman missed his shot. "*Chyaila!*" he yelled out, outing his frustration.

Arjun smiled, and stepped onto the grass. "Hey," Arjun started, walking up to the batsman.

Everyone on the field turned to Arjun. "Can I show you something?" Arjun smiled at the batsman.

The boy scanned the unshaven, rough-looking middle-aged man, clearly doubting Arjun's ability to play. As Arjun got close, he whispered, "Let's try a sweep shot with this guy. May I?" Arjun asked in a friendly tone, holding out his hand. The boy hesitated for a moment then handed over the bat.

Arjun got ready. "*Chal, ball tak!*" Arjun shouted, telling the bowler to give it a go.

The others on the field laughed at Arjun's sudden enthusiasm. The bowler nodded seriously and took a few steps forward and threw the ball. Arjun swept the floor with his bat soon after the ball landed and smashed it high into the fence with ease. The kids across the field cheered, shocked by Arjun's technique and skill. Arjun gave the bowler a relaxed smile, unsurprised at the outcome. "That's a nasty spinner!" Arjun said approvingly.

Arjun turned to see the boy behind him look impressed. "Come!" Arjun urged him, making the boy stand in front of him. "It can be a leg spin, off spin, arm ball, or googly, but a low sweep often works for all." The boy now listened intently. "Lower your top hand a bit on the handle," Arjun said, moving the boy's hand. "Switch your stance the moment the ball hits the ground," he instructed, showing his shuffle. "And lower your knees and sweep across," he explained as he demonstrated the movement.

The boy nodded. "Thank you, uncle," he said.

"Try it," Arjun urged him.

The boy nodded at the bowler as Arjun stepped away. The ball came, and the boy switched his stance but was too late and the ball passed him.

"Again, and now change immediately as the ball hits the ground," Arjun instructed from behind.

The bowler took a few steps and again threw the ball aggressively towards the batsman. This time, the boy switched his stance quickly as the ball hit the ground and swept the ball high up into the fence.

"*Wa, kay shot ahe!*" Arjun shouted excitedly, complimenting the boy on his shot.

The boy turned around, smiling broadly, pride showing across his face. "Well done, beta," Arjun said, patting him on the shoulder. "Make sure you switch up those spins and fast balls!" Arjun advised the bowler. The bowler smiled, looking determined.

"Have fun, boys!" Arjun shouted. He waved and walked off.

"Uncle!" the boy suddenly yelled from behind as he exited the field. "We play here every Tuesday and Thursday afternoon. Come visit us?" he said.

"Oh, thank you. Maybe I will," Arjun said with a smile and turned right to continue onto St. Andrew's Road.

One of the reasons I excelled was because of the strong team we had in Jalna and playing against older guys, he thought. *I wonder what those guys are all up to now. Varun was such a strong, ferocious bowler. I had no choice but to up my game quickly. That's what initially got me in the tournaments organized by the Marathwada Cricket Association,* he reminisced. *Would my talent have taken me to play in T20 leagues?* He wondered what ever happened to Varun. *I haven't seen his name come up anywhere.*

He stood on the corner of Master Vinayak Road and Chimbai Road, suddenly reliving the moment of teaching that boy the sweep. *That was really fun.* He stared ahead into Chimbai Road. The bodhi tree awaited, but he decided to continue on straight towards Carter Road. *Not today,* he thought.

Aditi

IN THE EVENING, Aditi sat with Vishal behind their dining table to review his schoolwork. Continuing to read the question on the page in front of her, she nonchalantly picked up her vibrating phone.

"Aditi, this is Anish from Bhavishya Sankalp Ventures," the voice said.

A shiver ran through her body, making her stand up instantly, surprising Vishal. "Yes. Hello Anish," she said, a lump forming in her throat.

"You mentioned that you felt someone had to take a bet on you," he stated.

"Yes, yes, I did," she stammered, her heart pounding.

"Well, I am willing to do that, and I hope you agree to becoming our new assistant consultant."

Aditi's eyes welled up instantly as emotions rushed through her entire body.

"What? Really?" she blurted out, unable to contain her excitement. "I mean… yes. Yes, I would like that very much."

"Aditi, you bring exactly what we need to our team right now. Passion, hunger, logical thinking, and great problem-solving skills. And you are someone I would like to work with.

I do think you will have a steep learning curve ahead of you, but I believe you can handle it," he explained, offering her encouragement.

"Oh, thank you, Anish. Thank you for this life-changing opportunity. I am sure to become a most valuable member of your team. I can promise you. Thank you for being willing to take a chance on me," she said, tears of gratitude running down her cheeks.

"You're welcome, Aditi. Lakshmi will call you to discuss next steps, and I look forward to working with you. See you soon." He hung up.

Aditi put down her phone and stood quietly for a moment to reflect on what just happened. She saw Vishal staring at her with worry as she wiped away her tears. Her eyes moved to her parents' picture on the wall. "Who would have thought? Look at your daughter now!" she said aloud, watching her parents. "Assistant consultant at Bhavishya Sankalp Ventures. This is what a simple girl from the Koliwadahs can achieve!" A surge of energy took hold of her as she turned to Vishal and shouted, "Baala! I got it. I got the job! Oh my God!" she yelled, bear-hugging Vishal.

"Which job?" Vishal asked, looking confused.

"The opportunity I told you about. The one I could not have even imagined in my wildest dreams," she said, releasing him. "My call center days are over! Your aai is hitting the big leagues!" she shouted, unable to contain her excitement. Tears started to stream down her cheeks again as she hugged him. Vishal felt her emotions, and started to well up too.

"Congratulations, aai," he whispered in her ear. "You're hugging me to death!" Vishal laughed.

"Let's celebrate!" Aditi yelled out. "If we're quick, we can still get to that fancy cake shop on Hill Road."

Sumeet

Two hundred meters south, across from St. Andrew's Church, Sumeet sat defeated in the same hole-in-the-wall bar on Hill Road, mulling over the embarrassment of tonight's meeting and the many setbacks he had faced all these months. Halfway through his second flask of Black Dog rum, he sighed deeply, paid, and grabbed the bottle on his way out. It was late at night, and St. Paul's Road was dark and deserted. He slumped by the Moorings apartment building, fighting off the assault of emotions attacking him. After a few minutes, he stopped and sat on the curb then dropped his head into his hands and let the tears roll down his face.

"What did I do to deserve this?" he wailed. *I'm trying so hard. I never intentionally hurt anyone. I never backstabbed anyone*, he thought. "Why are they after me?" he said aloud, wiping his tears. Disappointment and the feeling of injustice took hold as he continued to sob. After some time, his feeling turned into resentfulness toward everyone, until finally the accumulation of all his dark thoughts turned him numb and his tears stopped. He got up and walked home, drunk and stoic.

In his apartment building, he slumped out of the lift on his own floor, but instead of going to the front door, he pushed open the steel exit door and walked up the emergency stairs. On the rooftop, he headed toward the western side of the building overlooking Chimbai Square, just one floor up from his in-home office. He stood still for a while, without thought. After taking a big gulp from his bottle, he stepped onto the low parapet of the building. He spotted Jogger's Park then saw part of Carter Road further ahead, as well as the enormous Arabian Sea. Shoulders hunched forward, bottle in hand, and eyes hollow in his pale, drawn face, he gazed straight down and saw the car park. A security guard walked across. Staring ahead, the moon brightened up the water. "It's not just work… it's everything," he murmured. *I can't do it anymore. I'm done,* he concluded, looking down, his admittance of defeat comforting him.

"Don't do it, beta!" a voice pleaded behind him. Sumeet snapped out of his dream and turned around holding his bottle, barely balancing himself on the far edge. He bent forward and squinted his eyes in disbelief, saying, "Dada?"

"Yes, beta. It is me."

"How?" Sumeet asked.

"Please, beta, step away from the edge," the chaiwallah urged softly, extending his hand.

Sumeet, still in a trance, wanted to grab hold of the hand, but his mind and heart, desperate for relief, wouldn't allow it.

"Please, come here, beta," the chaiwallah pleaded one more time.

Sumeet continued to sway on the parapet, but he finally found the strength within to extend his arm. The chaiwallah grabbed it and pulled him down onto the rooftop tiles.

"How did you get here?" Sumeet asked.

"It doesn't matter, beta, the important thing is that I am here for you," the chaiwallah said, sitting down on the tiles in relief. "Let's sit here for a bit," he suggested. Sumeet followed, placing himself next to the old man against the low brick barrier. "I saw you stumble home, and followed you to make sure you got home safely. And now we are here." He smiled with a look of concern on his face. "Things are not well with you, beta," the chaiwallah remarked.

"Things have not been well, dada," Sumeet admitted, his gaze devoid of emotion.

"It's okay," the chaiwallah said. "Let's just sit here together and watch the moon. It's beautiful, isn't it?"

After a long moment of silence, Sumeet suddenly said, "I have told you some of my problems but not everything." The chaiwallah watched him, putting an arm around Sumeet's shoulder as he waited for him to continue. Sumeet's tears started to flow, and he covered his face with his hands. He sobbed and looked up at the sky, his eyes drowning in sadness.

"I feel I have been living my entire life for others," he finally admitted to himself and the old man. "I'm doing all the right things every day for validation from others, but I am not happy. I have not been happy for a while."

The chaiwallah nodded, caressing him.

"Why?" Sumeet yelled, fresh tears starting. "To make my father proud?" he shouted. "To keep up appearances? For social status? For society?" He put his head back down, tiredness settling in after his revelation. After a pause he said, "Now, I'm just out of gas."

"That is perfectly fine, beta. Really, it's okay," the old man affirmed, trying to comfort him. "I have been in your situation as well," the chaiwallah revealed. "For too long, doing the wrong things."

"I am questioning everything," Sumeet said. "Every day I wake up, walk, eat breakfast, sit in traffic, and attend meetings all day that I do not want to attend with people I do not like. I come home late, engage in superficial small talk with my wife, and sleep," he explained. "And on weekends, I try to follow my wife's plans, meet people I don't want to meet, and go places I don't want to go. What kind of life is this?"

"How did you meet your wife?" the chaiwallah asked.

Sumeet sighed deeply. "Well, my father introduced us after graduation. We had a grand wedding with mostly my father's guests. It was his wedding, not mine. My wife and I never really got close. The relationship got worse after Nandini left. We're housemates. There is no love, no intimacy," Sumeet confessed, feeling shame and guilt after the words left his lips. The feeling of despair made Sumeet put his face back into his hands.

"I'm sorry for your pain, Sumeet," the old man said. "But it is incredibly brave of you to admit all this."

"Brave? It is loss and failure," Sumeet replied with sadness.

"What makes you think that?" the old man asked.

"They love me for what I achieve and portray. Without that, I am useless to them."

"They would be wrong, beta," the chaiwallah responded. "You are now admitting your pain, which is brave and the first step to overcoming your fear. It means you are ready for a new phase. We are a spiritual nation, but most men journey through life without questioning themselves, fearful of embracing their true purpose. We usually just put our heads down and go on." The dark, rich, wrinkled eyes pierced into Sumeet's soul. "So, the question you need to start answering in the coming period is, who are you, beta?"

Staring at the rooftop tiles for a moment, Sumeet answered, "The only thing I know is that this is not it."

"That's a great starting point," the chaiwallah said with enthusiasm. "Take your time to think, discover, and experiment. Only you can do that for yourself. Others cannot do that for you. You cannot ignore what happened tonight on this rooftop. Be grateful. Embrace it."

"I'm scared," Sumeet admitted.

"That's natural. It's the unknown," the old man said.

"My mother and daughter may support me, but my father and wife will not," Sumeet said.

"Push through that, Sumeet. There is something magical on the other side that you will be deeply grateful for," the chaiwallah said as he stood. "Come. Let me walk you to your front door. First, you need a good sleep."

Walking down the stairs, Sumeet thought about what he had admitted and the chaiwallah's comments. When they stood in front of his front door, he suddenly felt an enormous relief along with intense fear and a hint of hope. He had decided.

The chaiwallah turned to look into Sumeet's eyes before he opened the door. "You are ready, beta. I will see you tomorrow morning for chai," the old man said.

"Thank you, Daasa-da. I don't know how to thank you," Sumeet said, realizing his life had just been saved.

"Find your purpose, beta," the old man pressed upon him, and then he strolled toward the stairway.

Aditi

ADITI CAME INTO the office early, hesitating slightly before knocking on Krish's office at Gupshup Kendra. "Good morning, sir," she greeted him softly.

"Ah, good morning, Aditi," Krish responded warmly. "I was going to check in with you later this morning to see how you are doing."

Aditi's expression grew solemn. "I am truly sorry, Krish Sir," she said, her voice apologetic.

"What is it?" he asked, concern etching his features.

"I've been offered another job," she confessed. "It's an enormous opportunity, and I must take it."

Krish's eyes widened with surprise. "Really?" A mixture of shock and disappointment was evident in his tone.

"Yes," Aditi replied, her voice laced with remorse. "I have been appointed assistant consultant at an investment firm in town," she added, trying to steady her voice.

"Oh," Krish said, his smile wavering. "Consultancy firm. Wow, that's big." He attempted a light-hearted laugh. "Can you get me in?" he joked, hoping to ease the tension.

Aditi managed a small, grateful smile. "Thank you for the opportunity you gave me," she said earnestly. "I really did appreciate it. For many years, I was unsuccessful in moving on, and then you offered me the role on your team, but now this consultancy opportunity came out of nowhere."

"When do you start?" he inquired, a hint of sadness in his voice.

"They want me to start as soon as possible," she replied.

"Ah…yes, I understand. I was the same with you," he murmured, wistfully recalling his own request. "Well, I guess there isn't much of a handover needed. And I don't want to stand in your way. You just go ahead, Aditi."

Aditi's eyes lit up. "That is very generous of you, sir. I really appreciate it, thank you," she said with gratitude and a touch of relief in her voice.

He paused, taking a breath to steady himself. "I was going to block some time for us this morning, so let's use that for you to walk Tanvee and me through your work with each client."

"Yes, great, let's do that," Aditi confirmed and walked back to her desk, her emotions a mix of excitement and guilt. She then quickly called Bhavishya Sankalp Ventures to inform Lakhsmi she could start tomorrow.

As she hung up, an enormous sense of accomplishment filled her. *I can't believe this is happening,* she thought. She searched for Sumeet's number and called, but no one answered. *I'll leave him a message before he hears this from Anish,* she thought, quickly typing, *Mr. Daruwalla, this is Aditi Sawant. I was successful in the interview with Mr. Chopra, and by some miracle they offered me the job! I will work hard and do my best, sir. I don't know how to thank you. Best regards, Aditi.*

With a deep breath, she sent the message, feeling the first wave of her new journey wash over her.

Sumeet

SUMEET WOKE UP later than usual and tried to avoid Manisha all morning. He now sat at the dining table having oatmeal, mulling over everything that led to the unthinkable tipping point he reached on the rooftop last night, and how he and his family were saved from tragedy. Anxiety settled in as Manisha finally approached him, and he had to face the inevitable confrontation.

"No walk this morning? Meetings starting late today?" Manisha questioned, her voice laced with curiosity.

"I'm not going to work," he said softly, trying to muster strength.

She scrutinized his face. "Are you sick? You don't look like it," she remarked suspiciously.

"Actually," he started, thinking about his explanation. "Actually, I am sick Manisha. I have been sick for a while." He paused and looked at her, hoping to see compassion but didn't find any. "Manisha, please sit, we need to talk." Instead of concern, her eyes showed irritation and confusion as to where the conversation was headed.

"What is this all about?" she asked.

"I'm taking a break from work," he confessed, feeling the weight of his decision bear down on him.

"Break? You started only six months ago. What will Radhika say?" she scoffed.

"I spoke to Radhika this morning. I've decided to quit my job, Manisha. I resigned, and I am no longer general manager," Sumeet said, trying to give himself strength by explaining his action in a few different ways.

"You did what?" she yelled, standing up, shock and anger intertwined in her voice. "Resign? Just like that! How can you do that? Have you lost your mind?" Her fury was palpable.

"Manisha, can you please sit and calm down?" Sumeet pleaded.

"I will not!" she shouted from behind the dining table.

"Manisha, I am completely burned out. I should have seen the signs earlier. The endless headaches were just the beginning," he explained, struggling to convey his inner anguish.

"Well, Sumeet, it's just a tough time at work. Most men in your position deal with that. It's normal. And they overcome. They don't give up like this!" she exclaimed. "You just started. You need to call Radhika back right now to apologize, tell her you made a mistake, and get your job back."

Sumeet knew deep down this conversation was futile, but he had to try. "It's not that simple…" he began, but his frustration cut him off. She wouldn't understand, he thought despairingly. "Look, Manisha," he said more sternly. "Last night something bad happened to me. I was no longer in control. Some sort of emergency autopilot took over," he revealed, his voice trembling. "I couldn't take it anymore," he admitted, feeling his chest tighten with the memory.

"Sumeet, both of our fathers experienced that stress too, but they pushed through the tough times," she argued.

Sumeet felt a tear slip down his cheek, surprising both of

them. "Last night, I walked up to the rooftop. My thoughts turned very dark."

"Dark thoughts? What are you talking about?" she snapped.

"I was going to jump!" he yelled, finally unveiling the dark truth.

"Jump?" she repeated, her voice a mixture of shock and disbelief. "What is wrong with you? Are you crazy? Have you lost it?" Her disappointment stung more than he expected. "What will our families say about all this?" she added, her concern shifting gears.

"It doesn't matter what they say," Sumeet replied softly. "I need to take a step back and do something else."

"Do what?" she yelled.

"Can you please calm down, Manisha," he requested again. "I don't know yet, but it won't be the same."

She sat back down. "What kind of responsible man just quits his high-paying job as general manager in one of India's largest companies?" she scoffed. "It's stupid, that's what it is. Think about your name. What will people think?"

Her words hit hard, but Sumeet was no longer surprised. "I don't care what they think. I need to take care of myself. I can't keep going like this," he said.

She got back up again and said, "What about Nandini?" Before walking off, sadness crossed her face.

"We've saved enough, Manisha. We can cover her studies," Sumeet reassured her, following her into the bedroom, but she stormed off into the bathroom, locking the door.

Disappointed with Manisha's strong reaction, Sumeet stood in front of his prominent wooden bookshelf in need of inspiration. He spotted the autobiography of Sachin Tendulkar, who lived around the corner and was widely considered India's greatest batsman in cricket. Anish had gifted him the book years ago, and Sumeet, like many Indians, had used Sachin's famous quotes throughout his adult life. Next to that stood a novel by Amish Tripathi, which now felt more relevant than ever, as the author left a highly successful banking career to become a full-time writer after his first book became a success. But Sumeet decided to pick up the teachings of Sri Ramana Maharshi on Advaita Vedanta, hoping its core philosophy on the principle that the individual self and the universal self are one would ease his mind. He slumped into his office chair, opening to the section on the nature of reality, which explored concepts of illusion and reality that transcend time, space, and causation without a beginning or end. After reading through, and desperately seeking the infinite peace and bliss the teachings alluded to, Sumeet considered the all-important core question: *Who am I?*

As he read on, immersing himself into the teachings, Manisha suddenly entered his office. "Here, talk to your father," she said, thrusting her phone at Sumeet.

Sumeet's face paled. "You called my father? How could you do that?" he whispered sharply to ensure his father didn't hear. Anger boiled inside him for putting him on the spot.

"Baba?" Sumeet said.

"What is Manisha saying, Sumeet?" his father queried.

"Baba, I'm not well. I have not been well for a while now. I need to stop and pivot," he explained.

"What do you mean?" his father countered, sounding concerned.

Sumeet took a deep breath and looked at Manisha, who stared at him with cold disappointment. "Baba, I started to realize I have been struggling for some time. Now it is time for change."

"I saw this coming," his father said.

"Coming? Or were you waiting for me to fail?" Sumeet responded angrily.

His father sighed, and said, "Not at all. What are you going to do now?"

"I don't know… something different," Sumeet replied, his resolve firm.

"You worked so hard for so long to reach this point. What was it for?" his father asked.

Here we go again, Sumeet thought bitterly. "This is all just about your reputation. It's not about me. It's about how others will perceive you for having a son that abruptly quit his career. Isn't it?" Sumeet shouted, anger and guilt taking hold of him.

"No." His father's voice was soft.

"Last night I was contemplating ending my life! Would you have preferred that?" Sumeet snapped.

His father paused, his silence telling. "Take a good rest today, Sumeet. Don't think about anything. We will talk again tomorrow," his father said and hung up.

"Happy now?" Manisha said coldly and walked off.

Sumeet sat alone, silently battling his despair, thinking, *The chaiwallah is right… this isn't going to be easy.*

Arjun

WALKING TOWARDS CHIMBAI Square, he squinted his eyes to stare into the distance and froze. *It's those bastards again!* he panicked. Arjun quickly pressed himself against the blue-painted wall of the apartment building, trying to stay out of sight. He ducked into the alley around the corner. *Is it really them?* he wondered, his head resting against the wall. He peeked out and scanned the road again. *Yes, it's them! Why are they back already? Did they see me?* Arjun turned around to see the alley was a dead end and there was no escaping. He quickly ran to the end of the lane so he could spot passersby but remain hidden from view. Minutes felt like hours, but then he caught a glimpse of the men speeding past going south, seemingly on a mission. *They will trash my room,* he fretted silently. Arjun realized he was cornered. *Life has trapped me,* he thought, despair washing over him. *No, not life... my own stupid actions.*

Peeking out once more, he realized the men had vanished, so he walked north.

"Where the hell have you been?" Rohit's angry voice cut through his thoughts as he saw his friend slumped underneath the bodhi tree. "How could you leave me there and run off without saying a word?" Rohit demanded.

"I just had to run away from those thugs again," Arjun said hastily. "I think they were looking for me, but luckily I was able to hide in time." Then he dropped down next to Rohit, his scare and subsequent concerns making him grab Rohit's bottle.

Rohit looked at him with disappointment. "What the hell happened that night?" he demanded.

"I am really sorry, bhai," Arjun said earnestly. "I had sudden stomach issues… terrible cramps, and had to leave in a hurry."

"Sudden cramps?" Rohit echoed, incredulous. "You don't ever leave your partner behind. Something's definitely off with you."

"I'll make it up to you," Arjun vowed.

"When I saw you were gone, I went after you and walked out with nothing!" Rohit fumed. "You owe me."

"Anyway, I managed to get a phone and a copper vase. Let's split it," Arjun offered.

"Keep it," Rohit dismissed. "You need it more than I do. Those guys will make you disappear. You cannot avoid paying them," Rohit warned.

Arjun nodded seriously. "I know, I know."

After a few gulps of Rohit's poison, Arjun's anxiety calmed somewhat, and he started to observe the few movements around the now dry, dusty square.

Arjun noticed two men in front of the fruit seller. One, approximately his age, was impeccably dressed in a dark grey suit, white business shirt, and green tie. He was holding the arm of the older man next to him whose mobility was impaired.

As they turned to make their way onto St. Joseph's Road, they had to go around the bodhi tree, but their path was obstructed by Rohit's stretched-out legs. Arjun watched Rohit picking his nose, unconcerned.

"*Rohit!*" Arjun hissed, pointing at his legs. Rohit sneered, but then sluggishly pulled his legs in. *They must be father and son,* Arjun thought, noticing their resemblance as they slowly passed. The man in a suit raised his eyebrows and pursed his lips as he held onto his father. Arjun felt embarrassment wash over him and lowered his gaze.

As Arjun watched them leave, he suddenly turned back to Rohit with an intense look.

"What?" Rohit reacted.

"I have decided. I am ready," Arjun said, determined.

"Ready for what?" Rohit asked, curiosity piqued.

"The big heist," Arjun affirmed. "No more small-time jobs. This will be the final inning, and then I'm out."

Rohit's nodded, his eyes wide, his excitement growing. "With proper planning, we can pull this off. I was waiting for you to finally come through, because I wouldn't trust anyone else to do this with me. They're all rats," Rohit smiled, his resolve firm. "Let me sort out the details."

Arjun nodded decisively, confident about the decision he had just made.

Aditi

THE FOLLOWING MORNING, Aditi stood in front of Vishal and beamed, trying to control her nervousness. "Well, how do I look? Today is your mother's first day as assistant consultant at Bhavishya Sankalp Ventures, baala." Saying it out loud suddenly made it feel more real for Aditi.

Vishal lookup up from his bowl and smiled approvingly at her new saree.

It all happened so fast, it's hard to believe, she thought, chuckling. She told Vishal to finish his breakfast, and that she would be back soon to take him to school, deciding she had to start this day on an auspicious note.

Moving through Koliwadah's labyrinth, she passed the shacks made of corrugated metal plates, wood, and plastic sheets that often housed three Koli generations in one home. The wind now started to hit her face more ferociously as she neared the beach. She saw it was low tide with many of the fishing boats beached, awaiting the night to head out. After turning down a few different alleys, she arrived at the beach.

The sea water was murky brown, and the beach was colored by empty bottles, pieces of plastic, parts of fishing nets, and debris. Aditi took a deep breath. The air smelled like sea salt, dried fish, rubbish, and masala from homes nearby. For Aditi, this smelled like home.

Seeing a fisherman work around the beach, she reminisced about her youth, thinking about her father taking out his boat, often away for weeks before coming back exhausted with his catch for her mother to sell. Aditi used to be so excited and proud whenever he came back. As a child, she helped him sort crabs, lobster, prawns, Bombay duck, catfish, and anchovies. On some days when he was home and the weather got rough, he would take her across the shore to find pomfrets, telling her they could catch them because they ran before the storm.

Deep in her thoughts, she took off her sandals and stepped forward until her ankles were submerged in the water. She suddenly remembered her thoughts of defeat that night after her first day at Gupshup Kendra; she felt guilt. *The mind, Diti,* she reminded herself again. *Your fears and doubts were based on the past and future,* repeating the chaiwallah's wisdom. *But now you got more than you could have dreamed of… embrace it wholeheartedly.* She closed her eyes, squeezing them shut tightly as if to make sure her message got through. She put her palms together and said a prayer to thank the gods and to ask for good luck on her first day as assistant consultant.

*

The entire Bhavishya Sankalp Ventures team gathered in the canteen. Aditi's face was glowing.

"Hello, everyone!" Anish said excitedly. "What a day! Two big things. First, you all know, we have Vikram Singhania speaking to us this morning. Make sure you are all in the big conference room after this. And two, we have a brand-new assistant consultant joining us. Let me introduce to you Aditi Sawant," Anish said, looking at her with pride.

Aditi repeated to herself; *Aditi Sawant, our new assistant consultant at Bhavishya Sankalp. Yes, Diti, this is happening,* she thought pinching herself.

Anish continued his speech. "As we grow our business, we need to grow our team of talents. After working in various companies in customer service and sales roles, Aditi is ready to use her passion, problem-solving skills, and customer service mindset for our mission to push India forward. She has a ten-year-old son Vishal, and they live in Bandra. Aditi is very keen to learn, and I am counting on all of you to help her with whatever you can to get her up to speed as soon as possible."

People around the room clapped and smiled at Aditi. She was beaming, never experiencing such a welcome when starting a new job. Then Anish looked at a young, composed man. "Aditi will work with Jahan." Aditi nodded and smiled at him. He nodded back, his expression professional. "You are in good hands, Aditi; Jahan has been with us for a few years and knows the business well. Okay, let's get back to it," he said.

After the introduction, Aditi walked up to Jahan. "It's nice to meet you."

"You too. Welcome, Aditi," he replied kindly. "Let's sit," Jahan suggested, pointing at one of the meeting rooms.

"Did you really move here from working at a call center?" Jahan smiled as he asked, but his voice held a hint of disbelief.

"Yes, in sales," Aditi answered, his question making her feel a little insecure.

"Do you understand what we do here? And the type of businesses we help?" Jahan asked.

"Yes, we invest in and help grow businesses that focus on improving health, well-being, people's livelihood, and the environment," she replied.

"Right. Lakshmi told me she gave you a general overview of the companies we are working with at the moment. Have you gone through the file on BUH, Bharat Urban Harvest?"

Aditi nodded confidently. "Yes."

"Great, that is now my most important client, others being Dhanjavad Vitt and Pharma Direct. You will support me on all three. We're meeting BUH tomorrow, and Mr. Chaudhary from Dhanjavad Vitt and Susmita from Pharma Direct later this week. I will send you the invites and all previous emails for you to understand the progress we have made. Please go through all the material today."

"Will do!" Aditi responded. "I'll try to catch up as quickly as possible."

"That's the expectation, because I only work with the best," Jahan smirked.

Aditi nodded confidently, eager to get going.

"To give you the quick summary on BUH. They came to us for three things: funding, to help with their strategy, and for us to identify and collaborate with partners to help them grow faster and more profitably. Usually, we are not involved in anything executional because we don't have the manpower, except for help to conduct research, etc. We already had a few meetings to work on their financial model to boost growth, but it still needs work, and we haven't yet found the right partners. We need partners that can provide services to expand their platform."

"Right," Aditi said, quickly repeating the information to herself. "I love the idea of popularizing urban farming," she stated. "Our cities need it. I think it would really help if I could visit a few farms to understand their business better."

Jahan gave Aditi a small smile and then said, "Yes, sure."

"Now let's move to the main conference room," Jahan said. "Vikram Singhania's session starts soon."

In the conference room, Anish walked up to Aditi excitedly. "You are so lucky to start with us this week, Aditi. Come! We have the legendary Vikram Singhania, a dear friend of mine, speaking to us right now. The team has really been looking forward to this the last few weeks."

Aditi decided to take a front-row seat.

Vikram was a tall man with a thick black mustache, wide shoulders, and a big belly with great posture. He gave off an air of possessing both knowledge and confidence. He would have been a very imposing-looking man if it wasn't for the kindness showing in his face.

Anish walked up to Vikram and turned to the team. "Everyone! I can see you are just as excited as I am. This is a story that I wanted to share with you for some time—the story about this gentleman that inspires me every day to do better. He is well known for being an early investor in Flipkart and our client PharmEasy, but he has invested in more than 100 companies to date, mostly companies that link to our purpose. Companies like Eco Health India, New Meds, and Wellness Planet Enterprises. However, he is most famous for his investment in people. It's really his intuition in identifying and working with the right founders that have made him successful. He has been my friend for more than twenty years, and he has been my mentor ever since I got into this business. I am very proud to have him speak to us today about his journey. Please give him your warmest applause to welcome Vikram Singhania."

Everyone stood up and clapped. Aditi was full of excitement. *The big leagues!* she thought.

Vikram walked forward, his presence immediately taking over the stage, demanding everyone's attention. He thanked Anish for the kind introduction and detailed his illustrious career. Aditi sat on the edge of her chair, incredibly impressed by his journey.

"Now you know a bit about me, but I want you to take away two things from my talk this morning. The first one starts with a story," he began.

"When I was twelve years old, my father and I stood in front of a coffee cart, a *kaapi kadai,* in Chennai. Behind the cart stood a young man. Friendly and relaxed, he struck up a conversation with my father. Then he started talking about his product. He exuded knowledge and passion while talking about his robusta blend and the importance of his chicory in the coffee-making process. He used a coffee filter that provided health benefits, and his rich coffee flavor and aroma were so good that you could enjoy it without milk or sugar. At the end of the conversation, the young man told my father he was convinced that in the coming years, his coffee would be enjoyed by all Indians. My father loved his energy and loved his coffee but didn't believe him. That man was, and is, Ravi Shankar Reddy."

He paused, seeing the audience in awe, knowing the man he spoke of was the founder of one of India's largest coffeeshop franchises.

"Right now, he has more than four hundred outlets. You know why I remember that encounter vividly as a young man? Not because he is now famous. There were four things that stuck with me.

"One, the man was naturally very friendly. He made you feel welcome and comfortable. He asked us about our day and told us about his. While my father waited for his coffee, he told us a comedic story, which made us laugh. The brief interaction made you want to come back.

"Two, he was very passionate about coffee and knew his product. While my father sipped his coffee, he explained about growing coffee beans, the different types, how it impacted taste and aroma, and what made his coffee so special compared to other vendors nearby.

"Three, he had positive energy. The man exuded optimism. How could a street vendor be so energized with seemingly— and I repeat seemingly—limited prospects ahead of him?

"Four, his forward thinking and commitment. The young man mentioned to my father that he expected to start a franchise and grow his brand across India. He had an enormous vision and knew what he wanted. It's unlikely he knew how to make it happen, but the dream was clear.

"My father was so infatuated by the man and his coffee that he drove past all other coffee stalls to get a coffee from him. These are the personality traits I look for in business owners, and I believe you should too. You want a personality that you can and want to work with. You want someone who knows their stuff. You want unbridled passion because things will get tough. You want someone with a big vision. There are many roads to get there, but you need to have grit and be able to think big. And, you know, many of the most successful people come from low-income, lower caste backgrounds who had to fight their way to the top."

Is that right? Aditi smiled, intrigued by his last comment.

"The second thing I want you to take from this talk is how to help these business owners as investors, consultants, and mentors. You will be getting married!" Vikram smiled and raised his voice. "You promise to support each other through thick and thin! And you see a beautiful, and, of course, profitable future together." He chuckled. "A vision! Are you aligned with that vision? A house with a garden in the hill stations with two children and a dog? Or an apartment in the city without children and pets? How will you achieve it? What are the goal posts? By when? And then, how will you make the journey together? What steps will you take? Will you provide the funds for your partner to work around the house? Or will both parties work? Or do you need external help?"

Aditi laughed within, now considering the chaiwallah her mentor.

"There are many questions you should answer together for this business marriage. For example, how often will we communicate? Should we sit down face to face once a week to give each other scores on how we are doing in different areas?"

I could have used that in my own marriage, Aditi thought.

"At what stages should we evaluate our partnership to decide if we should, one, continue as is; two, pivot; or—and it's sad but happens—three, stop this marriage?"

Not sad… heartbreaking, Aditi thought.

"I believe the seven keys to a successful business marriage are the following! One, an aligned vision. Two, agreed steps you will take as a team. Three, agreed timelines. Four, ways of working between parties. Five, a set decision-making process. Six, ways of communication. And seven, stages of check-in and evaluation."

With a big smile, he looked around the room, waiting for reactions.

"Any questions or thoughts you want to share?" Vikram asked.

Aditi turned and didn't see any hands, so she raised hers, which made Anish smile at her for taking the initiative. "Yes, madam in the front row!"

"Hello, Mr. Singhania, my name is Aditi Sawant. Thank you so much for your wonderful insights," she started. "I am very clear on the personality traits and how you feel about marriage."

Vikram laughed.

"In your experience, what drives these founders to start and run their business other than the financial incentive? Understanding their motive may help me work better with clients," Aditi said.

"Wonderful question Aditi. Usually," he paused, "it is not the financial incentive. They have an urge to drive change for the better. After they get success and money, they often start something else. To work better with your clients, I would advise you to spend time identifying their strengths and weaknesses to understand where you can step in to drive that change together."

Aditi nodded. "Noted. Thank you so much, Mr. Singhania."

"Any other questions or thoughts?" he asked.

Sumeet

Sumeet sat behind the dark oakwood desk in his home office late morning. He noticed the laptop sitting in his leather briefcase, feeling enormous relief there were no meetings for him to attend anymore. The day after the horrific breakdown on the rooftop, his body and mind had forced him to stay in bed without experiencing any of his usual headaches. This morning, he had shaved off his moustache, which he had kept for years, to enforce change as part of his new path ahead. He put on his shorts and a t-shirt and entered the living room when he saw his father calling him. A wave of apprehension washed over him as he sat down on the couch in the living room.

His father asked how he was feeling, and Sumeet answered that he needed time and rest. Then his father asked if he had come to the same conclusion, with Sumeet confirming he had. When they hung up, Sumeet noticed Manisha' eyes, hard and questioning, from behind the dining table.

"It's just irresponsible," she spat as he ended the call.

Donning his sneakers, Sumeet stepped out and closed the door behind him, the click of the lock almost comforting, until a voice disturbed his peace.

"You're starting late today," said his neighbor across the hall. He was dressed in an immaculate suit.

"Ah, yes, just a bit," Sumeet replied, pressing the lift button and hoping to avoid more probing.

"No more moustache. I've never seen you like that," the neighbor smiled.

Sumeet nodded with a forced smile. The lift doors opened, and they stepped in together.

"How's business?" the man asked.

"Hard to keep up with demand, as usual," Sumeet said, unwilling to reveal anything further. "And your practice?"

"Better than ever!" the neighbor said excitedly. "We're printing money!" He laughed. "That's important, right?" the man smiled arrogantly.

"Yes, good to hear." Sumeet managed a weak smile.

They said their goodbyes with Sumeet feeling the weight of the encounter drop off as they did so. The cool morning air greeted him as he turned into Chimbai Square, adding a touch of freshness to his troubled mind. As he passed the newspaperman, he saw the chaiwallah smiling at him.

"Good morning, beta! I didn't see you yesterday. I was a bit worried." The old man sounded concerned.

"I just took the day to rest," Sumeet answered.

"Come, sit," the chaiwallah urged. "You don't have to wait to come back from your walk for chai."

"Well, I guess I have no meetings today!" He laughed as the old man poured him chai. Sumeet gazed across the square like the newspaperman always did, seeing the supermarket staff flattening carton boxes and customers moving in and out of the different shops underneath the apartment building.

"Yesterday I quit my job and slept the entire day," Sumeet said, accepting the tea. "And, as expected, my wife and father are concerned and upset."

"You didn't quit. You started something new," the chaiwallah smiled.

"I'm scared to death," Sumeet confessed.

"Don't be, and don't force anything. Just let it come to you," the chaiwallah advised.

"What if it doesn't come?"

"There are some things you can do that may help," the old man began. "You can reflect on how you were as a young boy—your personality traits, what you loved doing, what you were good at. See if anything stands out. And it's important to keep talking to people so you get exposed to new ideas and thoughts," he said wisely. "Lastly, experiment with new things. Just take one step at a time. No need to hurry."

"Right." Sumeet nodded. "I'll go on one of my long walks today," he said, finishing his chai.

"Moving your body helps, too," the old man said with a smile.

The moment lingered, a brief pause in the relentless uncertainty in Sumeet's mind. "Daasa-da," Sumeet began, using the old man's real name. "I'm deeply grateful for what you did for me the other night. I still can't figure out how you knew to follow me up to the roof, but I'm glad you did. I really owe you."

"You owe me nothing," the chaiwallah said firmly. "But you do owe yourself."

Sumeet waved goodbye to the old man and walked onto the southern Chimbai Road.

"Strong, courageous, and devoted," he murmured upon spotting the small Hanuman temple further down the street. "I could use some protection right now." With a wry smile, he remembered driving past this temple daily but couldn't recall the last time he'd stepped inside. Descending the steps, he entered the simple space. Someone had already lit candles that flickered softly, casting a warm, sacred glow over the large, majestic statue of Hanuman, the monkey god. Sumeet observed the decoration on the platform in front of the god. Interestingly, someone had placed a small statue of Sai Baba, a revered spiritual leader, wrapped in saffron cloth and adorned with marigold garlands. *Am I making the right decision?* Sumeet wondered, ringing the temple bell and closing his eyes.

An hour later, Sumeet sat in a taxi driving along Lala Lajpatrai Marg and admiring the Haji Ali Dargah. *Majestic,* he thought, marveling at the shrine of Sayed Peer Haji Ali Shah Bukhari. Continuing his gaze, he observed the long narrow path leading to the five-hundred-year-old white marble temple of tranquility standing in the middle of the sea. *Breathtaking,* he thought. His journey continued down Peddar Road and through Beach Candy, past the famous hospital overlooking the sea, and further south past the Sri Sri Radha Gopinath Mandir, the temple devoted to the teachings of Lord Krishna and God Rama. Sumeet thought about a Sunday morning program he once attended there, remembering the melodious kirtans and delicious prasadam. Reaching Marine Drive, he got out and began walking south along the promenade. The sea was calm. *The chaiwallah is right, there should be no pressure now. I can just be myself.* The thought lifted weight from his shoulders, relaxed him as he passed many different people who were walking and sitting along the boulevard.

Then Sumeet got called over by a young man, asking if he could take a picture of him and his friends. Sumeet snapped a few photos and returned the phone. Before walking off, he asked the young man about his studies.

"Business management," a young man replied, introducing himself as Kabir.

"Do you know what you want to do next?" Sumeet asked, interested to talk to students his daughter's age.

"No idea, sir. And I am not sure I can get a job later," he

said. Now his friends gathered around. "The job market is too competitive. Everyone has a degree."

"Right," Sumeet agreed.

A young woman, his friend, joined the conversation. "It is very difficult for us, sir. I've been trying to get an internship but only got rejections."

The young man sighed. "And without work experience, we won't get a job later after graduating with our degree."

"Yes, it's tough," Sumeet acknowledged. "What do your parents do?"

The young man explained that his parents owned a small leather shop in the market nearby. And then his friend jumped in and told him her parents worked in a garment factory in the north of the city.

Sumeet pondered for a moment and then offered, "Would you like me to help you?"

The young man looked surprised. "What do you do, sir?" he asked cautiously.

"I have been working in automotive manufacturing most of my life," Sumeet replied. "If you send me your resume, the companies you're applying to, and your cover letter, I can take a look."

"Could you do mine too?" the women requested. "My name is Nandini."

Sumeet nodded, unable to resist helping the girl with the same name as his daughter.

They exchanged contact details, and Sumeet continued his walk along the promenade, his mind taking him to his daughter, comparing her to these students. *She has it relatively easy,* he thought. *With her degree from Canada and our family network, her future is guaranteed. These kids can't even get a relevant job after graduation.*

Arjun

THE SETTING SUN cast an orange hue over the street bricks on Chimbai Square, illuminating the varied stalls lining the road and glinting off the cars, rickshaws, and scooters passing through. Arjun sat with bloodshot eyes by himself beneath the ancient bodhi tree, his flask beside him almost empty, a storm of anxiety grabbing hold of him as he considered the upcoming heist. "Your purpose is revealed through your actions," he mumbled to himself, remembering the calligraphy on the doctor's wall.

Oh, dear God, just let me do this one last time, and that's it, he prayed internally.

"Beta?" the chaiwallah interrupted his thoughts, standing in front of him. "A cup of chai might do you good," he offered, extending a glass, steaming with a fragrant cloud of different spices.

The tang of alcohol clung to Arjun's clothes. "Please, not now, old man," Arjun dismissed him, though with a hint of warmth.

"It may help freshen you up," the chaiwallah insisted. "Sitting here and drinking every day won't help you get where you need to be."

"And where is that?" Arjun retorted, a little irritated by his kindness and confrontation.

"Toward fulfilling your purpose." the chaiwallah suggested, his dark eyes radiating kindness.

"My purpose is dark," Arjun replied sternly, resisting the old man's wisdom.

"Oh beta, even if you do not believe in *moksha*, you can create or find your purpose in the light. You just have to take steps in the right direction." He paused, but didn't get a response. "At least take my chai," the chaiwallah offered once more.

"No… leave me!" Arjun snapped. The chaiwallah set down the cup of chai and reached for the flask next to Arjun.

"Hey!" Arjun shrieked, losing his balance. He tried to stand up but collapsed onto his side. "Go! Just go!" he yelled drunkenly from the ground. "You don't know me! You don't know about my life!"

"We all need someone who believes in us," the chaiwallah said passionately. "You can do better than this." He set the bottle back down.

Arjun calmed down and clutched his bottle but continued to wave the man away. The chaiwallah walked off, leaving Arjun to brood over his words. *Not now,* he thought. *I am committed to evil and need to focus. There is no turning back.* A swell of immense fear and faint hope surged within him as he contemplated the danger and possible reward ahead of him. He took another sip of his tharra, trying to drown out his inner turmoil.

Aditi

ADITI'S HANDS WERE clammy as she held her laptop, and her heart raced with thoughts spiraling in her mind about this very first client meeting with Bharat Urban Harvest. She stood in the reception area to welcome her clients where she had waited for her interview only some days ago. After a few minutes of waiting, her nerves eased somewhat and she chuckled, remembering the first time she entered the building and felt she didn't belong. "Look at me now," she murmured, feeling satisfied. The lift doors opened and a man and woman stepped out. She quickly straightened herself and stepped forward.

"Hello, Mr. Patel, Ms. Sharma. I am Aditi Sawant."

"It's nice to meet you, Aditi. Anish told us all about you," the woman said. "And please call us Akash and Sucheta."

Aditi smiled, liking the informality. She guided them to one of the meeting rooms in the hallway alongside reception where Jahan was connecting his laptop. He greeted them confidently and asked them to be seated. Just as Aditi sat down, Jahan requested that she print some documents from his emails. Hurriedly stepping back into the room with her printouts, Aditi was somewhat disappointed to see they had started without her.

"...and keeping the last few slides in mind," Jahan said, "we feel it is now time to expand beyond Mumbai, starting with Delhi and Bangalore." Akash and Sucheta nodded in agreement.

Akash responded, "We started engaging with Delhi's government last year, and in Karnataka, we had our first talks with officials last month. They both love our online urban farming marketplace in Mumbai and our achievements, and they seem keen to collaborate."

Aditi had spent all of last night and this morning studying BUH's business model and urban farming and had made a long list of thoughts and ideas. She was now fully engaged in the discussion, but slightly feared overstepping in this first meeting.

As Akash finished his summary of next steps, Jahan noticed Aditi's intention to add her thoughts and subtly shook his head.

Aditi bit her tongue and decided to swallow her ideas.

"Can we run through the latest Mumbai financials now?" Jahan asked the BUH team, disconnecting his laptop.

As the meeting progressed, Aditi's thoughts lingered on several missed opportunities to speak up. She tried to quell the unease rising in her chest.

"Cool. Now, onto the actions for this week," Jahan said.

As they concluded, Jahan stepped out of the room, expecting Aditi to walk them back to the lift. Aditi approached Akash and Sucheta. "I was hoping you could spare thirty minutes so I can ask you some questions about the business?"

"Yes, we can do that right now," Akash answered.

Once alone with the clients, Aditi's nerves settled. "Your entrepreneurial journey is very inspirational. And I've seen myself how easy it is to grow aloe vera, *pudina, kadi patta, shimla mirch*, and lettuce in Mumbai," she shared.

"Oh, how come?" Sucheta asked, surprised.

"A few people in my neighborhood grow these things."

After talking to them a bit, Aditi realized both of them were highly educated and experienced techies from Mumbai's high society, which felt slightly intimidating as she was now the one who had to help and advise them.

Suddenly Sucheta asked her, "What are your thoughts on our expansion plans?"

Plenty ideas after all my research, but I shouldn't overstep Jahan, Aditi immediately thought. "Well, let me discuss that with Jahan first," Aditi replied with a smile.

"Come on, I saw you holding back your ideas and thoughts during the meeting. We really could use everyone's thinking to grow our business. Please, share your preliminary thoughts with us," Susheta requested without a hint of prejudice.

Aditi hesitated, feeling flattered, but then realized Susheta insisted and she couldn't deny such an important client.

After a moment, she smiled and said, "Okay, I think that before launching the marketplace into Delhi and Bangalore, we should review the products, services, and information we will offer in those cities based on climate and target audience understanding."

Seeing both Akash and Sucheta listening intently, Aditi's confidence grew and she continued. "Your goal is to popularize urban farming. I believe it will be good to understand the size, behavior, and needs of different audiences to customize content, services, and incentives. This would improve user experience and enable you to optimize the reward system that we propose to government."

"Yes. You are right. Everything now is very Mumbai-centric," Akash said.

"Great, practical thoughts, Aditi," Sucheta added. "Why didn't you just share this in the meeting with Jahan?" She laughed.

Aditi responded with a nervous smile. By the end of their discussion, Aditi and Sucheta waited in the lobby for Akash to return from the washroom. "Aditi, please join me at my wedding reception. Anish and Jahan will be there too," Sucheta said, handing her an invitation.

"Oh, wow. Wonderful. Congratulations!" Aditi responded. She loved grand weddings.

"Our entire wedding schedule got messed up due to my work," she laughed. "But finally, we managed to have our *Ganesh* and *Grah Shanti* poojas."

"How was it?" Aditi asked, intrigued.

"Beautiful," Susheta quickly said, her eyes lighting up. "The colors, the flowers, the incense, everything was perfect. It started with *prarthana*; we chanted the *Gayatri Mantra…*"

Movie scenes with weddings among well-off people ran through Aditi's mind.

"Our *kundali* show our differences", Susheta explained, referring to their astrological charts. She glanced back to see if Akash had returned, and continued. "For instance, my sun is in the tenth house in Aquarius, reflecting my ambition and leadership skills," she smirked. "However, my fiancé's sun is in the seventh house in Virgo. He is analytical, service-oriented, and values harmony. He finds his identity through his connections, whereas I am very different."

"Right," Aditi acknowledged, enjoying her openness.

"My man thinks I can be stubborn, so he was happy seeing me crush that coconut in front of him to break my ego, leaving only my soft and pure personality traits." Sucheta giggled and Aditi laughed. "And my *haldi* and then *mehndi* party afterwards were loads of fun."

At that moment, Akash approached. "Anyway," Sucheta went on, "we got it all done in the end." She laughed. "Let's catch up soon, Aditi, and if you have any more thoughts about the business, please share them. Your input is very valuable."

Aditi felt a surge of pride that her ideas proved to be valuable.

"You can bring your husband and son," Sucheta said, stepping into the lift.

"Thanks, Sucheta. It will be just me and my son," Aditi replied.

The lift doors closed, and they were gone.

Aditi beamed.

Sumeet

ON SATURDAY EVENING, Sumeet and Manisha walked out of the lavish Indian restaurant down the plush deep-red carpeted stairs of the glorious Land's End Hotel situated at the end of Bandra's bandstand. The carpet ran down from the stairs onto the main seating area of the hotel lobby with beige and red sofas and armchairs in front of a bar. The ceiling was a tessellation of squares two floors high that gave off a grand ambiance.

As they passed the small fountain next to the elevator, Manisha said, "The Mehtas are such an interesting couple, don't you think?"

"They're okay," Sumeet replied, annoyed she kept the appointment that forced him to keep up appearances.

"Well," Manisha continued, "she collects art from across the world."

"Sure, with family money," Sumeet noted, now exiting the hotel and going down the stairs where their driver was waiting. Sumeet could feel the disagreement between them, as they stepped into the car.

"Yes, but still," Manisha said. "She gets to travel a lot,

attend different auctions, and meet many interesting people. And he became CEO of the investment fund."

"Yes, his father's investment fund. His father pushed him into that role, and he couldn't refuse."

"Well, maybe you should also talk to your father."

Sumeet's eyes narrowed, feeling a familiar tension rise.

"He can get you another job. What else are you going to do?" she said dismissively.

Sumeet ignored the question. He checked his phone and said, "Oh, I got an email from this student Kabir I spoke to on Marina Drive the other day." He was excited to go through the attachments when he got home.

"They will think you are a strange old man harassing them," she said sharply.

"Not at all," he said calmly, browsing through Kabir's resume. "I asked two of them to send me their resumes and cover letters to help them strengthen their applications and use my network to get them an internship."

Manisha wasn't pleased. "You don't even know them," she said condescendingly.

"Yes, but they seem like nice kids. Who knows where they will end up with a little bit of help?" he replied with optimism, reflecting on the chaiwallah's comments about luck.

"This is what you're going to do? Help poor, random students for nothing?"

"Yes," he said firmly.

"That's not going to pay the bills, Sumeet. You're wasting your time."

"The bills are getting paid," he said sharply, her comment causing further irritation. *She's so bitter,* he thought. "Never mind, you won't understand," he said as they stepped out of their luxurious black sedan.

Upstairs, Sumeet immediately walked into his home office, flustered by Manisha's reaction. After a moment of editing

Kabir's documents and conducting online research, the tension from earlier gradually diminished. When he was done, he wrote the following message:

> Hello, Kabir. Find attached your resume and cover letter with my edits. I made your resume a little shorter and sharper. You don't have to draw out your limited experience too much.
>
> Your cover letter is critical, and needs to be tailored to the company and role you are applying for. To help you write a stronger letter, you need to conduct some research on the FMCG industry, the company, and their marketing position. I attached some links below about industry trends and the business.
>
> Point out the specific challenges they face in the industry. Explain that you understand with whom, where, and how they are battling for growth and market share. Buy their products and try them, as well as their competition. Point out your critical findings, whether they are right or wrong, and tell them what you would do to grow the business, with changing 6Ps or introducing a different product segment.
>
> Finally, tell them about the personality traits and motivation that will help you become successful during your internship, and what you expect to achieve in your first ninety days."

Sumeet ended his message by asking Kabir to re-write his letter and resend it for him to review. He leaned back in his chair, feeling accomplished.

Aditi

The following morning, Aditi and Vishal waited in the long queue to board the ferry near the Gateway of India, nestled in the southernmost part of Mumbai. Aditi had bought the luxury class ticket, and they now sat on the upper deck, enjoying the view on their way to the Elephanta Caves on the small island of Gharapuri. The warm sea wind blew in Aditi's face, and her mind swirled with thoughts about work. *So much to do… Jahan wants me to complete all his requests by end of today.* She glanced at Vishal, redirecting her thoughts. *Focus on the present, Diti,* she mused.

Vishal grinned as the wind tousled his hair. "Finally, we're off," he said, excited about the ferry ride.

"Yes, I know, baala," she replied with joy in her voice. "Sorry I've been so busy with changing jobs and preparing for interviews on weekends. But now, we are set to go," she announced, her eyes gleaming with relief.

"The last ferry back is three o'clock," Vishal mentioned.

"We'll have enough time," Aditi assured him.

After an hour-long journey through choppy brown murky water, they arrived. Vishal leaped out of the ferry and turned to her with a teasing grin. "I'm sure I will be at the top first!"

he said looking up at the one hundred and twenty steps ahead of them.

"Let's see, baala," Aditi shot back, her competitive spirit ignited. "I might be fitter than you!" she called out, speed-walking up the steps. "Come on, we'll head straight to the Shiva Cave."

When they reached the grand portal, Aditi's face lit up. "Isn't it beautiful?" she asked Vishal.

"It looks old," he said, taking in the massive sculptures and intricate carvings that adorned the cave walls.

"Some of the Buddhist stupas date back to the second century," Aditi said, her voice tinged with reverence.

"It's so big here," Vishal replied, his eyes widening in amazement.

"Come on, let's go further inside to see the Trimurti Sadashiva," Aditi urged, her excitement mounting. As they walked deeper into the cave, she marveled at the three-headed Shiva statue.

"Do you know why the statue has three faces?"

Vishal thought for a second, then replied, "Um… yes, each face represents something different."

"Yes, the three aspects of Shiva: creation, protection, and destruction," she explained and asked, "This statue doesn't show, but do you know why Shiva's throat is blue?"

"Yes, because he drank poison to save the world," Vishal replied promptly.

"Correct. People worship Lord Shiva for his strength, wisdom, and ability to balance the world," Aditi explained. "Come, let's eat something!" she suggested, seeing boredom across Vishal's face.

After returning from Gharapuri, Aditi had to work deep into the night.

*

THE FOLLOWING MORNING, she passed Jahan's desk with confidence; *everything he requested is in his inbox.* After getting coffee from the kitchen, she sat down at her desk, and with surprise, she spotted a new unread message from Jahan. The email read, *Aditi, set up a whiteboard and markers in the Pondicherry meeting room and print the attached document.* Browsing through the document, she noticed it was an agency's proposal for research in Delhi and Bangalore. *Wow!* she thought. *Akash and Sucheta followed up on my research ideas from last week.*

About an hour later, she spotted Akash in the hallway and greeted him kindly.

"Aditi, why weren't you in the meeting just now?" he immediately asked.

Aditi was taken aback. *What meeting?* she thought. "Oh, Jahan didn't tell me to join," she explained.

"Well, you should have been there, because we ran through the research you proposed," Akash said pointedly.

"Oh," Aditi started but switched tracks. "Yes, that's right," she said, trying to appear composed and professional. "I'm on top of it, Akash. I'm catching up with Jahan later."

Akash seemed skeptical. "Alright, please send me your feedback separately. We need your perspective too," he said.

"Definitely, Akash, I'll do that," Aditi replied, frustration building inside her. *My research proposal and I was not invited?* She was upset. *Anish instructed me he wants assistant consultants to attend all meetings, and work hand in hand with the project lead.*

As Akash walked off, Aditi swiftly walked over to Jahan's desk and said, "Hi, Jahan, do you have a minute?"

"Yes, Aditi."

"There was a meeting with BUH this morning, but I didn't get the invite."

"I'll let you know when you should attend, Aditi," he stated calmly.

"Okay, but the weekly meetings are fixed, right? Could you please forward those?"

"Sure, will do."

Aditi considered sharing Akash's comment with Jahan but decided against it. At least she had secured the weekly meetings, she thought.

"You must feel very lucky to get this job, right?" he smiled.

Aditi forced a smile, unsure of Jahan's intent.

"Well, you know," Jahan continued, "not many people like you are in this position."

Aditi decided the comment was well-intentioned. "Yes, I feel lucky and excited."

"I need one more thing," Jahan said sternly. "I want you to run through BUH's financials and give me an estimate of their net profit break-even point. And please include the two cities with current estimations," he added.

"Right, I am on it," Aditi agreed, completely overwhelmed by the request knowing she clearly lacked experience for such a task. *Besides, Anish mentioned that the finance director handles all financial analysis and proposals,* she thought. Just before she turned away, an idea popped up, and she suggested, "Jahan, should we wait for the research outcome to offer a more accurate overview?"

"No. I need a preliminary view by Thursday noon."

"On it," she stated confidently while stressing inside.

Arjun

ARJUN SAT SOBER on one of the stone benches on the Carter Road promenade in the early morning, watching the horizon across the sea as a fresh breeze blew across his face. Thoughts of his home in Jalna and his father flooded his mind. *Hopefully the drought didn't impact the farm too much these last few years. Did he remarry? Is my uncle still working with him? Did my father ever find out?*

"Okay, listen," Rohit said, snapping Arjun out of his daydream. "We're talking about more than four hundred employees. My friend who will buy them from us promised me at least fifteen thousand for each laptop, depending on the model. That would total sixty lakhs—thirty lakhs each."

Arjun felt his heart pumping wildly. "Thirty lakhs..." he slowly repeated.

Rohit nodded. "Your debt problem solved, and you buy some land in Jalna."

"Jalna?" Arjun echoed, taken aback.

"I know what you really want, bhai. I've seen it in your eyes since the first day we met."

"I don't think I can go back..." Arjun replied. The weight of Rohit's words settled heavily on him.

"How do we get in and out of the building? Security will be tight, twenty-four hours," Arjun asked, redirecting the conversation to the big heist.

"Like I told you, my friend's wife is a cleaner in the building and close to one of the guards. They earn next to nothing. She can convince him to pay off all others to turn a blind eye for one hour… for the right price of course," Rohit explained.

"We'll need a big van," Arjun remarked.

"I will get it," Rohit replied.

"How about a floor plan?" Arjun proposed. "That many laptops must be all over the place."

"Let me check."

"It's critical; otherwise, we will just be searching for the entire hour."

Rohit nodded. "Can you organize a dolly and flattened boxes?" he requested.

"Yes, I know someone at a moving company," Arjun said, now pondering the box size. *The boxes they use for books should fit about ten laptops side by side and a few on top. Bigger boxes will get too heavy.*

"Okay, guards, floor plans, van, two dollies, boxes," Arjun summarized. "How do we pick the drawer locks?"

"Easy, bhai." Rohit laughed. "With a simple thread cutter. You keep the tension on the cylinder by gently turning it while you pick." Doubt set into Arjun's mind. "Don't worry. You just load the van."

"Cameras? They must be everywhere."

"Yes, but there will be sudden power cuts lasting for one hour." Rohit gave Arjun an evil smile. "And coincidentally, they ran out of gasoline to run the back-up generators."

It's all about those guards, Arjun thought. *If we get caught, they will connect our DNA to other robberies and the murder Rohit committed. We'll be going away for life.*

"We may need another guy," Arjun proposed.

"No. He may rat on us. We can't trust those bastards," Rohit said firmly.

"Theek ahe. Let's get it all organized," Arjun agreed.

202

Aditi

Aditi and Vishal were on their way to Sucheta's wedding reception. They turned left at the Juhu circle, speeding ahead, the dazzling lights coming into view. "This is so exciting!" she said to Vishal. Passing here a few times, she had always wondered what a wedding reception would look like on these grounds. After seeing their names on the guest list, they entered the flamboyant makeshift hallway toward the open space, its fluttering silk sheets of ruby red and gold creating an ethereal atmosphere. *How glamorous for an outdoor wedding!* Aditi thought.

Strolling along the red-carpet entrance lined with tall vases brimming with white roses, they emerged into the main area where hundreds of guests mingled. Waiters in white suits roved about, while off to the right, an enormous catering setup featured countless Northern, Southern, and Mughlai dishes displayed in shiny copper crockery. The center of the grounds hosted a vast tent with round tables trimmed in red and white silks where guests ate, drank, and enjoyed the entertainment from the grand podium adorned with the bride and groom on a golden couch like royalty.

Wow, just like in the movies, she marveled, thinking that her own Koli wedding paled in comparison. As she moved through the crowd searching for colleagues, she spotted Anish standing by one of the high round tables and walked over.

After they greeted each other, Anish said, "And this must be Vishal."

Vishal extended his hand shyly. "It's nice to meet you, Mr. Chopra. Thank you for hiring my mother."

Anish laughed. "What a friendly and caring young man," he said to Aditi, who smiled in return.

"We are very happy to have her, Vishal," Anish said with his hand on his shoulder. A waiter passing by offered a glass of red wine, which both Aditi and Anish accepted. "Aditi, I know we are catching up tomorrow, but how is your onboarding going?" Anish asked.

"It's going great. Jahan has been showing me the ropes, and I absolutely love the projects. And it was exciting to see Sucheta and Akash follow up on my research proposal for Delhi and Bangalore. I believe it will help us make better decisions and scale faster compared to Mumbai," she explained.

"That was your proposal?" Anish asked, surprised.

"Yes," Aditi replied proudly.

"Wonderful. Good to hear you are settling in quickly. But," he paused, laughing, "that was my expectation, Aditi." Aditi let out another smile, feeling valued. Anish then asked her and Vishal to follow him to the rest of the team waiting in line to congratulate the bride and groom. They walked to the side of the stage and stood in line to greet the couple.

Aditi took in the resplendent decorations. When her eyes landed on the happy couple on stage, she thought, *Where is Vishal's father now? With another woman? More children? He knew I was ambitious. He knew I wanted to continue to work. Why couldn't he handle that after Vishal was born? How could he not miss his son?* She looked at Vishal and smiled, though a hint of bitterness and disappointment lingered, unnoticed by him.

Akash suddenly joined the group. After an exchange of pleasantries, he excused himself. "See you tomorrow, Jahan."

Meeting? Aditi thought. *If I get left out of meetings and information, I will look incompetent in my weekly catch-ups with Anish,* she thought, stressing. She turned to Jahan. "Um, excuse me, Jahan. Is there a meeting tomorrow?"

"Akash and I will just go through a few things," Jahan responded.

Aditi let out a shallow sigh, feeling somewhat disheartened on being left out again but decided not to confront him here. "Okay, please let me know if you need me to prepare anything," she offered.

"Yes, I was going to send you a message. Before my meeting at eleven, I need you to give me the top twenty-five largest flower shops in both cities based on annual revenue, their top twenty best-selling products from last year, and their delivery reach," Jahan requested.

"Shall we wait for Friday's research outcome so that we have the right data? Otherwise, the analysis will include lots of unverified assumptions," she noted.

"Just give it to me in the morning, Aditi," Jahan said, turning his back to talk to others.

Aditi put her arm around Vishal's shoulder. "It is beautiful here, isn't it, baala?"

Sumeet

This morning, Sumeet decided to pick up a paper from the stall next to the chaiwallah and stroll leisurely along the footpath on the Carter Road promenade. Instead of his usual fast-paced walk up and down, he decided to sit down on one of the stone benches to read. There was an update on the national Make in India initiative with the government rolling out a series of incentives and reforms to attract global investors, such as tax breaks for the manufacturing sector. For a moment, Sumeet got tense thinking about the possible impact on his manufacturing sites with increasing competition in the automotive sector, but then he quickly realized that it no longer impacted him. When he finished reading the key headlines, he continued his walk north until reaching his usual cue to turn. Just then, his phone buzzed with a message from Manisha. "Sumeet, I am leaving you."

Sumeet's heart dropped. What? his mind raced, but he forced himself to read on. "We cannot continue on like this. Deep down, you know this too. Our relationship was always cordial but never loving. After Nandini left us, our relationship deteriorated further. I am now on my way to my parents. When you come back from your walk, I won't be here. I hope you find your way, Sumeet."

Her parents? Dubai? he thought. Immediately, he called her number, but there was no answer. Then, in a rush, he ran toward a rickshaw parked next to the road, yelling to the driver to quickly drive him back to Chimbai Square. After jumping out of the rickshaw in front of his building, he hurried across the parking area into the lobby, waiting anxiously for the lift. Opening the door of their apartment, he went into the hallway shouting, "Manisha!" There was no answer. Manisha!" he shouted again, opening their bedroom. Afraid to discover the truth, he hesitated to open the closet. Reality kicked in when he saw all her clothes were gone. In the bathroom, her usual collection of perfumes, makeup, and cotton balls were no longer there. *This can't be happening,* he thought, his heart pounding with disbelief.

"What do I do?" he muttered to himself, the migraine that disappeared after quitting his job now re-emerged. He picked up his phone again to call Manisha's mother, but she didn't pick up either. *When did she plan this? When did she decide on this? Was there nothing we could do?* he wondered, as he began to search for flights to Dubai. He found a plane departing in twenty minutes. *Maybe she is on that flight,* he thought slumping down on the couch in despair. *Has she really left me?* he pondered, and then he broke down in tears.

After the initial shock and tears, he picked up his phone.

"Anish? It's Sumeet. Manisha left me," he blurted out, his voice cracking.

There was an initial silence on the other side.

"What do you mean she left you?" Anish asked.

"She sent me a message. She left and went back to her parents," he said, sniffing slightly.

"Dubai?" Anish asked. "Where are you now?"

"Home," Sumeet answered.

"I'll be there in an hour."

After they hung up, Sumeet reflected on the message. *You knew this could happen one day,* he told himself. *Would therapy have helped us? We never had open, honest conversations,* Sumeet thought. *We never shared common hobbies or interests. We just kept it going.*

He then thought about his next steps. *Do I fly to Dubai to get her back? Would our future be very different from our past?* His thoughts tangled. *Unlikely, but think about the family,* he urged himself.

How will Nandini respond to this? Poor girl, he sighed.

Think about the shame in the family, he told himself. *First my career, and now this! I will be the first in our family to ever get divorced. This will impact my father's reputation—the one he has been building for decades. I will let everyone down.*

How can I face people after this? What do I tell them? he asked himself. *I quit my career because I burned out, and then I gave up on my marriage? What kind of man am I?* he questioned.

"Selfish, pathetic bastard," he muttered to himself.

This is happening because deep down in my heart, I have been feeling lost for a long time. I lived my life thinking about others, he argued within, his father on his mind. *It was not sustainable, and this is the outcome. These are all messages from above for me to find meaning,* he thought.

But then he began to second-guess himself. *Are they from above? Or is this all just my own doing?*

Perhaps, he thought, closing the door behind him. *But does that make it wrong? Isn't the purpose of life to follow your heart, to find love and happiness?* He waited for the lift to come up. *Or am I going against my path of Darma? Turning my back on duty, honor, and loyalty?* As the lift doors opened, he glanced back at his front door, feeling emptiness.

At the chaiwallah's cart, Sumeet sighed deeply and slumped down on the plastic chair. "Life has just become a lot more complex than it already was, dada," Sumeet said before the old man could greet him.

"Tell me, beta," the old man replied, his voice concerned, showing immediate willingness to listen and help.

"Well," Sumeet paused, struggling to articulate it out loud. Finally he sighed and said, "My wife left me, dada."

The chaiwallah stayed silent, looking at Sumeet, waiting for more.

"She packed her bags this morning and went back to her parents in Dubai."

After a short pause to see if Sumeet wanted to share more, the chaiwallah said, "It is all happening to you now, beta," the chaiwallah responded. "When it's the will of the gods, everything comes forward," he added with comfort in his voice.

"That is what I have been wondering," Sumeet replied. "The gods? Or am I just destroying everything around me?"

"Oh, beta, you are overestimating your own powers," the chaiwallah smiled. "Sure, we make choices and decisions, but sometimes we just have to accept karma. There are many schools of thought, but I believe that eventually, the will of the gods prevails. Accepting that is the only path to *moksha* and any spiritual fulfillment. Think about all the things that happened at your work that you had no control over but impacted you significantly," the chaiwallah continued.

Sumeet thought about that for a bit.

"Are you in control of your wife's feelings, her choices, and decisions? Or a cyclone preventing you from driving to work? A colleague that calls in sick? The stock market collapsing?"

"True," Sumeet agreed.

"The question is, now that the gods have revealed your new path and everything is coming forward, what does it mean to you and how do you respond? Remember we spoke about reflecting on your personality traits, things that warm your heart, and getting exposed to new ideas and thoughts?“ the chaiwallah reminded him.

Sumeet pondered, taking a small sip from his chai.

Aditi

I ᴎ ᴛʜᴇ ᴏғғɪᴄᴇ, Aditi sifted through online content to improve her financial literacy and grasp the balance sheets before her. The many pages were cluttered with page markers and hand-written notes in different colors. *Are macchi! Who am I kidding?* she suddenly thought anxiously. *I don't know how to do this, and I am running out of time.* She suddenly reflected on the interview and the knot in her stomach seeing the balance sheets. *I got away with it that time being street smart, but now I will get exposed. I had some practical thoughts for BUH, but come on! This is an investment firm.* Resting her head inside her hands, she sighed deeply and stared outside.

Suddenly, she jumped up and rushed to the door when she saw a familiar face walking past.

"Hi, Kunal?" she said, peeking out of the meeting room.

"Oh, hello, Aditi, how are you settling in?" he asked, turning around. "Jahan did not yet send an invite for us to catch up."

"Yes, probably because I have been flooded with work for BUH," Aditi smiled. "Actually, I was really hoping I could pick your brain today," she asked somewhat sheepishly.

"Sure, actually, I have a little less than an hour right now," he proposed.

"Oh, that would be very helpful," she said, feeling a surge of relief.

For the next thirty minutes, Aditi tried her best to summarize all her observations, and Kunal answered most of her questions, promising to give her some more time at the end of the day. He explained BUH's contractual expenses and promotional buckets that showed net sales once deducted from revenue. He also listed all the different marketing and overhead expenses that revealed the reasons behind BUH's low margins.

In the early evening, Aditi stood smiling in front of one of the windows near her desk, watching the sun set across the many skyscrapers. *Amazing! You see, Diti!* she encouraged herself. *Now you can formulate those projections Jahan is looking for,* she thought confidently. Working through the various formulas, another email from Jahan popped in—the invite for her to take him through the analysis.

"I accept!" she said aloud, with a sense of purpose.

Aditi hurriedly collected all the notes in front of her and speed-walked toward her last meeting with their microfinance client Dhanjavad Vitt. *Our Koli community could really benefit from these services,* Aditi thought, hurrying through the hallway. When Aditi walked in, Jahan was seated and making small talk with Ankur Chaudhary.

"Please sit, Aditi," Jahan urged her. "You can just listen and take notes," he instructed her.

"Sure," she responded, feeling somewhat sidelined.

"What are the latest numbers, Ankur?" Jahan asked authoritatively.

"The last three months, our disbursements were 38 million rupees, repayments 26 million, and net interest income at 2.1 million," Ankur explained.

"Growth remains stagnant," Jahan noted quickly.

"Yes, nationwide," Ankur confirmed. "But we are growing Bihar, Uttar Pradesh, and West Bengal. Our investments in other regions are not yet paying off. Let me take you through the next slides that show our findings, challenges, and subsequent actions for the next three months."

"Okay, I think I am clear," Jahan said after the full update. "Let me set up a meeting to brainstorm with the entire team. We need to unlock that incremental growth fast because competitors have been making aggressive moves lately." He got up to wrap up the meeting.

As Jahan left the room, Aditi hoped to make a connection and said, "Your business made me think about my own community."

"Tell me," Ankur responded, intrigued.

"I'm from Bandra's Koliwadahs," she began. She noticed his friendly nod. "When I was younger, I remember my father having lots of business ideas as a fisherman and handyman. For example, he always wanted to start his own seafood consortium. If he had access to funding at that time, he could have started his own instead of joining someone else's outside our community. Having one could have helped other Koli fishermen in our area." Ankur nodded attentively. "Another example is my aunt. She is a well-known cook and sells pre-made meals, like curries, at the market with the fish from her husband. It's a small market stall, but with some investment, I believe she would thrive having her own restaurant."

"That's what we do, Aditi. And even today, only about 5 percent of the population has access to microfinance loans, although around 50 percent nationwide qualify," Ankur explained.

"What are the eligibility requirements?" Aditi asked, intrigued.

"Well, our business focuses mostly on helping women—women who already have income-generating businesses so that we understand their capability to repay. We check if they have paid back any historical loans. Eighty-five percent of our revenue comes from joint liability loans where members guarantee each other's loans. Our borrowers can only access the funding after going through basic personal finance literacy training. And of course, we need identification, like the Aadhaar and PAN card."

"Right," Aditi replied, pondering the implications. "I was just thinking, Ankur," Aditi said, "most of the Kolis are not very digital savvy. Have you experimented with on-the-ground marketing activities?"

"Not much, Aditi. It's expensive and reach is limited."

"Yes, but I think the quality of engagement will be high for each person you reach. For instance, it would be really interesting to educate a woman in our Koli community about the loans and options, give her monthly targets, and let her sell door-to-door. Those women listen to each other, and she could answer all their questions on the spot. And you would be giving someone much needed employment."

"Interesting. We could test this," Ankur said, visibly pondering.

"Another way is to create roadshows. Trucks that move around busy areas in low-income communities, to educate through fun and games and sell on the spot."

"Right," Ankur said, considering her idea.

"Do you also offer a one-stop WhatsApp service, like some banks do?" she asked.

"Our team is working on that right now," he said.

"Oh great," Aditi said.

"You've got lots of ideas, Aditi," Ankur smiled.

After a short pause, she continued, "How about Bangladesh and Pakistan?"

"How about them?" Ankur asked, surprised.

"They are enormous untapped markets in which we could replicate your model with a strong partner on the ground."

"You're thinking big! I like it," he smiled. "But I believe we can still drive enormous growth within India."

Aditi hesitated but then said, "If you agree, I will identify partners for the door-to-door sales and roadshow activities and work with your team."

"That will be great," Ankur said, concluding the meeting.

*

LATER THAT NIGHT Aditi reviewed some of BUH's presentations from the last two years at home. *It's a bit like the online marketplace Flipkart, but for urban farming,* she thought. *They need users. With more users, they can attract more advertisers. Initially, they invested in educating people and free giveaways to get people started. They continue to highlight growth, but rising costs are making it hard to break even.* Unable to find the answer, she stepped out to walk toward Chimbai Square. *If the chaiwallah has left, I will just get something from the supermarket,* she thought. The square was dark and deserted, except for light coming from the supermarket and the chaiwallah's cart.

Look at him, she thought. *Who is he waiting for this late?* "Namaste, dada, you are staying late," she said, walking up to his cart.

His face lit up. "Namaste, beti! How is your new job?"

"Oh, it's great!" she said. "It really was a miracle for me to get it, and there is much to learn."

"Be like a sponge, my dear…soak it all up," he said, smiling proudly, handing her a glass of chai.

"The people there are so smart. I can't help but sometimes feel I don't belong," Aditi admitted, taking a sip. "They are all so professional and well-spoken, and I'm obviously the one with the least experience. It sometimes triggers negative self-talk."

"Learn, but don't let this new environment change who you are, dear," he told her.

"What do you mean?" she asked, curious. "I need to work hard to try and fit in."

"Yes, work hard and do your best, but don't try to fit in. I imagine that most or all of your colleagues come from privilege, which helped them get into their positions," he said. "With your background and personality, you are a wonderful anomaly, beti," he added proudly.

"Well, yes, it's clear that I am different," she confessed, reminding herself that's how she passed the interviews.

"That is your strength," he said. "But, you may come across people who don't want you to succeed, and they will test you, possibly even try to get rid of you," he warned.

"Right," Aditi said. Jahan crossed her mind.

"When something like that happens, you have the choice to become docile, retaliate, or let it empower you."

Aditi saw the old man reflecting for a moment, and then he admitted, "I learned this myself a little late." He smiled sheepishly. "There was a time in my own life that I gave up and became docile in response to things happening to me, but it didn't help me one bit," he smiled. "You are already there. You have the job, you have already proven to yourself that you are good enough and that you belong there, beti. Tell yourself regularly, and feel empowered."

Aditi nodded gratefully. His advice and comments lifted her up and gave her food for thought.

"And keep in mind that the people who hired you, picked you—an intelligent, ambitious young woman from the Koliwadahs, over all the other candidates. They must have seen the same potential that I see in you. They need you there."

Aditi's face lit up.

"Well," he said. "With that, I guess my day's work is done," he concluded and started to clean up his cart.

Sipping her tea, Aditi thought about Jahan. *Is it too soon to be direct with him? Should I just continue to work hard until he gives me recognition? Or should I mention it to Anish? I will not become docile,* she decided, reflecting on the old man's advice. *I must continue to deliver as much value as possible, but I need to become a bit more assertive.*

"Thank you, my wise counselor!" she chuckled.

Sumeet

A FEW DAYS LATER, Sumeet sat on a bench at Bandstand, the southernmost tip of Bandra West near the Bandra-Worli Sea Link. He had the sea in front of him and the luxurious Taj Land's End Hotel and the home of famed Bollywood actor Shah Rukh Khan behind him. A man on the bench next to him lit a cigarette, the flame making him reminisce.

Diwali after my graduation... that was special. Sumeet reflected on that particular year of India's joyous festival of lights that celebrates the triumph of righteousness over evil. He vividly remembered there were firecrackers and chants from the nearby temple that woke him up that day, completely free of worry. Sumeet sighed and closed his eyes to go back in time. With his father, he decorated the front door with circular rangoli using different colored powders, rice flour, flower petals, and sand. Just as they tried to place the marigold door hangings in the shape of Ganesha, it fell. They laughed hysterically. Sumeet gazed across the sea, remembering that specific moment he held so dear with a smile. *Baba told me that he was proud of me, and that he thought I was going to be a better man than him,* Sumeet thought, reflecting on the happiness and hope the comment had given him.

I never really understood what he meant with that, Sumeet thought. *But I know I am not like him. I admire him, but it is now clear I should not try to follow his footsteps,* Sumeet thought. *I need to find my own path.*

Watching the waves hit the shore, Sumeet reflected on the chaiwallah's comments about the danger of overestimating his own powers, and that it was the will of the gods that had led to the end of his career and marriage. He let that perspective simmer. *Interestingly, the gods also gave me an unlikely friendship with a chaiwallah. Why did he suddenly show up at this point in my life?* Sumeet mused.

The man next to Sumeet stood up, wishing him a good afternoon, and walked away. Sumeet's thoughts continued. *My recent dramas also helped me reach out to Anish and rekindle our friendship. And that led to Aditi getting her opportunity.* He smiled at the feeling of helping her. *The gods also introduced me to Ananya, which led to lecturing those wonderful kids in Dharavi. And I got to meet those students on Marine Drive.* This thought excited him.

Wait!? Isn't that it!? Passion to help others?

The epiphany made him stand up and start a fast-paced walk along Bandstand. *I said yes to everything that appeared in front of me that could help grow and develop others. I derive energy from that. Dharavi in particular was inspiring… that is a goldmine of undiscovered talent. How can I use that passion to help those kids in Dharavi and students like Kabir and Nandini?*

A few steps later, he suddenly remembered Ananya's comment. *They need school supplies, facilities, structure.* Then he connected another need. *Work experience,* he thought. *A person's performance at school and on the job often differ dramatically,* he realized from his own experience nurturing talents in his long career. Then he remembered Anish's comment that talent should be used to make the world a better place. Sumeet was now at the far end of Bandstand, nearing Bandra Fort, overlooking the water and the Bandra-Worli Sea Link.

Companies are increasingly pressured to improve people's lives and care for the planet, but they must continue to grow revenue.

Everyone loves the underdog story… a child from the slums becoming CEO, he thought. *If companies can help nurture talent, monitor progress, and get easy access to that talent, it solves their recruitment requirements. And if that talent has a story, they can tell the world as part of their sustainable business practices.*

"That's it!" he said aloud, his voice carrying across the water. Buzzing with newfound energy, he thought, *I need to speak to Ananya and Anish.*

Aditi

IN THE PANTRY area of the Bhavishya Sankalp Ventures office, Jahan walked up to Aditi as she made a cup of Red Label black tea. "Are you sure you're ready to go through today?" he asked standing behind her, doubt seeping into his voice.

She turned around immediately and answered firmly, "Yes, I am ready, Jahan." *Ready to pass your test,* she thought. "If you prefer, we can do it right now," Aditi proposed. Jahan's face registered surprise for a fleeting moment before his expression hardened.

"No. I'm busy right now. Let's stick to our slot later," he suggested.

"Sure," Aditi said, smiling politely.

That afternoon, while Aditi was connecting her laptop to the projector, Jahan entered the room.

"Okay, let's do this," Aditi said confidently, hoping to diffuse any lingering tension.

Jahan nodded and sat down, the authoritative air of a superior hanging around him.

"First, I'd like to take you go through BUH's Mumbai numbers to show how and why they are growing fast but continue to operate at a loss. Then I'll show you what I think needs to change to hit break-even. Right now, it is looking like they won't get there anytime soon." Aditi could see Jahan's surprise at her insight. "Then we can run through the launch models for Delhi and Bangalore and what I believe should be the financial targets for each city," she added. *Here goes,* Aditi thought, steeling herself.

"Sure," Jahan affirmed, his attention piqued.

"You can see here," Aditi pointed to her first chart, "we can forecast that at the end of this year, 60 percent of BUH's income will come from advertising through their website, 30 percent from sales commissions, and the rest from product listing earnings and government funding." She could feel Jahan's scrutinizing gaze.

"Based on what?" Jahan inquired.

"Here is the correlation from advertising spend and user growth versus advertising income and product sales," Aditi pointed out on her next slide. *I am well prepared, Jahan,* she thought.

"Okay, makes sense," Jahan conceded after checking the chart.

Aditi continued, "Sales commission will continue to grow faster than any other source of income as they attract new users, and with user growth, they can charge vendors more for advertising on their website. Their subscription-based services and consulting commissions are growing fast, but remain less than 1 percent. As you can see, they operate lean with low overheads due to their small team and co-working space." Aditi paused. "However," she continued towards her conclusion. "Net profits have dwindled because their advertising spending has gone through the roof."

Jahan nodded. "Yes, that's right."

"Their advertising spending doubled after using online influencers. User growth increased, but sales per user declined.

My forecast shows this will drive net earnings toward a negative 35 percent in the next two years."

"I see," Jahan said, critically examining the numbers displayed. Aditi sensed that Jahan was trying to compose tough questions, but none came. "But we already knew this. Explain your assumptions for Delhi and Bangalore," Jahan said.

"We can learn valuable lessons from Mumbai's launch to improve profitability in Delhi and Bangalore. I propose we increase the costs to advertise on our platform by 20 percent from day one. Our Mumbai sales data can persuade vendors it's worth the investment. Sucheta and Akash kept prices too low for too long, worried that customers might back out." Jahan nodded in agreement. "But Delhi and Bangalore will need localized content," she suggested.

"That's costly," Jahan noted.

"Yes, but both cities experience much less rainfall, and Delhi gets much hotter. For example, okra, tomatoes, and pumpkin thrive in Delhi's hot and dry climate, but they are more difficult to grow in Mumbai."

Jahan nodded again.

Aditi presented the projected financials for Delhi and Bangalore for the next three years, illustrating how BUH could match Mumbai's current net earnings in just over one year. "That's it," she said with a broad smile, feeling a great sense of pride.

"Right," Jahan replied neutrally. "Send me the slides and assumptions. I want to double-check."

"Yes, of course," Aditi answered. Jahan stood up. "Please follow up on the actions for Ankur, because he mentioned you promised him a few things. And, next time, run them by me first Aditi. I'll see you in Anish's office later."

"Okay, sure, I will," Aditi said, feeling a familiar knot of anxiety.

A few hours later, Aditi and Jahan sat across from Anish in his office. "Okay, team. Let's make this quick," Anish said.

"Yes, sure, Anish," Jahan responded, quickly taking charge and moving closer to Anish's desk.

"I have reviewed the Mumbai launch and found ways to start their expansion more profitably," Jahan began. Aditi's mind echoed back his words, feeling a twinge of indignation. "Let me show you the ideas," Jahan continued. *Did he make changes?* Aditi thought.

As Jahan talked Anish through, Aditi noticed he used her exact data and explanation, and he had just repackaged some of her slides to make it his own. *He is taking all the credit,* Aditi thought. She wanted to speak up, but a part of her urged restraint. *My job is to support the lead consultant,* she reminded herself. *That is what I am doing. Patience, Diti.*

"Did you align this with Kunal?" Anish asked skeptically. Jahan hesitated. *This is the moment to be assertive,* Aditi told herself, reflecting on the decision she had made in front of the chaiwallah's cart. "Yes, Anish-ji," Aditi jumped in, summoning her courage. "Here is the supporting data," she said, turning her laptop to show her slides.

Anish looked at her with surprise and a flicker of newfound respect. "Great. This gives me confidence. Really well done, both of you," Anish said after reviewing the assumptions and formulas.

Aditi felt a slight relief from the encounter.

Jahan got up, throwing Aditi a displeased glance before leaving.

Arjun

ARJUN VISITED HIS acquaintance at a moving company in Powai, northeast of Mumbai, to organize the dolly and boxes. They would be delivered to Rohit later in the day. Powai felt like a city within a city with its new, well connected roads, parks and greenery, and many more footpaths compared to other suburbs. Afterward, he walked along the lakeside promenade at the southern end of the artificial lake that was surrounded with new modern high-rise residential buildings.

The British had created the lake in the late nineteenth century by constructing dams across the Mithi river. The river was a crucial waterway originating from the Vihar Lake located in the Sanjay Gandhi National Park, one of the world's largest inner-city parks. The park was home to the Kanheri Caves and wildlife such as leopards, deer, and monkeys. The Mithi River ran southwest through the city until it emptied into the sea at Bandra's Sea Link Bridge, near Chimbai.

Strolling along the lake, Arjun considered taking the bus up to the park but decided instead to go to Juhu Beach on the east side of the city. The bus took him from Powai through the suburb Andheri East. On the Western Expressway, moving through traffic, he glanced at the office buildings in Gundavali, his feeling balancing between optimism and apprehension. *Everything is ready to go, but I'm putting my life at risk by trusting Rohit that all those guards will play along.*

He got off at the Juhu Hotel bus stop near the impressive JW Marriott Hotel with its stunning sea-view rooms, outdoor seating, and pool areas often visited by Bollywood's celebrities.

Arjun strolled into the side street next to the hotel until he stepped onto the sand and started walking south barefoot with the wind in his face to the Chowpatty with its many food stalls. He bought a samosa, briefly thinking about his father, and sat down.

The final inning, Arjun, he thought, now determined, watching the white tops across the water.

*

DEEP INTO THE night, the dark Carter Road promenade was deserted, except for some lazy dogs slumbering around the footpath. Arjun could hear the waves break across the shore beside him. He crept along until he spotted a white van underneath one of the streetlights in the distance. Recognizing the license plate number, his pulse started to quicken. "That's the one," he murmured to himself. Approaching the front of the van, he saw Rohit sitting behind the wheel. Arjun opened the door and slid into the passenger seat, meeting Rohit's gaze with a determined nod.

"This is it?" Arjun asked, breaking the silence.

"Yes. Everything is set. Ready?"

Arjun's heart raced, but he kept his voice steady. "The dollies and all the boxes are in the back?"

"Of course," Rohit confirmed.

"Are you confident about the guards?" Arjun asked as they sped off.

"I've been very generous," Rohit said confidently.

After driving along the highway at Golibar, they passed the airport and Vile Parle until they exited the highway into Andheri East. After a few minutes, Rohit pointed ahead. "Here we are." Carefully, he turned the van into the tree-filled narrow side street and drove straight down.

"This is the moment of truth," Arjun said seeing the gate house of the company compound in front of them. Rohit remained calm and collected, and stopped to keep his distance from the gate house, letting the darkness swallow them whole. Rohit flashed his lights to signal the guards as per plan.

The barrier opened.

"Amazing," Arjun remarked excitedly.

"Bastard!" Rohit laughed aloud, and drove through, passing the seemingly empty guard house. They reached a garden area in front of an enormous glass building and parked underneath a large bodhi tree, the branches covering the van. "That's the path that leads toward a door we can enter, right next to that palm tree," Rohit pointed out. "Our one hour starts now…"

Walking alongside Rohit, Arjun noted the ambient lights seeping through the building's glass walls.

"Will all these lights stay on?" Arjun said.

"It works to our advantage," Rohit reassured him, nearing their entry.

"You said there will be a power cut," Arjun noted anxiously.

"They said they can only turn off CCTV for the hour," Rohit said. "Don't worry. You'll see," he proclaimed proudly, opening the door for them to enter.

Rohit stepped inside the enormous building first. After a brief moment, he told Arjun behind him, "Now go back and pick up the dolly and boxes and wait downstairs. I'll go up."

Arjun hesitated, sticking his head in the doorway to glance up. "Up? Stairs? You never mentioned stairs!"

"Four hundred laptops are not all on the ground floor!"

Rohit retorted. "I will go up, crack the locks, and toss them down one by one. You catch them, pack them up, and load them into the van. Hurry up!"

Arjun's anxiety bubbled to the surface.

"Hurry!" Rohit urged him.

Arjun took a deep breath, steeling himself. *No time to hesitate. It's all or nothing,* he thought. Stepping back into the quiet, shadowed garden, a sense of foreboding crept over him. *We would be trapped if any guard turned on us.* He ran across the footpath, opened the van's backdoor, took out the dolly and boxes, and pushed it all back to the building. Once inside, he gasped at the sheer size of the place. His eyes stood wide with awe. *Their canteen is bigger than any restaurant I have seen,* he mused. He panicked as he looked up. *Where is Rohit!?*

"Hey!" came a call. Rohit stood ready on the walkway. "Catch!" he said, tossing down the first laptop. Arjun caught it, the weight lighter than expected. "Careful! We don't want to drop fifteen thousand rupees!" Rohit laughed. Arjun carefully placed the laptop into one of the boxes. He repeated the process, swiftly packing the loot into boxes.

"They also have monitors!" Rohit called, dropping one down. "Join me," he urged Arjun. "While I pick the locks, you can carry some down."

On the first floor, Arjun saw Rohit frantically move around the countless rows of desks, some with monitors.

Jackpot, Arjun thought, unplugging a monitor.

Forty-four laptops and fifteen monitors later, Arjun's heart thrummed with energy. "That's more than seven lakhs already," he calculated, moving the dolly back to the van, the garden lights casting eerie shadows around him. *How can no one be here?* he thought.

Through the dark, dead-quiet, Arjun moved to and from the van with silent efficiency. There were no guards, no interruptions. "Let's go!" Arjun finally called out from the ground floor. Rohit's face poked out from the walkway. "After this load, the van is full, and time is almost up!" Arjun suggested. Rohit nodded and disappeared.

They had stacked the last boxes along with the dolly, and now they sat together in the van squinting their eyes to catch any movement ahead. They both sighed deeply. "So far so good," Arjun said.

Rohit started the engine and drove slowly along the leafy lane towards the gate, seeing the guardhouse aglow. "The last piece of the puzzle," Rohit whispered.

Arjun's heart pounded as they approached, eyeing one guard standing near the barrier that was left open. Closing in, the guard strolled to the back of the guardhouse, seemingly oblivious. "Go, Rohit," Arjun urged, the tension palpable.

Both held their breath. "*Aaicha gho…*" Rohit then muttered with a sigh of relief as they merged onto the main road, excitement simmering between them. They turned onto Cardinal Gracious Road and onto Sahar Road until they were forced to stop at a traffic light. Rohit's sudden laugh punctured the silence, but Arjun remained cautious. "We did it, bhai!" Rohit exclaimed, as the light turned green, allowing them back onto the highway.

"Not yet… not yet!" Arjun countered, although he felt a glimmer of relief.

"From here, we're just fifteen minutes away from Kala Nagar," Rohit said, brimming with confidence.

"Keep to the speed limit," Arjun said.

"Woohoo!" Rohit yelled out, punching the ceiling of the van. "My guy is waiting. We'll count and take photos of everything, and hand it over."

"Let's do this!" Arjun finally yelled, letting his guard down. A flood of thoughts came rushing in. *This could be it—free from debt at last, a new life awaiting,* he thought. They continued south onto the expressway.

Suddenly, out of nowhere, lights and sirens pierced the silence. "We're screwed!" Arjun screamed, looking frantically in the rearview mirror.

Rohit floored the gas pedal. "Bastards! They tipped them off!" Rohit said furiously.

Fear gripped them as the van sped onward. "You missed the exit! Where are we going!?" Arjun yelled.

"We need to keep going!" Rohit shouted, panic threading through his voice as the van barreled past a hundred twenty kilometers per hour. "This van's too heavy. I can't go any faster!"

Sirens wailed, closing in as they reached the Bandra-Worli Sea Link. "We can't escape in this van, Rohit!" Arjun's voice quivered with terror. Police cars swarmed behind them, a relentless surge of flashing lights. The van smashed through the Sea Link toll booth, shattering the barrier.

"Slow down!" Arjun shrieked. "You're going too fast ahead of the turn!" The van shuddered violently, but Rohit remained resolute, determined to evade the screaming sirens.

"No!" Arjun hollered feeling Rohit losing control.

Tires screamed in protest as Rohit slammed on the brakes, but the van launched through the stone guardrail of the bridge, the earth vanishing beneath them as they plunged into the abyss below.

Aditi

THE NEXT MORNING in the office hallway at Bhavishya Sankalp Ventures, Aditi bumped into Saanvi from their communications team. "Excited for your BUH meeting today?" Saanvi giggled, her eyes twinkling with mischief.

This puzzled Aditi. "Sure. Why? Is there something special?" She couldn't fathom what was so amusing.

"Well, you know..." Saanvi laughed cheekily, her tone almost teasing.

Feeling a mix of curiosity and unease, Aditi forced a smile. "I don't know; tell me." She smiled, trying to keep her voice light.

Saanvi's grin widened. "I heard about you and Akash."

Aditi's mind raced, searching for an explanation. "What do you mean?" she asked, her voice tinged with confusion.

"Come on," Saanvi continued, trying to get her to admit.

"No. I really don't understand what you mean," Aditi replied firmly.

Saanvi's face fell slightly, a shadow of guilt passing over her features. "Oh, maybe I misunderstood," she mumbled.

Sensing an opportunity to clear the air, Aditi asked,

"Misunderstood from whom? Who told you that, Saanvi?" Aditi asked, feeling a surge of frustration.

"Oh, you know, water cooler talk," Saanvi smiled weakly.

Aditi's patience wore thin. "It's a total lie. And very unprofessional," she pointed out, her voice firm.

Saanvi seemed visibly taken aback by Aditi's strong response.

"I am really sorry, Aditi. Really. I didn't want to make you uncomfortable. I thought it was common knowledge. Maybe I misunderstood," Saanvi apologized, her tone sincere.

Aditi's face reddened with a mix of anger and embarrassment. "Please, Saanvi, can I request you not to spread this kind of gossip? I work here to build a career to support my son," she said with seriousness.

"Yes, of course. Sorry, Aditi, I didn't mean to embarrass you," Saanvi replied, her own face reflecting shame.

"Who did you hear this from?" Aditi pressed, but Saanvi seemed eager to end the conversation.

"I don't want to cause any more issues, Aditi. Please accept my apologies," she said, quickly walking away to avoid further questioning. "I will see you later," she added over her shoulder.

I never gave anyone a reason to think that. Where did this come from? Aditi thought, frustrated by the undeserving gossip after just beginning work here. But then she thought about the conversation with the chaiwallah about our power to decide our response to anything at any moment. *This is one of those moments.*

*

IN THE WEEKLY meeting with Sucheta and Akash, Jahan took them through the slides he showed Anish. Both Akash and Sucheta seemed to appreciate the suggestions for Delhi and

Bangalore—Aditi's slides and suggestions. Aditi didn't feel like adding much to the conversation after the encounter with Saanvi. *Remember what your wise counselor said Diti... you choose your response,* she thought, trying to inject herself with positive energy.

After the meeting ended, Aditi walked out and found Anish waiting. "Do you have a second?" he asked.

"Yes, of course," Aditi replied, following him back into the same room.

"How is everything?" he asked, his tone concerned.

"Good, Anish-ji. I'm learning a lot."

"Good," he smiled reassuringly. "Listen, normally I don't get involved in my team's personal life, but I wanted to let you know that I heard about you and Akash."

Aditi's face paled. Her mind raced with anxiety and a sense of injustice.

"Sorry if this offends you. As your boss and mentor, I just want to ask you to tread carefully. BUH is an important new client, and you are their consultant. I would like you to continue to work with them. You have supported Jahan well so far."

Aditi sighed deeply. "Anish-ji, I do not know where this gossip is coming from. This is a complete lie that someone is spreading about me," she said sternly.

"What?" Anish responded, clearly taken aback.

"There is nothing between us. Not even friendship. We have been completely professional." She sighed. "This is very distressing," she added.

Anish pondered quietly for a moment then said, "Okay, Aditi. Gossip like this is totally unacceptable. I will get to the bottom of this. Just leave it with me."

Aditi could see the embarrassment on his face. He was about to walk away, but hesitated. "Aditi, I am really very sorry about this," he said earnestly.

"Yes. I just started here, and I don't want people to think of me that way. I just want to deliver great work and build my career," Aditi said, her voice firm yet pleading.

"I will handle this and keep you up to date," Anish assured her.

You choose how to respond! she yelled inside, holding back tears as Anish walked off down the hallway.

Sumeet

SUMEET'S EXCITEMENT WAS palpable as he moved himself through the alleys of Dharavi. *Why am I so nervous right now?* he wondered, his eyes scanning the ground meticulously to avoid the numerous hazards. *Is it just because of my plan, or something else?* he mused, reaching his destination. Then he heard her voice.

"As you can see from this chart, the standard deviation is..." Ananya paused, then addressed her class, "One moment, please." She stepped out of the classroom and spotted him. After showing her initial surprise upon seeing him, she asked him to come back in thirty minutes during her break. Sumeet jokingly told her that would be perfect, giving him enough time to enjoy that paav bhaji nearby and come back.

Sumeet saw the students gathered outside when he returned. He entered the class and approached Ananya.

"Well, Sumeet, it's such a surprise to see you today. What is it that you wanted to talk about?" she asked him kindly.

"I quit my job," he announced. "Well… I think I quit my career actually," he corrected himself. Ananya's eyes opened wide and her eyebrows rose, but she waited for Sumeet to finish before responding. "I want to start a college to help young adults like Anjali in your class find success in the workforce. And I need your help."

Her mouth was now agape in disbelief. "What? Really? How?" she asked, clearly astonished.

"Large companies invest a lot of money to get and nurture talent. And those same companies often battle with their corporate social responsibilities. We can give them both," he smiled. "They invest their funds in our college, get access to talent, get to exercise influence on their preparation for the workforce, track their progress, test and hire them, and get to tell their story to the world."

Ananya's eyes sparkled with astonishment. "I am really flabbergasted," she said. Sumeet couldn't help but smile at her reaction. "Firstly, I am elated that you took inspiration from my teaching and my students. Secondly, I am shocked you have the courage to pivot your career like this. And thirdly, I am honored that you want me to join your mission," she said with admiration.

He smiled broadly in response to her summary.

Ananya sat down on the only plastic chair in the room next to the desk, her eyes still wide with amazement. She explained that she had seen many students come and go with enormous potential, but that they were not given the opportunities to change their lives around. She tried to attract more funding and expand but couldn't pull it off.

Sumeet started to take her through his plan. They would need one hundred students in their first year studying a business curriculum built between college and companies. From that pool of students, they needed to ensure at least five high-performing students got an internship in different companies afterward. The internship should have the possibility of leading to employment to prove the model and attract more funding. He would use his network to start working on the curriculum.

Ananya proposed she could reach out to the few universities

she had worked with to get their affiliation and help with their unique curriculum to get approval from the University Grants Commission and the All-India Council for Technical Education. Sumeet said that the registration as an entity and the various no-objection certificates and licenses would take some time. He told her he calculated they would need one hundred eighty lakhs to cover the building rent, desks, seats, desktop computers, stationary, projectors, whiteboards, staff, and website in their first year.

"I'm a teacher, my expertise on running a business only comes from books, not actual experience," Ananya replied, doubt showing on her face."

"Don't worry," Sumeet assured her. "I will draft a five-year business plan based on all the information I have and talk to my best friend who is an investor and get his input. With his feedback, we can finalize the proposal and start approaching those universities and different companies.

"It all sounds so simple, doesn't it? Now we just need to turn the dream into reality!" He laughed.

"We?" she repeated. "How do you see my role in all this?" Ananya asked. "I don't have money to invest," she confessed.

"Co-founder and head teacher? You will get shares for helping me set this up, and a salary once we get funding," Sumeet explained. "You inspired me, Ananya," he said earnestly. "Many things led me to this change in my life, and it feels right. How does that sound?"

"This could help many more people and create real impact," she said, thinking aloud. "Sounds like an opportunity of a lifetime. Count me in!" she exclaimed.

"Wonderful! Let's change lives!" Sumeet replied with pride.

Aditi

"WHAT IS IT?" Jahan responded brusquely as Aditi walked up to his desk.

"I'd like to catch up and discuss ways of working with BUH," Aditi said, trying to sound casual.

"Okay?" Jahan responded defensively.

"Can we go into a meeting room to discuss?" Aditi suggested.

Jahan sighed, his impatience evident. "How long will it take? I only have a few minutes."

"It should only take five minutes," Aditi assured him.

Jahan reluctantly followed Aditi into the meeting room where he sat across from her. The tension in the air was palpable.

"Thanks, Jahan. Could you tell me when the next meeting is with BUH?" Aditi asked, deliberately choosing her words to avoid confrontation.

"You have the weekly meetings in your calendar, right?" Jahan said.

"Yes, but you have been having separate meetings with them outside the weekly meetings. Anish mentioned that he wants me to attend all meetings with them," Aditi explained.

Jahan opened his calendar, his expression indifferent. "I am meeting them later today."

"Okay. Could you please forward that invite and include me in all future meetings?" Aditi asked.

"Well, okay, but today I am just going through some administrative things."

"Yes, but please include me, because that is what Anish requested from me. If I attend all meetings, we'll be sure to always be on the same page," Aditi insisted.

"Okay," Jahan said dryly.

"With that, please include me in all project email correspondence," Aditi added.

"You want it all, don't you?" Jahan replied sarcastically.

"It's just a lot easier. There might be questions and comments from BUH that I can respond to directly," Aditi reasoned. "And, one last thing, Jahan. I hope you can help me…" Aditi began hesitantly.

"With what?" Jahan asked, his tone a mixture of curiosity and impatience.

"Someone told me they heard I like Akash romantically," Aditi said, watching Jahan's reaction closely.

"No, really?" Jahan asked, surprised.

His uncharacteristically excited response made Aditi feel he wasn't truthful. *I think you know exactly what I mean,* Aditi thought bitterly. "Yes, someone has been telling this lie to others, and it now has become such common knowledge that even Anish is aware. As you know, my relationship with Akash is purely professional. The story is false and is damaging to my reputation."

"Well, I didn't hear anything. Who told you this?" Jahan asked.

"It doesn't matter. But I hope if you hear anyone talk, you will let them know this is absolutely false," Aditi said firmly.

"Sure," Jahan replied.

"Okay, thank you," Aditi said, deciding it was best to end the conversation there. "That's all."

They went their separate ways but tension lingered.

Arjun

A RJUN NOTICED SOME brightness across his eyes and opened them slowly to reveal a slither of grey concrete.

He was disoriented, but then noticed the familiar smell of sea salt filling his nostrils. *Where am I?*

While keeping his body still, he slightly lifted his head to find a large palm leaf covering his upper body. Using his hand to move it aside, a bolt of excruciating pain followed by a wave of heat forced him back down.

His upper body was a mass of fiery agony while his lower body felt freezing cold and numb. He moved his hands onto the gritty texture beneath him. Then his hands moved across his upper body and he discovered his shirt was ripped open and his chest and stomach were cut and sore.

Pushing himself through the screaming pain, he lifted his head again to see his torso pressed in between jagged black rocks and his lower half enveloped in water. He willed his legs to move, but they refused, trapped in the wet, torn denim of his jeans with his feet dangling lifelessly in the murky water.

What happened? he thought.

He rested his head for a moment and slipped into unconsciousness.

When he stirred awake sometime later, a renewed sense of urgency gripped him. With his hand, he grabbed onto one of his legs and pulled it towards him, out of the water. When his knees bent, he started to regain feeling in his legs and feet.

Using his hands against the rocks as leverage, he lifted himself upright. He looked around but didn't see anyone or anything except a stone wall adorned with steps behind the black rock formation. *I need to get up those stairs,* he thought. His toes twitched as he focused. "Come on, you bastard," he said aloud. As soon as his weight shifted to his legs, an excruciating pain shot through him and he collapsed with a strangled cry.

Gritting his teeth, he attempted to stand again. Once initial dizziness subsided, he steadied himself on his hands and knees and slowly moved across the rocks. Inching forward, another blitz of hurt made him rest with his face flat against the rocks. He kept his eyes on the stairs and alternated crawling and resting until he finally reached the wall beside the stairs. He sighed deeply, his breath ragged and full of pain. *What the hell happened?* he wondered, frustration mingling with bewilderment. *How did I get here?*

Using the steps as support, he crawled up the stairs on his hands and knees, his fingers scraping the rough stone. *I need help*, he thought, sensing his broken body. As he reached the top, he miraculously discovered a rickshaw driver in the distance, lounging in his seat. "Help!" he called out, waving weakly. The driver watched him for a moment. The hesitation enhanced Arjun's desperation, but then the rickshaw moved toward him. The relief weakened his arms, making him drop down and roll onto his side. The driver stepped out and helped him up into the backseat. Arjun muttered, "Chimbai," and instantly lost consciousness.

A yell from the driver roused him. "Where?" he heard.

Arjun opened his eyes and dizziness overwhelmed him. His head lolled as he struggled to take in his surroundings.

"I will take care of you, Arjun," a new voice said as someone slid into the rickshaw beside him. "Sion Hospital. Chal!" the voice urged as Arjun surrendered to unconsciousness once more.

Sumeet

I N THE EVENING, Anish and Sumeet enjoyed a glass of Black Dog rum in Sumeet's apartment.

"Bhai! When and how did you come up with this?" Anish called out after Sumeet finished his presentation. "This is quite random, seemingly coming out of nowhere," he laughed. "I mean, you told me you did that lecture, but this is different."

"What do you think about the plan?" Sumeet asked. He was nervous. Having Anish's support would be invaluable.

"I absolutely love it! And that's exactly the kind of business we would invest in at Bhavishya Sankalp Ventures… if you were going to make a lot of money with this," Anish smirked.

Sumeet's eyes fell down, realizing his idea wouldn't qualify.

"But," Anish said, "because I expect this business not to make much money … I am happy to invest my own money to make this happen."

"Really?" Sumeet asked in disbelief.

Anish nodded confidently from across the table. "Now tell me, how did all of this happen? I know you always liked to coach people at work, but this is different."

Sumeet told him about his friendship with the chaiwallah,

meeting Ananya, his lecture, Kabir and Nandini on Marine Drive, and the recruitment insights from his career. "I know how companies think and work, which helped shape my plan. That, and the realization that I can no longer continue with my career and need to make a drastic change," Sumeet said, his voice soft but resolute.

"A chaiwallah, a random teacher, and conversations with students on the street… yes, this sounds like the old you—the real you that I remember from college," Anish responded, smiling broadly at him. "This new endeavor fits you perfectly, Sumeet!" he added, pride evident in his tone.

The comment made Sumeet feel hopeful and even more determined.

"This college will need investment," Anish said, "but I am confident it will pay off for the organizations we approach, which will attract more companies and funding. Let me look over the business plan during the next few days."

Then Anish playfully hit Sumeet on the shoulder. "You really found me a diamond, you know?"

"I'm glad you think so," Sumeet said.

"Yes, your business idea too, but I am talking about Aditi. In no time at all she has become an incredible asset. All the clients she works with are raving about her," Anish said, clearly excited.

"Oh, really?" Sumeet looked up, intrigued.

"She is performing much beyond expectations. She has even made an enemy, a senior staff member who is jealous of her work. She is that good," Anish said.

"That is so good to hear. Well, not about the enemy," Sumeet said, concern flickering in his eyes.

"Don't worry, I am handling that," Anish replied confidently.

Standing up from the couch to get some water, Sumeet spotted an email from a law firm. He opened the message, wondering what it was about. The email read:

Mr. Sumeet Daruwalla, we are writing to inform you that our law firm Kalbadevi Family Legal has been retained by Mrs. Manisha Daruwalla to act on her behalf in the matter of seeking a divorce.

Sumeet's heart sank and he felt his body was about to give in. He leaned against the wall in the kitchen, his mind racing. *She is going all the way. And so fast,* he thought.

"Are you okay, bhai?" Anish asked, observing his body language.

Sumeet walked back and showed him the email.

Anish read the message and said, "Were you expecting anything different?"

"Not really, but it still hits hard," Sumeet admitted, the weight of the situation pressing down on him.

"She is probably going to live either permanently in Dubai or join Nandini in Canada to start her new life," Anish said, placing a comforting hand on Sumeet's shoulder. Sumeet sighed deeply, but there were no tears.

"I will get you in touch with a good family lawyer who will handle all this for you," Anish said, "so you can focus on executing your plan. That is what you need to concentrate on now."

"Almost twenty years," he sighed again, feeling a lump in his throat. *Nandini needs to know about this. Hopefully Manisha didn't say anything yet. We need to do this together. Poor Nandini, she will be incredibly sad,* he thought looking around the house as Anish continued to review his presentation. *We will need to sell this apartment,* he thought. *As long as Nandini can continue and finish her studies, that's all that matters.* His thoughts were a storm of worries. *I need to tell my parents.*

"Sumeet?" Anish said, trying to get his attention. "I'm sorry, man, but I need to go. Let me have another look at the plan over the next few days, give you my input, and get some preliminary feedback from a few of my friendly partners. See what those companies think about all this. I will get back to you on this, okay?"

"That will be great, Anish. Thank you so much," Sumeet replied, a flicker of hope in his weary heart.

"Your slides didn't show the actual name of the college. Do you have one?" Anish asked.

"Dharavi Future Leaders College," Sumeet said proudly, the name rolling off his tongue with a sense of promise.

Aditi

A DITI STROLLED THROUGH the office hallway late at night. She had not yet heard anything from Anish. *Who spread this gossip?* she thought, disappointment lingering. *Working with all these different people in an office can really be painful,* she sighed, tired from another long day.

In the lift, she admired the sprawling display of city lights and messaged her aunt that she would be there in forty-five minutes. In the basement, she stepped out into the dimly lit parking area and noticed she was one of the last people in the building. Unhurried, she walked toward her kinetic in the far-left corner where some other motorbikes were parked. *Well, a dream job must come with some obstacles,* she told herself.

"Aditi?" a voice came from behind.

Aditi turned around and was surprised to see Vikram Singhania, Anish's friend and the investor who had given such an inspiring speech on her first day. "Hello, Mr. Singhania. It's nice to see you again!" she exclaimed. "You remember my name..." she smiled.

"I remember the names of everyone who asks good questions." He smiled broadly, which lifted his prominent black moustache. "I was just catching up with Anish tonight.

He mentioned you're working on Bharat Urban Harvest, Dhanyavad Vitt, and Pharma Direct?"

Anish mentioned me? Aditi thought, happily. "Yes, it's been very exciting, Mr. Singhania," she replied.

"Anish also told me he thinks you might be the company's new superstar." Vikram smiled.

"Did he?" Aditi laughed, brushing off the compliment. *He didn't really say that, did he?* she thought, astounded. "I'm learning so much… it has been amazing so far," she admitted, forgetting the gossip. "And talking with all these founders is so inspiring. They make me think about all the possible business opportunities out there."

"Like what?" Vikram asked.

Aditi hesitated, surprised by his directness. "Um… well, please know that I am fully dedicated to my job day and night, but I did come up with an idea on my own," she admitted somewhat sheepishly.

Vikram's eyes lit up. "Tell me, I'd love to hear it," he urged.

She hesitated for a moment, thinking it may not be appropriate as she had just started working for Anish, but then she thought sharing her idea wouldn't hurt. "Actually, my idea comes from combining all the different projects I am working on."

Vikram moved a little closer, visibly intrigued.

"I think there's an opportunity for an online agricultural platform," she said. "A platform localized by state that connects independent agricultural product sellers with buyers, helps with transactions and insurance, integrates micro-finance solutions for sellers, and provides agricultural product insights and analytics for both parties."

Vikram nodded. "Well, that's a mouthful," he smiled. "Why?"

"Well, I'm from Bandra's Koliwadahs. I think it could really help people like our Koli fishermen find funding, find buyers, create networks, get better prices, and build sustainable growth. I would first focus on Maharashtra because of its diverse agricultural sector and high GDP."

"I love the idea, Aditi. It's big, though, and will require a big business plan to make it happen."

"Yes, and I hardly have the time," she laughed, relieved to get a positive response from such a legendary investor.

"Well, let me know when you progress. I'm happy to have a look at it sometime," he suggested.

"Really? Wow, that would be an honor," Aditi exclaimed, slightly intimidated by the offer. "Thank you. I will make sure to keep working on it whenever I can," she promised.

Vikram handed out his card. "Reach out when you are ready," he smiled. "Goodnight, Aditi."

"Goodnight," she said, as Vikram walked off.

Ha! This is unexpected, Aditi thought, smiling broadly as she walked towards her scooter.

Arjun

"You are awake…"

Arjun saw the chaiwallah grinning at him warmly.

"Where am I?" Arjun strained to lift his head, struggling to survey his surroundings.

"Don't worry about a thing, beta. Just rest—you're in good hands now," the chaiwallah said.

Arjun laid his head back down, exhaustion claiming him.

The next time Arjun awoke, darkness had blanketed the world beyond the window. The chaiwallah sat slumping in a chair, an empty glass on the side table next him. Seeing Arjun's body move, the old man inquired softly, "How are you feeling?"

Arjun took a moment to scan his body. "An inch from death." He slowly turned his head from left to right. On his left were two empty beds, the room desolate except for the persistent hum of hospital equipment. Arjun shifted his body to the right, every movement accompanied by a symphony of pain. "Everything hurts…"

The chaiwallah rose and approached his bed. "The doctors removed many glass shards from your body. Your lower back had fractures, your ribs were broken, and your nose was reset." He paused for Arjun to absorb the information. "You had a blood transfusion because of severe blood loss from all the lacerations and ruptured vessels. But with rest and medicine, you should recover just fine."

A sudden image of Rohit screaming behind the wheel right before the nosedive flashed by. Panic seized him. *Where is Rohit? Is he alive?* A heavy sense of doubt clouded his thoughts.

"Did anyone else come looking for me?" Arjun asked the chaiwallah anxiously.

"No... do you want me to call someone for you?"

"No, please don't," Arjun responded hastily, paranoia creeping in. *Why haven't the police come to get me?* he wondered, piecing together the foggy memories of that night. *They will come soon, and I won't be able to run away... Karma.*

Time seeped away in silence, his thoughts oscillating back to the present.

After a moment, Arjun fought through the pain to force himself up. The chaiwallah quickly got up too and put his arm around his shoulder. "It's okay, it's okay," Arjun said, but then accepted the help.

On their way to the bathroom, Arjun's attention suddenly shifted to the television screen at reception, seeing a picture of the shattered barrier on the Bandra-Worli Sea Link Bridge. Shocked at seeing the scene of the accident, Arjun immediately let go of the chaiwallah's arm. Fear and anxiety coursed through his aching body.

Then he heard the news announcer say, "The burglar appeared to be operating by himself with inside help from the security guards. The man was able to spend an undisclosed amount of time inside the compound taking electronic equipment."

A headshot of Rohit from his previous bid in jail appeared on the screen. "After a wild police chase, he lost control of his vehicle and shattered through the barrier into the Arabian Sea. Divers found his body in the van at the bottom of the sea."

Oh my God, Arjun thought. *That poor bastard.*

Arjun turned back toward the chaiwallah.

"Are you okay?" the old man asked. "You look pale."

"Yes, yes, I'm fine." Arjun said, trying to hide his emotions.

Once in the bathroom by himself, he broke down in tears, thinking about Rohit. After a moment, he remembered the announcer's comment. *The burglar operated by himself? They probably missed seeing me because I was tucked away in between those large rocks with that palm leaf underneath the bridge.*

Back in the hospital bed, Arjun turned to his side, thoughts racing through his mind.

What do I do now? How do I pay off my debt? First, I must get better, he told himself. *I almost died without seeing my father one last time. And for what?*

In his mind, he started to list all the challenges he had faced in life and then thought about where he had landed… broken, with nothing to his name. Tears welled up and cascaded silently down both cheeks. Murky memories from the distant past surged forward, dark and oppressive.

This is all because of him! Arjun suddenly concluded. *My father trusted him, his own brother.* He seethed internally. *But he ruined my life!*

The chaiwallah edged closer to Arjun's bed. "You will be alright, beta," he whispered consolingly. "You will recover." Arjun's sobs grew louder, tears flowing freely now.

"Can I help you with something, beta?" the chaiwallah whispered kindly.

"No, dada… I cannot be helped. I am hopeless," Arjun replied between sobs.

"What is it, beta?"

Arjun turned his back to the old man and wailed uncontrollably. He looked up at the ceiling, his eyes swimming in agony. "It cannot be corrected, and it cannot be undone…"

"What is it?" the chaiwallah asked gently.

Arjun's face twisted, fighting against the emotions that overwhelmed him, threatening to crack the internal dam he had built up over the last twenty years. He wiped his tears with the sleeve of his gown, but the flow went unabated. His body was consumed with heat and tension, intensifying the wails.

The chaiwallah took his hand. "Let me help you, beta," he whispered. Arjun recoiled, but the old man held on tightly. "It is okay, Arjun. You can let it all out. Let it go," he urged.

Arjun began to accept the chaiwallah's grip and squeezed back before suddenly letting go and bawling out, "That bastard! That sick man!" he screamed across the room.

The room hung heavy with silence before Arjun yelled again, "He should be killed!"

The chaiwallah continued to steady his hand, which trembled violently. "Who, beta?" the old man whispered. "What happened to you?"

Arjun's pillow was drenched. He turned away, embarrassed.

"You are in much pain, beta. It is okay to let it out," the chaiwallah coaxed.

The deep-rooted shame, guilt, pain, and sadness that had festered within Arjun for decades battled for escape. Shelled up, he continued to wail.

Then, in a voice reminiscent of his eight-year-old self, he finally stammered, "He... touched... me. My uncle." Then he cried out, "My father trusted him and that bastard touched me! I was just a child!" Arjun sobbed. His voice cracked. "My father didn't know. Never knew. I couldn't become the son he wanted. My rage wouldn't let me. I just couldn't stay there anymore."

After a moment, Arjun said through his tears, "I... I could have been a cricket player, but he ruined it for me! Once in Mumbai, I needed to earn money and I couldn't practice anymore. I couldn't play anymore..."

The chaiwallah squeezed his hand. "Now you are safe,

beta," he said softly. "You are safe," he repeated. "Now you can take control. You can become the man you want to be."

Arjun pondered the old man's words but responded, "I can't," he said. "I have debt... it's haunting me. They are looking for me. They will kill me. They will find me. And if not me, they will find people around me."

"Don't worry about that for now," the chaiwallah said. "Now you are safe, and you need to rest. You need to recover."

Arjun gazed up at the ceiling, wiping his tears before exhaustion claimed him and he drifted back to sleep.

Sumeet

Late Saturday afternoon, there was light rain. To avoid getting wet, Sumeet hurried through the prominent gate of the large house on the hilly Nargus Dutt Road near the Pali Market. Walking across the well-maintained garden, he tried to avoid the many puddles of water to reach the heavy wooden door with its luxurious copper handle. Standing underneath the canopy, his mind swirled with anxiety. *This news will give them a heart attack,* he thought as he opened the door.

"Baba? Aai?" Sumeet called out, stepping inside of the house, dreading the task ahead.

"I'm in the kitchen!" his mother yelled back.

Sumeet hesitated for a moment in the living room. His father was sitting on the couch, absorbed in the newspaper. "Hey, Sumeet," his father said, looking up. "What have you been doing? Any ideas about the work front?"

"Oh, I have been busy with various things," he answered, trying to steady his racing heart. One of the maids was laying an array of dishes on the table.

"Are you hungry?" his mother called, her voice filled with a warmth that contrasted sharply with Sumeet's growing dread. "We're having a simple dinner tonight," she added.

"It doesn't look that simple," Sumeet murmured, eyeing the multiple dishes and breads spread out on the table. He ignored her last question.

"I need you to eat well," she said, as if nourishing him could shield him from any discomfort. "*Aho*, come," she beckoned to his father. "How is Manisha?"

Sumeet ignored the question. After they sat down, he could feel the words forming a lump in his throat. "I need to tell you something…" he blurted out, his heavy heart evident as their eyes met.

They immediately felt it was bad news. "What is it?" his mother asked, panic in her voice.

Sumeet sighed deeply, feeling the weight of what he was about to say out loud. "Manisha and I are getting divorced…"

His mother's reaction was instant and visceral; she spat out her curry, her face a mask of shock. "What?" she screamed.

His father remained silent, but Sumeet saw his shoulders slump and his gaze drop to the table. The room felt suffocating. "I know what you think. It's shameful for the family and that it will be horrible for Nandini."

"Damn right!" his mother yelled, her voice trembling with anger. "What happened?" she demanded.

Sumeet looked at both their faces, his heart aching. "It's not about something specific happening. We have just grown apart over the years. And it got much worse after Nandini left us." He paused, feeling apologetic, but continued; "Honestly, we never truly loved each other. We were just living together."

His mother's face softened slightly. "Well, there's nothing wrong with being married and feeling like good friends."

"Yes, but we aren't even good friends. We're just house-mates," Sumeet confessed, glancing at his father as he mechanically served himself some food, wondering what he was thinking. *Somehow he doesn't seem as disappointed and upset,* he thought. His father's composed demeanor puzzled him.

"I was on my walk and got a message from Manisha. When I came home, she was gone. She had packed most of her stuff and taken a flight to her parents in Dubai."

His mother's eyes widened in disbelief. "Oh my God," she whispered.

"And then I received a letter from her lawyer requesting a divorce." Sumeet's voice wavered, the reality of his situation crashing down on him.

"Just like that?" his mother asked, her voice strained.

Sumeet nodded.

"Well," his mother said. "Manisha and I were never very close, but she should have at least come talked to us," she said, her voice tinged with hurt. "Just out of courtesy… don't you think, aho?" she added, looking at Sumeet's father.

Sumeet looked earnestly at his parents. His father's face remained unreadable, a blank canvas amid the chaos.

"Did you speak to Nandini about this?" his father asked, finally looking up.

"No, not yet. I want Manisha to agree that we tell her together."

The rest of the dinner was silent, except for the occasional sigh of disappointment from his mother who was trying to process the news. Despite having more news, Sumeet felt it was not the right time to tell his father he wouldn't get another high-paying job because he wanted to start a college. *Let's save that confrontation for another day,* he thought.

Aditi

IN THE MORNING, Aditi led Susheta and Akash towards their meeting room down the hall. Eyeing Akash, she was reminded about the gossip that had spread about them throughout the office. As she opened the door to let them in, Aditi thought about the chaiwallah's comment about her power to control her response. *I will not be docile,* she decided, stepping into the room.

"Aditi, Jahan just messaged me that he will be delayed," Akash said, and then added, "By the way, we missed you in the website design meeting the other day."

Damn it! Aditi thought, fuming. *Jahan continues to have meetings without me.* "I will catch up with Jahan about that separately," she smiled. "While we wait for Jahan, shall we just start?" Aditi proposed, remembering her vow for assertiveness.

"Yes," Akash said, visibly appreciating Aditi's bias for action.

After twenty minutes of discussions, Jahan walked into the room. "I am sorry, my previous call overran by a lot."

"No problem," Sucheta responded. "Aditi just took us through her partnership ideas for the rewards programs for Delhi and Bangalore."

"Okay…" Jahan responded as he sat down, casting a critical eye over the occupants of the room.

Aditi noticed the slight irritation on Jahan's face when Sucheta listed all her ideas. *Jahan continues to downplay my ideas and involvement,* she thought silently.

"Aditi and I will review once more before we finalize our recommendations," Jahan said, sitting forward, his tone and body language exuding authority. "What are the next steps?" he added.

"Sucheta and Akash already provided their feedback," Aditi said, stepping in. "And, I have answered their questions, as per the proposal I sent through," Aditi said steadily. Aditi saw Jahan's confusion as he waited for a detailed run through to stay informed.

He didn't read it, Aditi thought.

"I believe we must now decide our monetary or point rewards and finalize the reward tiers to ensure we quickly move customers from competition with our wider range of products, services, and superior localized content."

"Um… yes, that's right," Jahan added, trying to insert himself into the discussion.

"Akash and Sucheta already agreed as per my proposal," Aditi replied, maintaining her composure.

"Great," Jahan replied, his face strained.

"Thanks, Aditi, I'm very happy with the progress we're making," Akash jumped in, breaking the tension.

Aditi smiled, feeling validated.

The meeting was over. As Sucheta and Akash walked out, Jahan turned to Aditi with a frown. "Aditi, what was that?"

"What do you mean?" Aditi asked, trying to keep her tone neutral.

"You were trying to run the meeting," Jahan said angrily, his voice rising.

"You were a bit late, so I took them through the rewards program that was exchanged by email," Aditi explained calmly.

"Well, yes, I get that..." he stammered. "But I am the lead here, Aditi," he pointed out, visibly frustrated. "Aditi, you are the assistant. I lead the meetings and you assist," Jahan said condescendingly.

"I am sorry, Jahan. Did you disagree with anything from my proposal? You confirmed by email it was good to go."

"Yes, it was. That is not the point."

"Okay," Aditi said, struggling to keep her emotions in check. "I thought it would okay to take them through the proposals, which I compiled and we signed off on," she said.

"BUH is my client. I am responsible for leading the client-investor relationship effectively."

"I thought they were our client?" Aditi noted, irritation creeping into her voice.

"No. My client. Know your place, Aditi," Jahan added.

Aditi felt her emotions boiling inside but decided to keep her composure. "Sure, Jahan, I understand. I was just trying to help." She swallowed her pride. "Apologies, if I made you feel uncomfortable," Aditi added, her voice calm despite the storm inside.

Jahan stood up. "Make sure you support me from now on. I don't want to tell Anish you are disrupting client relationships and being unsupportive to the project lead."

Aditi nodded, simmering with restrained anger.

Sumeet

DHARAVI WAS LIVELY and crowded as usual. Sumeet and Ananya strode purposefully along the now dusty, vibrant Station Road, their steps kicking up little clouds of dirt with each stride as the sun and heat dried up the city after all the rain. They were deep in discussion about the many challenges of the new venture, their voices occasionally drowned out by the bustling sounds around them. The air was thick with the scent of street food and the cacophony of vendors, rickshaw drivers, and the distant rumble of a passing train.

Listening to Ananya's ideas for the curriculum, Sumeet suddenly found himself noticing her almond-shaped eyes sparkling with determination. Her thick, chocolate brown lips contrasted beautifully against her lighter caramel skin complexion, and her shoulder-length, curly black hair with highlights caught the sunlight just right. Her big smile, which she flashed at the end of her explanation, lit up her entire face, accentuated by her prominent high cheekbones and large white, even teeth.

Sumeet nodded, feeling a sudden pang of embarrassment and guilt for his observation. He quickly averted his gaze across the train tracks that led to Parel and Churchgate near the majestic Gateway of India on the southern tip of Mumbai. A few minutes afterward, Sumeet pointed at a small coffee shop on their right. "Here it is." Ananya followed him as he pushed open the door and the rich aromas of sweet donuts and coffee beans enveloped them. In the corner, they saw Anish seated comfortably.

"Hey, bhai!" Sumeet called out, his excited voice mingling with the soft hum of the shop.

Anish stood up, greeted Sumeet, and introduced himself to Ananya. After small talk, Sumeet got up and ordered coffee and donuts. Returning back to the table, he enjoyed watching Anish and Ananya talk. He sat back down and turned to Anish. "The reason I asked you to come here is because I found a really great building within walking distance from Sion Station. After our talk, we can have a look."

"Perfect," Anish replied, leaning forward with interest.

Ananya jumped in. "We had our initial meetings with the international school where I used to work. They were all interested in the college concept and wanted to be affiliated, so we will have follow-up meetings for next steps. One of them mentioned that their affiliation could possibly offer international exchanges, which could significantly raise our profile. I can build the curriculum with them and the business partners we get."

Sumeet and Anish nodded excitedly, then Sumeet added, "I'm expecting we will get about ten to fifteen thousand rupees per student per year from the Ministry of Education. The rest will need to come from partners."

"That's where I come in," Anish started. "I have spoken to several companies who said they are ready to invest…"

"Really?" Sumeet interrupted.

"… once we show the results of year one," Anish smiled, finishing his sentence.

"Right," Sumeet nodded. "Once we prove that our students from class can turn into high-performing talent in the office."

"Yes, however, they are keen to co-design the curriculum from the start to give guidance on their expectations."

Sumeet paused, worry on his face. "How will we get all the funding to kick-start this thing? Going to banks and the government will be difficult and time consuming."

"As promised, I will put down twenty lakhs." Anish said. Sumeet smiled gratefully. "For shares, of course! But I won't get involved whatsoever," he added.

Sumeet laughed. "Of course."

"That means we need another one hundred sixty lakhs," Anish pointed out. "I am going to talk to a few businesses later this week and keep you posted."

Sumeet considered his divorce settlement, Nandini's studies, and ongoing costs. After a few minutes of silence, Sumeet said, "I can add about fifty lakhs. *That leaves one hundred ten lakhs. It will be hard to get a loan without income and investment commitments,* he thought, somewhat troubled.

Anish observed Sumeet's contemplative expression. "We need to prove the model works. Funding will come."

"Yes," Sumeet replied, standing up. "Come, let's have a look at that building."

They all stood up and walked towards the door of the café. "Sumeet, I have class soon so I won't be joining you," Ananya interjected when they stepped outside. "It was great meeting you, Anish. Bye, Sumeet." As Ananya walked away, the gentle breeze played with her kurti, hinting at the graceful curves of her silhouette.

Anish turned to Sumeet as they headed toward Sion Station. "Do you have feelings for her?"

Sumeet paused for a moment and answered, "I don't even know what that is. I married after graduation to someone I didn't love. I don't know about love, except for the puppy love

I felt for Samina in college. But we knew our parents would never agree to an inter-religious marriage, so we just broke up."

"Oh yeah, I remember," Anish chuckled.

"Let's cross," Sumeet said, noticing the cars stopped in a traffic jam.

Aditi

A FEW WEEKS LATER, Aditi was sitting behind her desk analyzing BUH's performance when Anish messaged her that he wanted to see her in his office.

"Please come in," Anish said, as she walked up to his door.

Aditi entered and sat in front of him, thinking he needed information about one of the projects she was working on with Jahan. "How can I help Anish?" she asked eagerly.

"I spoke to Akash and Sucheta," Anish started. "While discussing BUH's progress and action plans, both Ankush and Sucheta were praising you."

Aditi managed a smile, giving herself a mental pat on the back.

"In fact," he continued, "they advised me it would be more effective if you could lead the entire project."

Aditi blushed, feeling both apprehensive and excited. "Oh... really?" she said, her voice shaking. "That's a big compliment," she added, feeling a surge of pride.

"Yes, it is," Anish smiled, but stayed professional.

"In fact, Ankush and Sucheta told me they felt you were being held back by Jahan."

Aditi listened intently, holding her breath.

"They even told me they considered hiring you, but that they respected me too much to make you an offer."

Anish paused again for effect, and Aditi's mouth opened slowly in astonishment.

"Digging deeper, I found that you've basically done all the work on BUH's expansion plans, including asking Kunal to teach you about financials. He was very impressed by your insights, analysis, and your financial literacy improvement from one meeting to the next. Way beyond the level of other assistant consultants."

Aditi chose not to respond and kept looking at Anish, her mind racing.

"And despite your leadership on this project, Jahan kept you from attending some critical meetings. Is this true?"

Aditi was startled by his directness. "Well," she hesitated. "some meetings Jahan held on his own, but I attended most of them," she explained, deciding not to betray her lead consultant. "It was teamwork," she added.

"No, Aditi. Don't protect him. He intentionally left you out because he felt threatened, while continuing to present everything as his own doing, severely understating your leadership on this project."

Where is he going with all this? Aditi thought, anxiety gnawing at her.

"Last week, I had meetings with Ankur from Dhanjavad Vitt and Susmita from Pharma Direct. They both praised your questions, ideas, and output. Ankur called you a breath of fresh air due to your on-the-ground knowledge and insights, and Susmita told me to unleash you. Her exact words." Anish laughed out loud.

Aditi raised her eyebrows, trying to hide the joy bubbling up inside her.

"It's clear to me that you have been leading, not assisting, despite the hurdles you have faced. "Therefore," Anish's tone shifted, building the suspense, "I have decided to make you lead consultant."

"What?" Aditi exclaimed, her voice echoing in the room.

Anish laughed again. "Yes, Aditi. You are our new lead consultant!"

"But I've just joined the organization!" she blurted out, still trying to process the unbelievable news.

"I knew you had much more in you, but I expected you would need more time to develop. But I—and our clients—believe you are ready now. As lead consultant, you can add much more value to our business. What do you think?" he asked.

Aditi was overwhelmed by everything Anish just said. "Well, it will be an incredible honor, Anish. I will make you proud. I know I will," she said with tears in her eyes. She couldn't fathom what had just been offered to her.

"I have no doubt," Anish said, satisfied. "I want you to take over all of Jahan's projects, starting now."

"Jahan's projects?" Aditi asked, her voice laced with disbelief.

"Yes, he no longer works here."

"Excuse me?" she said, stunned.

"Yes," Anish said. "He was already under-performing and had been for some time. Then I found out the way he treated you, which is completely in conflict with our culture. But the last straw was hearing that the gossip about you and Akash started with him."

Aditi's face paled, her silence speaking volumes. "I will do my best, Anish," Aditi said, overcome by emotion. Then, shifting to a more confident tone, she added, "You can count on me."

"We will announce your appointment later this morning," Anish affirmed.

Aditi nodded, beaming, thinking, *You belong, Diti, you belong.*

Sumeet

About twelve kilometers east of Chimbai Square, Sumeet and Anish strolled out of an apartment building in Chembur. "Have you told your father about your plan yet?" Anish asked.

"No, I think the news of my divorce was bad enough. It was strange. As expected, my mother freaked out, but my father remained mostly stoic. I thought he would be very upset, but I just spotted a little disappointment."

"Well, I can tell you one thing, bhai," Anish said. "I have really seen your energy change. For the longest time you had a bit of a gloom hanging over you. Your project has made that disappear." Anish smiled. "Keep pushing forward."

"Thanks, I have no doubt that this is what I need to do. I've never been so clear," Sumeet smiled, the resolve in his voice unmistakable.

Sumeet turned around to take another look at the building. "I know this is a big downgrade, but it's not too bad. What do you think? Should I take it?"

"Definitely!" Anish responded with a playful glint in his eye.

"What? Why are you so enthusiastic?" Sumeet laughed, the

sound blending with the distant chatter of street vendors and children playing nearby.

"Well, as an investor, it tells me you are making personal sacrifices for your business. And we like that," Anish replied, his tone both serious and encouraging.

"I am definitely putting to work whatever resources I will have."

As they turned a corner, the streetlights flickered on against the dusky sky. Anish asked, "By the way, what is the latest?"

"As you know, we continue to speak with Ananya's previous employer, the international school, as our potential affiliation," Sumeet began, his voice rising over the din of a nearby construction site. "I still say potential and not definite, because they are unsure, but very curious, about the corporate inputs into the curriculum."

"I imagine they feel they are putting their reputation on the line," Anish commented.

"Yes. Ananya will finish the draft curriculum she co-created with them by the end of this week to start working with the potential donors you proposed. We will have an ongoing weekly meeting with both parties," Sumeet explained.

"That should comfort both sides," Anish agreed.

"That is the priority, so we can submit the curriculum and get through the paperwork, which will enable us to apply for government funding."

"Awesome," Anish stated.

Sumeet's eyes lit up as a thought crossed his mind. "I spoke again to the building manager in Dharavi, but they want a significant deposit. I'm hesitant to put that up until we get clarity on funding."

"Yes, don't rush," Anish nodded. The sound of a distant train added to the urban symphony around them. "I'm still talking to other potential donors, but the real money is going to come when they see we've created a talent machine that produces wonderful stories."

"It is all coming together, bhai," Sumeet said, feeling optimistic about the tremendous progress they had made in such a short time. *But we still need funding for our first year,* he thought.

Arjun

THE FOLLOWING MORNING, Arjun stepped outside the hospital for the first time on crutches, wearing a back brace. He scanned the parking area. *No police or gangsters waiting to pick me up?* he thought anxiously. Then realization hit him like a cold wave—he could move, but he couldn't run if anyone came for him.

A mixture of fear and hopelessness washed over him. *What should I do now? Where should I go?* Arjun contemplated. Returning to the shelter of the bodhi tree or his home felt like a death sentence. His assailants would show no mercy next time. He imagined his room, likely destroyed by now, and some hidden cash probably found. Rohit's absence left him paralyzed. *I can't do it alone,* he thought. The kindness of the chaiwallah, who had slipped money into his pocket, felt like another undeserving act of grace amidst all the chaos he had caused.

"Hill Road," he instructed the rickshaw driver in front of him, his voice barely steady.

Half an hour later, Arjun stood amidst food carts, savoring his favorite buttery, spicy masala vada paav. The traffic blurring past him seemed to mock his moment of peace. Just as he took his last bite, a voice to his left pierced his bubble of temporary normalcy.

"Hey!"

A man blocked the path on his right. Fear froze him mid-chew. It was the man in black, accompanied by his accomplice. Arjun's heart raced. His mind screamed for escape, but there was no escape.

The leather-jacketed man chuckled, "How did you do it, you bastard?"

Confusion clouded Arjun's face. They weren't attacking him. They were... smiling? Was it the crowded street that restrained them? Arjun scanned the area around him. *They might drag me into a nearby alley. Or into a car,* he thought. "What... what do you mean?" he stammered.

The man laughed harder, shoving him lightly. "You're a funny bastard. Tell us how you paid it all off at once?"

Arjun could only smile weakly, bewildered.

"And using an old man to deliver it for you—scandalous!" the man said, startling Arjun.

Paid off? An old man? He swallowed.

"Good for you! Didn't want to beat you up again." The man laughed.

How? I don't understand, Arjun thought. To get confirmation of the miracle, he stammered, "My debt is gone? Right...?"

"Yes, done," the man sneered, pushing him again before walking away. "Hey, thanks again for that bat; my son loves it!" he added, laughing across his shoulder.

"Don't get in trouble again, bastard." The accomplice grinned and followed the man in black.

Arjun's mind reeled. *This can't be true.* The weight on his shoulders felt lighter, but he couldn't grasp what just happened. *Did they confuse my debt with someone else's? An old man delivering on my behalf? It's impossible.* He began making his way toward Chimbai Road. Though his debt had miraculously vanished, and he wasn't wanted by the police, Rohit's faith cast a dark cloud over his relief.

Arriving at St. Joseph's Road, he saw the empty space under the bodhi tree and walked past it, heading toward the chaiwallah's cart. "Good afternoon, dada," he greeted.

The chaiwallah beamed. "I knew you'd be out soon! You're walking well. Want some chai?" He quickly handed over a steaming glass.

Arjun stared, many questions swirling his mind. "How are you, dada?"

"Wonderful, seeing you walk again," the old man smiled.

"Dada…" Arjun turned his question serious. "Were you the one that took me to the hospital?"

The chaiwallah's smile widened.

"Okay, that answers it." Arjun smiled back. "You saved my life, dada. I don't deserve your kindness," he admitted, feeling guilt for his previous angry outbursts.

"Everyone deserves kindness, beta. You look much better," the old man said.

After a few sips, Arjun turned around to face the old man. "Dada… I owe someone a lot of money."

The chaiwallah nodded knowingly.

"And that debt led me down terrible paths. It almost killed me."

"Everyone makes mistakes… be kind to yourself," the chaiwallah said gently.

"Did you meet with my debt collectors?" Arjun probed directly, still unable to believe this could be a possibility.

"I may have…" he replied. "I meet many people every day, beta," he added, evading the question.

"Right…" Arjun smiled, doubt lingering.

After another sip, he glanced back at the chaiwallah, skepticism gnawing at him. The assumption felt absurd.

"Impossible!" Arjun suddenly laughed, still staring at the old man.

"Good to see you laugh, beta!" the chaiwallah responded warmly. "Perhaps now it's time for you to go back to Jalna," he said.

Arjun let the idea float, imagining his father's reaction, wondering if he'd be loved or shunned. His thoughts darkened when he thought of his uncle. *Maybe it's time to confront the past... the gods have given me a chance I don't deserve.*

Aditi

A DITI STOOD IN the center of Chimbai Square and looked up, her eyes sparkling with pride. The sun softly bathed the building's beige exterior, casting playful shadows across the large glass windows of the apartment.

"This is the same place you were staring at the time of the Talent Festival, right?" Vishal said.

"That's right, baala," Aditi said proudly. "Come, let's go up," she added, her voice laced with anticipation. They passed through the lobby. The echo of their footsteps resonated as they climbed the cool, stone stairs. On the second floor, Aditi paused to retrieve her keys. The metal jingled softly, and the locks clicked open.

"Wow," Vishal breathed, stepping into the living area. He marveled at the spaciousness, the way natural light flooded the room through large windows, casting a warm glow. "This is really where we will live?" he asked, eyes wide with awe. "This is so much bigger than our room," he said.

Aditi smiled proudly. "Come, Vishal, have a look," she said, stepping into the room next to the living area.

"The bedroom?" he asked.

"Your bedroom," she corrected gently.

"Then where will you sleep?" he asked with sadness in his voice.

"The living room. Don't worry, baala, I will snuggle up to you sometimes," she assured, pulling him close. "Think about how you will decorate your room. We need to replace this old-fashioned wallpaper! How about we make it look like a jungle?" she suggested, suddenly seeing Vishal's eyes sparkle with imagination.

Aditi returned to the living room and lingered in front of the enormous window that framed Chimbai Square like a living picture.

Sunlight danced on the leaves of the bodhi tree to her right. Shoppers moved in and out of the supermarket on her left. The newspaperman sat slumped half-asleep straight ahead, right behind the white crucifix. Next to the newspaperman, the chaiwallah was serving customers. Watching him for a while she thought, *ever since I met this chaiwallah, my luck has completely turned around. It started with his comment to Mr. Daruwalla, and then his continued advice helped me thrive at work. Now I am a lead consultant, working on my own business idea, and we live in this unbelievable apartment.* She laughed out loud.

"We should put our table here," Vishal said, interrupting her thoughts.

After scanning the square for a brief moment, Vishal turned to her. "This is like watching TV!" Aditi nodded in agreement. Vishal smiled, showing his large front teeth. "You look very happy, aai," he said.

Aditi smiled, hugging him tightly. "I am, baala..." she replied. "I'm happy with you." She watched some joggers cross the square, their footsteps a rhythmic cadence.

Vishal's hands suddenly covered both her eyes from behind her. "How many guys are sitting on top of the supermarket racks?" he quizzed her.

"Two?" she guessed, laughing.

"Three!" he pointed out triumphantly. "Now can we get an ice cream on Hill Road?" Vishal asked, tugging at her hand.

"Sure," she said, but then thought with a touch of excitement, *Later this afternoon, I need to continue working on my business plan... I still can't believe Mr. Singhania gave me such quick feedback on that.*

Sumeet

Just as Aditi drove off with Vishal behind her, Sumeet walked across the square.

"Good to see you, beta!" the old man replied cheerfully as Sumeet sat on the plastic chair next to his cart.

"Yes, dada. Unfortunately, I won't see you on my daily walks anymore," Sumeet announced with sadness.

"I guess you found your new path?" the old man smiled kindly, the lines in his face deepening. "I was expecting change, but not this soon," the chaiwallah said, his tone encouraging.

Sumeet sat down then revealed, "I'm selling the apartment to live somewhere cheaper."

The chaiwallah nodded, stirring the chai thoughtfully.

"It has been a whirlwind of change since our moment on that rooftop."

The chaiwallah nodded.

"I ended my career, my marriage ended, my parents are upset, and I need to inform my daughter about everything that has happened. But at the same time, I met an inspirational teacher, experienced teaching children, and now plan to set up a college to help underprivileged young adults succeed in the workforce," he said. Hope flickered in his eyes.

The chaiwallah offered a reassuring presence.

"Impressive, beta," the old man said, his eyes twinkling with pride. "You have discovered a new path swiftly. It means it really could not wait any longer, and you had to begin immediately."

"I guess you are right," Sumeet replied. "I sense an opportunity, an entry into embracing who I should be and what I should be doing." He stood up and touched the chaiwallah's shoulder softly as if to transfer his gratitude. "You have no idea how much you have impacted me," he said earnestly. "Even though I will be moving to another municipality, I will stop by every now and then to see you," he promised.

"You are ready to take on the path that has been revealed, beta. That gives me great fulfillment," the old man said, his voice laced with warmth and hope.

Sumeet waved and walked off, his mind brimming with a hundred thoughts and emotions.

Stepping out of the taxi on Laburnum Road in the south of Mumbai, Sumeet marveled at the brown, reddish-colored low wall with a circular black plaque that read, "Mani Bhavan. Gandhiji's residence in Bombay 1917-1934." *It's this place from which the Satyagraha was launched in 1919, and the civil disobedience movement in 1932,* Sumeet thought, standing in front of the three-story building with its myriads of windows, feeling a surge of inspiration mingled with respect for the great leader.

The outside walls at the ground level were entirely brown colored, while the upper floors were beige with contrasting brown window casings. He ascended the stairs with anticipation. As he explored the library, picture gallery, and memorabilia, he read, "The only tyrant I accept in this world is the 'still small voice' within me. And even though I have to face the prospect of being a minority of one, I humbly believe I have the courage to be in such a hopeless minority."

In awe he thought, *Such an incredible belief, devotion, and determination. That is the key to creating change. My father has also shown these kinds of qualities. That made him have the career he had. And he deeply feels that he contributed to society by helping develop India's banking system.*

Wandering around, Sumeet absorbed the significance, thinking deeply about the impact Gandhi made. *The man achieved all that with utmost humility,* he contemplated. Then, standing in front of one of the leader's statues, Sumeet thought, *I should also find my strength within, be proud of my decisions and share them with him. Rather than being afraid, I should embrace the new me and stand up to him.* In making his decision, he picked up his phone and sent a text: *Baba, when can I come and see you? I want to talk.*

He probably expects me to ask him for help in finding a new job... he will be very surprised, Sumeet thought. *Go with an open mind,* he urged himself.

Tonight, Sumeet. Come for dinner, came the reply.

"That was quick," Sumeet murmured to himself, his heart pounding with anticipation and uncertainty.

From here I will make the same walk along Marine Drive, he resolved, continuing his sense of opportunity and new beginnings.

Arjun

THE COOLER MORNINGS now lasted longer, with a crispness that lingered each day. The square's small bricks, newly cleaned of dust from an out-of-season downpour this morning exuded a faint earthy aroma mixed with the tang of salt from the nearby sea. The shops beneath the large apartment building, perched between the sea and Chimbai Square, were all open but eerily empty, their usual early morning and evening bustle overtaken by a muffled silence.

The newspaperman was napping, the rustling of the few remaining papers the only hint of his presence. Beside him, a rickshaw driver lounged lazily in his backseat, the sound from his phone barely disturbing the quiet. Diagonal across from the newspaperman, the bodhi tree was deserted, its branches swaying gently, contributing a soft whisper to the serene atmosphere.

Arjun's footsteps disturbed the square's tranquility as he put down a large duffel bag next to the chaiwallah's cart.

"Going somewhere, beta?" The old man smiled.

"Home!" Arjun replied with pride gleaming in his eyes.

"Wonderful. I think that's right, beta. You may have been

distracted, but now you know what to do. I am proud of you," the chaiwallah said.

"Yes, it's time." Arjun sighed and a wave of relief swept over him.

"Final cup of chai before you go?"

"Sorry, my bus leaves soon," Arjun said, staring at the old man. "I can never thank you enough for everything you have done for me," he said, pulling the Ganesha statue from his pocket which he almost lost to those thugs. He handed it to the chaiwallah, and the old man marveled at the gift. "I brought it with me when I left Jalna decades ago. I want you to have it… wishing it brings you luck and protection."

"It's beautiful, beta." The chaiwallah thanked him and reverently placed it on top of his cart, facing out.

Arjun felt a lump forming in his throat as he walked to the old man's side of the cart and gave him a heartfelt hug. His eyes began to water, but he blinked away the tears and stepped back. "Take care, dada." Arjun walked toward the rickshaw behind the newspaper stand. There would be time to get emotional later; he had a journey to begin now.

"Sion East Bus Station!" he said to the rickshaw driver.

Soon Arjun was on the long-distance bus going toward Jalna. "Twelve hours," he thought. He stared out the window as the bus drove through Mankhurd in the east of Mumbai, his thoughts hopeful and resolute. *I left with nothing, and after twenty years in this city, I am going back with nothing. But the chaiwallah is right. It's time to go home.* He sat there smiling. *Besides helping my father, I can start coaching one of the youth teams in Jalna.*

When the bus turned onto the Old Vashi Bridge, seeing the water below, he suddenly felt a tightening in his chest. Images of Rohit and the van crashing through the barrier and plunging below flashed vividly in his mind. *Aaicha gho!* he thought. He closed his eyes, his heart pounding. *Come on, Arjun,* he thought forcing himself to calm down. *By some miracle from the gods, you got away from death and debt.* As the bus reached the end of the bridge and entered Vashi itself, he opened his eyes and felt a rush of relief. He slumped in his seat. Mumbai was now behind him.

*

THE NEXT DAY, Arjun woke up near the Sri Hanuman Mandir in New Mondha, Jalna.

After arriving late at night, too late to continue the journey and surprise his father, he opted to stay next to the temple he had visited many times with his father in his youth. Arjun had entered the temple, removed his sandals, and bowed deeply. "Oh, holy Hanuman Ji, I bow at your feet. Grant me the fortune of my future; let your grace be upon me. Victory to Hanuman!" Sitting down, he prayed aloud, "Dear Lord, I don't deserve this chance. But, please let me embrace my past with humility and acceptance. Let my father forgive me. Let me forgive myself. And let me be the man I was supposed to be. I will take this opportunity with both hands and work to rectify all I have done wrong in my past life."

Afterward he sat in the bus heading north on Rajur Jalna Road passing Gundewadi. Noticing the dry fields, he wondered about the state of their farm. In the next town, Tatewadi, he stepped out of the bus and was immediately confronted with his past as he stared across the road at the two-story house. The dirt road beside it led to his youth, his father's farm. Arjun spotted clothes hanging out to dry on the balcony of the first floor, and the ground floor of the house had been converted into a grocery store. A mix of fear and anger rose within him, leading to a strong shiver going throughout his body and the feeling of uncertainty about his willingness to follow through just yet.

Hoping no one from the house would see him, he quickened his walk along the dirt road, noticing again the dryness of the land. Scanning the field, there was no sign of his father. Closing in on his childhood home at the end of the dirt road made him walk even faster, fighting off the wave of emotions washing over him. He imagined holding his father's face and their first embrace. Finally, he wept.

"Baba?" he screamed, wiping his tears before opening the door. The living room was empty. The sight of the long wall hanging with photo frames took him back. "Baba?" he yelled out again, dropping his duffel bag. He glanced at the pictures, showing him and his father in different places, and the memories came flooding back. *He didn't forget about me...* Arjun walked out the backdoor, thinking his father might be in the shed. But he wasn't. *What happened here,* he wondered, his anxiety mounting.

When he re-entered the house, he noticed his father had kept everything the same way. All his trophies stood on the wooden side table they had constructed together with all the pictures from his games hanging on the wall above it. He laughed out loud, tears welling up. The air in the house smelled a bit different, but it felt good to be back. "Where is he?" he wondered aloud, moving through the rooms.

Standing outside, he scanned the field once again for any sign of his father, but there was none. He decided to face the inevitable. *Will I kill my own uncle on sight?* he thought, walking back along the dirt road. Then he saw a woman moving amidst all the clothes hanging on the balcony. *Kaku?*

When he neared, the woman yelled from above, "Can I help you?"

"It's me!" he shouted back, walking closer to the house. He saw her eyes widening, realizing who he was.

"No!" she yelled. "No! It cannot be!" Her cries pierced the air and she started wailing. "Baala…? It is you!" she shouted, affectionally calling him 'son'. "Come! Come inside!" she yelled turning into the house.

Arjun waited anxiously at the bottom of the stairs, feeling sick to his stomach being in the house. From the top of the stairs, his aunt descended slowly. She held tightly to the handrail, staring at him in disbelief. Tears streamed down her face and a flood of nostalgia washed over him. When she reached the last step, she immediately grabbed him and hugged him, sobbing uncontrollably.

"Where have you been?" she whispered with sadness. "We have been looking for you our entire lives!" she cried out.

"Mumbai," he answered, his tears falling onto her shoulder.

"Oh, baala. Your life must have been so hard. So hard! I am so sorry for you. I am so very sorry!"

"It's okay, kaku…. it's okay. I am here now," he whispered. "Where is baba?"

She leaned back for their eyes to meet. "Come, sit." She pointed at the couch. "I have been waiting for this moment for twenty years, Arjun. I have been wanting to tell you for so long." She sighed deeply.

"Tell me. What is it?"

"Your father found out, Arjun."

"Found out?" Arjun's eyes widened, thinking, *Is it what I think it is?*

"Yes… what my husband did to you."

Arjun's body froze, his heart racing, unable to respond to her revelation.

His aunty dropped to her knees and sat in front of him with her palms together, tears flowing uncontrollably. She explained that she knew all along, but didn't have the courage to speak out. The knowledge haunted her in her sleep until one day, she could not bear it any longer, and she told his father what happened. Soon after, her husband disappeared after working on the land with his father. She decided not to ask any questions and let it be. It was resolved. She continued to sob softly, an enormous weight falling from her shoulders.

Arjun felt his own tears streaming down. "Where is baba?" he screamed angrily.

His aunt put her head down and sat still for a moment.

When their eyes met, Arjun saw pity. "Where?" he yelled again.

She then admitted, "I am so sorry, baala. After years of drought and the pain of missing you, he couldn't take it anymore. He is no longer with us."

Arjun instantly fell off the couch to the floor, unconscious.

"There you are," he heard from above. A cloth cooled his forehead.

"Are you okay?" his aunty asked with a smile. "It's a lot to take in," she said.

Poor baba… Arjun thought, lying on the floor, his eyes teary.

"You are home now, Arjun," she said, petting him gently. "This is your home. And that is your farm. You need to rebuild it, Arjun. For your father."

After having lunch with his aunt, Arjun walked back along the dirt road toward his childhood home, thinking about his father. In front of the shed behind the house, he scanned through all the tools and equipment, imagining his new path ahead, unsure how and where to begin. His eyes welled up when he spotted his father's work gloves on top of a wooden plank. Gently, he put them on and went back to the front of the house. Gazing across the land, he took a deep breath, filling his nostrils with the smell of hibiscus and jasmine he had been longing for all this time. His thoughts suddenly drifted to the chaiwallah for a moment, triggering immense gratefulness. *This is where I am supposed to be,* he sighed.

He took off his sandals and walked on the soil with his bare feet.

Sumeet

IN THE EVENING, Sumeet sank anxiously into the luxurious plush, familiar cushions of their family couch. The room was dimly lit, and the soft glow of the evening sun filtered through the curtains, casting long shadows. His father sat across from him, his brow furrowed with curiosity and concern. The air in the room was thick with unspoken words.

"Some water, Sumeet?" his mother asked, her voice a tender balm in the tense atmosphere.

"Yes, thank you," he replied, attempting a smile.

"Did you hear anything from Manisha?" his mother inquired hesitantly.

"No," Sumeet replied, shaking his head.

His father interjected in his deep, authoritative voice. "*Aamchi bayko*, Sumeet came here to talk to me about something." With a stern yet compassionate look, he asked, "What is it you want to talk about, Sumeet?"

Sumeet was momentarily taken aback by his father's straightforwardness.

"Uh..." he hesitated, gathering his thoughts. He took a deep breath and braced himself for the potential backlash, then announced, "I decided I will not just find another job to continue my corporate career."

Sumeet saw his mother had overheard, and she turned around, showing concern.

"Okay," his father responded, moving forward to sit at the edge of his chair.

Sumeet paused, surprised by his father's mild reaction. "Over the years," he said, "I have noticed I have a passion for discovering people's potential, coaching them, and helping them thrive."

His father nodded encouragingly. "Yes…"

"Recently, I met a teacher who works with young adults in Dharavi who can't afford formal education, and I had the opportunity to give a lecture. Shortly afterward, during one of my walks, I met some students from lower income families and listened to their challenges in getting into the workforce."

His father was listening intently, making Sumeet confident to continue on.

"All this, along with my experience in the corporate world, made me connect the dots. It gave me an idea—an idea that propels my passion for coaching, and the desire to help others to a whole new level." He took another deep breath before revealing his plan. "I want to start a college." His father nodded, encouraging him to continue. "A college that helps identify and unlock talent among underprivileged students, giving them a recognizable degree and helping them get into the workforce, to even the playing field with people like me who have always had easier access to opportunities." Sumeet paused, his heart thudding in his chest.

"That is very ambitious, Sumeet," his father commented, a hint of a smile playing on his lips.

Sumeet felt a wave of relief wash over him, making his excitement rise. "Yes, and I've already discussed the business plan with Anish, and that teacher, Ananya. He's shared the proposal, and there's strong interest from potential sponsors who want to build the curriculum with us and fund our college once we show results. We also found several universities that support the idea and can provide us with the affiliation required and help in building the curriculum with those sponsors to create a unique proposition in the education industry."

"Really?" his father said, sounding genuinely impressed. "How will you get the funding? I can imagine this will not be cheap," he said thoughtfully.

"Yes, Anish and I will contribute significant amounts, and we will rely on some government funding. For the remainder, Anish and I need to continue to find sponsors willing to take the gamble before our results come through."

"What is the remainder?" his father asked.

"We estimate it will be around one hundred and ten lakhs. We're confident we'll find a way."

His father nodded. "Well, count me in!"

"I'm not asking for your help, baba." Sumeet smiled, grateful for his father's excitement and his offer to help financially. "I just wanted to share my idea and tell you what I am working on."

"I know that, but this is something I really want to be part of. Will you accept my donation of one hundred and ten lakhs?"

Sumeet's eyes widened with astonishment and gratitude. "Really? That's amazing, baba. Thank you so much. I really didn't expect you to be so excited about this."

"Why not?" his father asked, his eyes twinkling.

"I thought you wanted me to get another high-paying job and continue my career. With this venture, I'm not expecting to earn a lot," he smiled.

"Yes, highly unlikely," his father chuckled, shaking his head.

Sumeet paused, the weight of unspoken emotions pressing down on him. Questions circled his mind until he could no longer hold back. "Baba… I was quite surprised by your reaction when I told you about my divorce. I thought you'd be furious and disappointed, but you haven't said anything. And now, you are excited about my idea in a way I have never seen you before. Why is that?"

"Your mother is upset about the divorce, but I am not," his father replied calmly. "It is just unfortunate. But that's life, beta. I introduced Manisha to you, hoping you'd be happy together. It hasn't worked out. I also feel I pushed you into engineering and kickstarted your corporate career. I did all that to help you be happy. But I feel you never were."

Sumeet's eyes started to well up.

His father continued, "I then hoped you would eventually take control of your life, but you didn't. Until now."

Sumeet's tears rolled down his cheeks.

"Do you remember the Diwali after your graduation?"

Sumeet nodded.

"I told you I saw something in you. But in all these years, I felt you never embraced who you really were. Perhaps I am partially to blame. But now, for the first time, I am seeing you take control and follow your purpose. You came here on a mission, even though you expected us to disagree. That's strength. That's passion. That's what I always wanted for you," his father said.

Sumeet wiped his eyes with a sleeve.

His father paused then looked at him with immense pride as he placed a hand on Sumeet's shoulder. "You've decided to accept this divorce and face backlash, and now you're leaving a stable career for a very uncertain adventure. That really takes guts, my boy, and I love it."

Sumeet's tears spilled over again as relief and love filled his heart. They stood up and he hugged his father. "Thank you, baba. Really, thank you."

His mother, standing silently between the couch and the kitchen, also wiped away her tears.

"What is the name of your college?" his father asked.

"Dharavi Future Leaders College."

His father smiled broadly. "Wonderful. Go and make yourself proud, Sumeet."

Aditi

Two weeks later, Aditi sat across from Anish's desk for their regular weekly catchup. She had prepared updates on all her clients and was excited to take him through the progress she had made with her new assistant consultant.

"Aditi, I need you to start working four days per week." Anish smiled.

"What do you mean?" she laughed.

"Well, only if you want to, but I hope you do."

"Four days? Come on, what is this about?"

"Do you remember your first day here?" he asked. "Vikram spoke about the personality traits to look for in an entrepreneur."

"Yes," she said, recollecting his comments. "Someone you want to work with, who knows their stuff, has passion and a big vision."

"Correct!" he said. "And usually, the most successful ones have a strong urge to drive change for the better."

Aditi nodded.

"That's you, Aditi," he exclaimed.

Aditi laughed, still unclear about the four-days-a-week comment. "Thank you, Anish. I am trying my best."

"Vikram shared the business idea with me that you gave him. BhaskarBridge.co.id?"

A lump formed in Aditi's throat. She nodded, feeling caught.

"And…" he continued. "I would like you to spend one full day a week in this office dedicating your time to building out the idea further."

"What?" she blurted out.

"Yes, Aditi. We love your idea. And, who knows where it will lead… perhaps to becoming one of India's unicorns." He smiled. "This could be the start of your entrepreneurial journey."

"But, Anish, I can't. You gave me this life-changing opportunity… I feel I need to dedicate every single hour to helping your business. I owe that to you," she explained.

"Aditi, first and foremost, I am an investor who supports entrepreneurs," he said in a serious tone. "You can continue your work here, but when I see a good idea, I have to support it. I realize with the hours you are putting in on your work here, you wouldn't have enough time to develop your idea. Besides, you could use the help from our team," he explained.

"Anish, I don't know what to say… I am just really honored," Aditi stammered, completely overwhelmed by Anish's offer and support.

"Of course," he replied. "Aditi, before you go," he said as she got up from the chair, "who is Bhaskar in your website name 'Bhaskar Bridge'?" he asked.

"It's my father," she said with a proud smile.

*

Driving her scooter onto Chimbai Square that night, Aditi wanted to share the unbelievable news with her wise counselor. She parked in front of her building and walked across the square. The chaiwallah waved, seeing her closing in.

"You are radiating, beta," he said as she stood in front of him.

"I am!" she replied with a laugh. "It's almost difficult to grasp what is happening," she said, speaking much faster than usual.

"I can't wait to hear it," he said, pouring her a cup of chai.

"So many things have happened to me since I met you," she said. "I was just a Koli girl in a call center, struggling to move her career forward. Then you gave Mr. Daruwalla the idea to introduce me to his friend Anish. By some miracle, I got hired as an assistant consultant with very limited experience. Even more miraculously, the dots somehow started to connect as I started to dig into my projects, and somehow, I got promoted to lead consultant in no time. And now," she paused, somewhat out of breath, "my boss wants to support the business idea I developed on the weekends."

She waited for the old man's reaction. "That's your purpose, Aditi." The old man smiled.

Her emotions didn't allow the old man's message to come through. "And you turned into such an invaluable mentor, dada. Your ideas and advice helped me countless times, but I don't understand where you get this knowledge from, and why you have been helping me achieve all these things."

"Beti…" he replied.

Aditi took a deep breath, trying to calm herself down.

"Who answered all the questions in that interview?" he asked.

Aditi didn't answer, waiting for him to finish.

"Who worked countless hours on your projects at work?

Who built rapport with your boss? Who created that business idea?" he asked, raising his eyebrows.

"I did," Aditi answered.

"And who is going to turn that idea into a flourishing business?"

"I will," she replied.

"Exactly," he concluded.

"I know that you have been helping Mr. Daruwalla too, because he mentioned it to me when I spoke to him about hiring interns for our office. And I have also seen you talking to that drunk who used to sit underneath the bodhi tree. Are you some sort of a secret saint?" she laughed.

The old chaiwallah laughed too. "I am just paying my debt forward," he admitted. After a short pause, he said, "Everyone needs a little help in life, dear. A word of encouragement, a little push, an introduction to change their perspective or get into a new situation that ignites an internal fire." He spread his arms wide in front of Aditi and beamed at her. "Look what can happen! Someone once did that for me, too."

Aditi nodded, grateful for the blessings she received.

"Hearing this wonderful news gives me closure, dear… my work is done." He smiled, but his voice held a note of seriousness, and Aditi wondered what he meant by his work being done.

"Anyway, dada, before you go home, I wanted to thank you from the bottom of my heart for your wise counseling thus far," she said, her hands folded at her heart. "I can't wait for your thoughts as I try to build this business." She was excited with the thought of getting started.

The chaiwallah's rich dark, deeply wrinkled eyes exuded warmth and love. "You will do great, Aditi."

*

THE FOLLOWING MORNING, the newspaperman parked his bicycle against one of the wooden pillars on the dark, quiet square. The air was cooler than usual. Wiping down his board, the newspaperman felt something amiss. Turning to his right, he noticed the chaiwallah wasn't there. *Ha! This is the first time I am earlier than him,* he thought. Two young men sat in front of the supermarket waiting for the delivery to come. As usual, he pulled out all the papers from his bicycle and started folding.

Aditi woke up feeling uneasy, instantly thinking back to the chaiwallah's comments from last night about closure and being done. She jumped up from bed to look outside. *I knew it!* She panicked. After ensuring Vishal was still fast asleep in his own room, she put on her slippers and walked down without freshening up. Crossing the square, she hastened her steps toward the newspaperman.

"Good morning," she said, glancing at the emptiness next to the newspaper stall.

The newspaperman looked up, surprised at the women in pajamas. His first customers were always joggers. He handed her a paper.

Aditi declined. "Have you seen the chaiwallah?"

"No," the man replied, continuing to read one of his papers.

Aditi stared at the spot where the chai stand used to be, and then asked, "Do you have his phone number?"

"No," the newspaperman replied. "Normally he leaves a few things behind in his spot, but now it's all gone. The old man disappeared the same surprising way he arrived sometime back." The man laughed.

"Right…" Aditi said. "Okay, thank you." She turned around and walked slowly back to her building, feeling a deep loneliness. All the conversations she'd had with the chaiwallah raced through her mind as she walked up the stone stairs. When she reached her apartment, she opened the door and made herself a cup of masala chai.

Sitting down behind her dining table that overlooked Chimbai Square, she took a sip.

I will miss him, she thought with sadness. *His patience, generosity, and knowledge.* After a brief moment, her demeanor changed, thinking, *Out of nowhere he showed up and guided me to reach this new path. I guess all those obstacles were just steppingstones toward this moment. I'm lucky to have Vishal. And I am now lead consultant in an investment firm and starting my entrepreneurial journey... just like baba.* She turned to glance at the photo of her parents on the wall and smiled at her clear sense of purpose.

Her eyes turned back to the now empty spot on the square, and she took another sip of her chai.

"I'm proud of you, Diti," she said aloud.